Robbins was still in the middle of the autopsy, and Warrick and Sara were in the midst of processing various elements recovered from the carpet, when the Candace Lewis story took over the air waves. The local news interrupted a soap opera so Mobley could give his press ●●●●●●●rence about their real-life drama. Grissom ●●●●●●●● ●●●● interruption was merely for the Ve●●●●●●●●●●●●●●●●● ●●ne national.

"I hav●●●●●●●●●●●●●●●●●●●●●●●●●y said, unfolding a sin●●●●●●●●●●●●●●●●●●●●●●●●ng it out onto the lecter●●●●●●●●●●●●●●●●●●●●●●s."

The rep●●●●●●●●●●●●●●●●●●●●●dn't interrupt.

"Most of●●●●●●●●●●●●●w that the body found on North Las Vegas B●●●●●●nd this morning was that of Candace Lewis, the missing personal assistant of Mayor Darryl Harrison. The sheriff's department—as well as my family and myself—wish to extend our deepest condolences to the Lewis family. I would like assure them, in fact to promise them, that the LVMPD will do its very best to bring her murderer to justice. . . . Questions?"

Original novels by Max Allan Collins in the CSI series:

CSI: Crime Scene Investigation

CSI: Miami

CSI:

CRIME SCENE INVESTIGATION ™

BODY OF EVIDENCE
a novel

Max Allan Collins

Based on the hit CBS television series
"CSI: Crime Scene Investigation"
produced by Alliance Atlantis in
association with CBS Productions
and Jerry Bruckheimer Television
Executive Producers:
Jerry Bruckheimer, Carol Mendelsohn,
Anthony E. Zuiker, Ann Donahue,
Danny Cannon, Jonathan Littman
Co-Executive Producers: Cynthia Chvatal, William Petersen
Series created by: Anthony E. Zuiker

POCKET STAR BOOKS
New York   London   Toronto   Sydney

An Original Publication of POCKET BOOKS

 A Pocket Star Book published by
POCKET BOOKS, a division of Simon & Schuster, Inc.
1230 Avenue of the Americas, New York, NY 10020

ISBN: 0-7434-5582-7

First Pocket Books printing November 2003

10 9 8 7 6

POCKET STAR BOOKS and colophon are registered trademarks of Simon & Schuster, Inc.

Front cover illustration by Franco Accornero

Manufactured in the United States of America

For information regarding special discounts for bulk purchases, please contact Simon & Schuster Special Sales at 1-800-456-6798 or business@simonandschuster.com

For Paul Van Steenhuyse
computer king

M.A.C. and M.V.C.

*What can be done with fewer assumptions
is done in vain with more.*

—WILLIAM OF OCKHAM

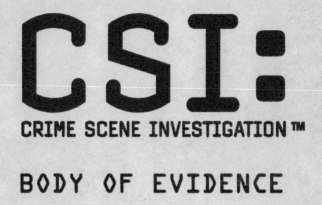

CSI:

CRIME SCENE INVESTIGATION™

BODY OF EVIDENCE

A ranch in the desert—that's how Las Vegas began. As years passed, and fashions changed, the ranch evolved into a town, albeit of the one-horse variety. And as time continued to crawl by, with a slowness the desert climate only exaggerated, the world changed even more, cars and buses and trains replacing steeds as the main mode of transportation. Men of hope and vision rode those vehicles to the tiny bump in the dusty road and saw not what was, but what could be. . . .

Among those wayfarers was a bigger-than-life gangster out of Los Angeles (by way of New York), a wiseguy with movie-star good looks who hated his nasty nickname—Bugsy—which in the street parlance of the day suggested nothing insect-like, referring instead to the handsome thug's ugly temper.

Ben Siegel envisioned a city where the hamlet stood, could make out a neon mirage in the desert, with casinos in place of barns, hotels instead of hovels. He preached this vision to others—investors who ran in his same left-

handed circle—and these hard-nosed businessman heeded the gospel according to Bugsy, which led to the construction of the famed Flamingo on what would become the Strip.

But hope is often tempered by frustration, and such was the case with Ben Siegel. The mobsters who backed his play weren't known for patience and had no understanding that, like any new plant, hope needed nurturing and time to grow. Impatience grew, too, as the mob absorbed budget overruns, time lags, and Bugsy's bugsy behavior (he was always one to live up to his nickname).

In the end, frustration won out, and Bugsy slumped in blood-soaked sportswear, weighted down by bullets in his Beverly Hills living room, hit before he ever got the opportunity to watch his vision, his hope, take root and bloom into the desert flower that would be Las Vegas.

Even now, the sparkling lights are its petals and the Strip its stem; but as Ben Siegel always knew, the roots were then—and forever will be—the gaming tables. And though the flower has changed, mutated, multiplied a thousand times over, and leafed out into branches known as Venetian, Bellagio, and MGM Grand, the fertilizer that feeds them is, as always, hope . . . one more turn of the wheel, one more roll of the dice, one more deal of the cards, bringing instant riches and fulfilling the worker bees hovering around the tables, pollinating the process with what seems an endless supply of dollars.

And always lurking in the background, ready to cut off the flow of green nourishment, is Ben Siegel's old pal, frustration. The losers who walk away, perhaps turning to other, even darker forms of hope, might threaten to overgrow the flower's beauty; but will never cause it to wither, for hope (as Ben Siegel knew if never admitted) never reaches fruition without encountering frustration . . . and Vegas is a city where hope forever blossoms, even as frustration reaps its constant harvest.

1

A SENSE OF FRUSTRATION RARELY REGISTERED ON THE PERsonal radar of Catherine Willows. Frustrating situations were so much a part of the fabric of her life by now that she could have long since gone mad had she let such things get to her. But at the moment, the sensation was registering, all right. In fact, she felt herself growing quietly pissed.

This was the tail end of yet another shift, and she and fellow Las Vegas Metro P.D. crime scene investigator Nick Stokes, who was at the wheel of the Tahoe, had been dispatched to take a 404 call—unknown trouble—at a business past the south end of the Strip. Unknown trouble could mean just about anything from petty theft to multiple homicides.

But what it definitely meant was another Monday morning where Mrs. Goodwin, the sitter, would have to get Lindsey up and off to school. Catherine's own childhood had often been spent waiting for her mother to come home, and she had hoped to do better for her own daughter. But she was a woman with many responsibilities. Once again, she would just have to tough it out. And be quietly pissed.

The Newcombe-Gold Advertising Agency, their destination, occupied a two-story, mostly glass building on West Robindale just off Las Vegas Boulevard, a couple miles south of the Mandalay Bay and the unofficial end of the Strip.

Newcombe-Gold had joined the new construction craze hitting that part of the city and even though the agency had been a fixture on the ad scene since the seventies, the building was a recent addition to that expanding urban landscape. Tinted windows gave the building a blackness in the morning sun, imparting a vaguely ominous vibe to Catherine, as she and Nick pulled into the gray-white welcome mat of a concrete parking lot, stretching across the building's blank black facade.

The small lot had room for between twenty and thirty cars, but aside from a dark blue Taurus (which Catherine recognized as a LVMPD detective's unmarked car), two patrol cars, and their own CSI Tahoe, only three other cars took up parking spaces.

Nick Stokes parked the Tahoe in a VISITOR'S space near the front entry and Catherine crawled down while her partner hopped out on his side—Nick was young enough, she guessed, not to feel the long night they'd just finished.

The tan and brown silk scarf—a Mother's Day present last year from Lindsey—flipped momentarily into her face, as if the breeze couldn't resist laying on another guilt pang. Her shoulder-length strawberry blonde hair whipped in the wind and she grimaced, wishing she were home. She stood nearby as Nick opened up the rear doors of the Tahoe.

Tall, muscular in a fashion befitting the ex-jock he was, Nick Stokes smiled over his shoulder at her, for no particular reason. His short black hair barely moved in the wind and the eagerness in his face made him look like a happy puppy. Catherine sometimes wondered if maybe he liked his job a little too much.

"Too early for admen to be at work?" Catherine said, casting her gaze around the mostly empty lot.

"Not even eight yet," Nick said, glancing at his watch. "Big shots'll be at least another hour—rest should be filtering in, any time."

"What kind of trouble, I wonder," Catherine sighed.

"Unknown trouble," Nick said, a smile in his eyes.

"Don't tease me at the end of shift."

"I would never tease you, Catherine. I have too much respect for you."

"Kiss my . . ." Catherine began, but she found herself almost smiling—damn him.

She grabbed the tool-kit-like stainless steel case containing her crime-scene gear, and led the way to the entry. A painfully young-looking patrolman, whose nametag identified him as McDonald, opened the door for her. The uniform man was tall and broad-shouldered, and you could smell recent-police-academy-grad on him like a new car. His brown hair was clipped high and tight and his smile also seemed a little excessive, considering the hour.

"Morning, guys," he said, with a familiarity that didn't negate the fact that neither CSI had ever seen him before.

"Thanks," she said as she entered, making her own smile pleasant enough but of the low-wattage variety.

"What's his problem?" she asked Nick when they were out of earshot.

"Aw, lighten up, Cath. He's chipper, that's all. You know these young guys. They haven't had time to get cynical."

Neither have you, Catherine thought, then said, "Well, I wonder how long it'll take him to stop opening doors for CSIs."

"CSIs that look like you, probably never. . . . You'll make it up to her, you know."

The non sequitur caught Catherine's full attention. "What?"

Nick shrugged, and his smile was tiny, without a trace of smirk. "Lindsey. She's cool. You'll be fine. Let's do our job—maybe I'll even buy you breakfast, after."

She gave up and smiled at him. "Maybe I'll even let you."

They were in a spacious lobby, and even though the building glass was smoked, sunlight flooded in. Four chairs, three sofas and two tables arrayed with trade journals and newsmagazines dotted the long, narrow area inside the door. In the far corner, a wall-mounted counter held neat little towers of styrofoam cups and a coffee pot that filled the room with the fragrance of fresh-brewed Columbian-blend. Catherine knew that this—unlike the sludge back at HQ—would be the first pot of the day.

A high counter, reminiscent of a hotel check-in desk, crossed the opposite end of the room, the receptionist's tall chair empty; on top of the desk rested an appointment book and a telephone system that looked to be capable of launching missiles across continents. The wall behind was replete with various awards from the Nevada Advertising Council, the Southwest Advertising Coalition and two awards Catherine recognized as the Oscars of the ad game, Cleos.

To the left of the reception counter, far off to the side, another uniformed officer stood at the aperture of a hall leading into the warren of offices.

Something was in the air besides that Columbian blend.

The pleasantness of the uniformed man on the front door had been replaced by a chilliness that had nothing to do with air conditioning. Catherine wondered if Nick sensed it, and she glanced at him. He too was frowning.

They moved through the room without touching anything. Though they had been dispatched here, the reason for the call had been obscured behind the "Unknown Trouble" tag. Sometimes the term means just that: the nature of the crime was unknown, possibly because the person who called it in had been vague or hysterical, but troubled and insistent enough to get a response.

Other times, a crime was considered sensitive, and the officer on the scene made a decision not to broadcast its nature over the police band.

Was that the case here?

At any rate, as they made their way over to the second uniformed officer, they did their best to not contaminate anything that might later turn out to be evidence.

So much for a cup of that coffee.

"Detective O'Riley's in the conference room at the end of the hall," the uniform informed them. This officer—Leary, the nametag said—was perhaps five years older than the one posted outside, and he was dour where McDonald had been chipper. Maybe five years on the job was all it took.

Catherine thanked him, and they walked the corridor, which was wide and long and lined with framed print ads; at the end, a set of double doors yawned open.

Along the way, the artwork on the walls depicted some of the company's most successful campaigns. She was familiar with all of them. When they got to what appeared to be the conference room, another hallway peeled off to the right.

Through the open door of the conference room, Catherine could see a large ebony table that consumed most of the space, surrounded by charcoal-colored, high-backed chairs. Nothing was marked off as a crime scene, so neither CSI put on rubber gloves, as they approached. When she ducked in the room, with Nick just behind, Catherine saw, crewcut Sergeant O'Riley standing at the far end, hovering over a blonde woman, seated with her head bowed, the thumb and fingers of her left hand rubbing her forehead.

"Ms. Denard," O'Riley said, in his gruff second tenor. Whether this was for identification purposes, for the CSIs, or to get the woman's attention, wasn't quite clear.

In any case, the woman jumped a little, looked up at O'Riley, then her eyes tensed as Catherine and Nick entered deeper into the room, moving to O'Riley's side of the massive table.

"It's all right, Ms. Denard," O'Riley said as he placed one of his hands on her shoulder. "These people are here to help."

The woman seemed to relax, thanks to O'Riley's touch and reassurance.

Catherine had come to revise her feelings about O'Riley, over the years; once she had overheard him dismissing the CSIs as "the nerd squad." But such adversarial days were long gone.

As usual, the detective's suit looked like he had fallen naked from a plane into a clothing store, only to rise and find himself fully if haphazardly dressed.

"Ms. Denard," the sergeant said, "this is Catherine Willows and her partner Nick Stokes from the crime lab."

The woman started to stand, but O'Riley's friendly hand on her shoulder—coupled with Catherine saying, "No, no, please, that's all right"—kept her in her seat.

Catherine stuck out her hand and the woman shook it delicately, then repeated the action with Nick as O'Riley said, "This is Janice Denard—she's Ruben Gold's personal assistant and office manager."

Ms. Denard didn't seem to know what to say, then she finally settled on, "Would either of you like a cup of coffee?"

"No, thanks," Nick said. "We're fine." Catherine nodded her assent to Nick's call.

Denard wore a sleeveless black-and-white polka dot dress that showed off slim, tan shoulders, the high collar—which Catherine thought should have shortened the appearance of the woman's throat—instead seeming to elongate it, giving the woman a supple swan neck. A simple silver cross hung on a tiny chain and she wore a slim silver watch on her left wrist, her only other jewelry a silver ring on the fourth finger of her right hand. She was in her early to mid-thirties and beautiful, her wide-set big blue eyes bearing lashes long enough to give Catherine a flash of envy.

"Really," the woman said, unconvincingly, "I'm fine—it's no trouble, if you change your mind."

Moments later, Catherine and Nick had taken seats on either side of Janice Denard, who began, "I came to work early today."

"Is that unusual?" Catherine asked.

"No. I do that most days—especially Mondays. I like to have everything up and running . . . you know, before Mr. Gold comes in."

"What time is that usually?"

"That Mr. Gold comes in? Just before nine."

"And what time do you get here?"

"Between seven and seven-thirty most days, but six-thirty on Mondays."

"And that's when you came in this morning?"

"No. It was more like . . . six-forty-five. I was running late, because of a traffic accident on Maryland Parkway."

Nick, who was taking notes, asked, "Where do you live, Ms. Denard?"

"East end of Charleston Boulevard. There are some houses at the foot of the mountains . . . ?"

"Yes," Catherine said, thinking, *Nice digs for a secretary.* "I know those houses. Very nice."

Nick bulled right in, though his tone was gentle. "You are Mr. Gold's secretary, I take it?"

Denard bristled. "Personal assistant to Mr. Gold and office manager. It's an executive position, and I do very well, thank you very much. Not that I see how it pertains to anything."

Catherine's frustration was very much on her radar now; neither O'Riley nor this woman had as yet indicated what kind of situation they were dealing with, so whether or not something "pertained" remained as "unknown" as the "trouble."

"No offense," Nick said, and he shared with the woman the boyish smile that had melted frostier types than Denard. "But you gotta admit, those are really nice houses."

Wouldn't you know it, Denard smiled back at Nick, showing lots of white teeth. *Caps?* Catherine wondered.

"My ex," Denard said, "was a divorce lawyer . . . but not as good as mine, as it turned out."

Nick gave half a grin and a head nod, and Catherine chuckled politely, thinking, *Shark.* Then Catherine asked, "So, back on point—you came in around six-forty-five, and then?"

A shrug. "I went about my routine."

Their silence prompted her to continue.

Denard did: "I shut off the alarm, I went to my office, took off my coat and hung it up, then turned on my computer."

Catherine could almost see the movie Janice Denard seemed to be watching in her own mind, as she retraced her morning.

"While the computer booted, I went through Saturday's mail, which was piled on my desk."

"How did it get there?" O'Riley put in, lurking on the sidelines, on his feet.

Denard blinked at him. "How did *what* get there?"

"The mail."

"Oh! An intern put it there."

"When?"

"On Saturday."

O'Riley frowned, mostly in thought. "You weren't here on Saturday?"

Nodding, Denard said, "In the morning, but I left before the mail came. Most of the staff works Saturday—"

Catherine put in, "Isn't that unusual?"

"Not in a competitive, deadline-driven business like ours. We're just that busy, and that includes the interns. One of them would've been in charge of making sure the mail was on my desk, before he, or she, left."

Nick asked, "Which intern?"

"I don't know," she said, with another shrug. "I could find that out for you. I can give you a list of all the interns, far as that's concerned."

"If you could."

"But not right now," O'Riley said, with just a little impatience. "Go on with your account, please, Ms. Denard."

She took a breath, and dove back in. "After I went through the mail, and my computer was up, I went online. I checked the e-mails of both myself and Mr. Gold. After that, I checked the fax machine in my office, and then went to the rear office and checked that fax, too. Once I had done that, I went out front and started the coffee."

"*You* started the coffee?" Catherine asked, sitting forward. "Not one of the interns?"

"The interns'll just be shuffling in about now. I'm here first and starting the coffee is just something I like to do myself. Anyway, after that . . . that's when I found . . . found those . . . *things.*"

Catherine and Nick exchanged glances, and O'Riley said, "Show us, if you would, please."

The woman took a moment to compose herself—as if preparing to do something very difficult; then, rising, Janice Denard said, "Come with me."

They followed her down the hall into a huge room divided into a colony of cubicles that seemed to be set off in squares of four with perhaps four central squares taking up the bulk of the space. The outside walls of the work area were the glass windows of offices that formed the room's borders.

Except for the framed advertisements, Newcombe-Gold looked to Catherine more like an insurance company than an ad agency, at least until they rounded a corner and she glanced into one of the corner offices and saw a giant slot car setup, and in an adjacent office an array of action figure toys surrounding a work station.

Two doors later, Janice Denard took a right into a spacious office, outfitted in a sleekly modern fashion, accented with splashes of color via framed abstract art. A starship of a desk—wide, gray and fashioned of an indeterminate substance—jutted from the left wall at a forty-five degree angle, envelopes and papers in three neat stacks, a mini-missile-launch phone setup roosting nearby; adjacent, a small credenza was home to a computer monitor and printer.

"This is my office," Janice Denard said—gesturing to file cabinets and chairs as if addressing loyal subjects in passing. Sensing that her little safari group had slowed to take in the impressive surroundings, the personal assistant/office manager paused to make sure they were all keeping up before she led them into Ruben Gold's office.

Nearly a half again as large as Janice's office, Gold's quarters were tan and masculine—the only wall decorations a trio of framed ad magazines with Gold's picture on the cover; the expansive area was dominated by a mahogany desk for which untold trees had given their lives. A speaker phone capable of defending against any missile attacks the lobby or Ms. Denard might launch perched on one corner, a silver airplane on a C-shaped silver base hovered on the other. Two leather armchairs faced the desk and a massive oxblood leather throne loomed behind it.

A glass cutout in the top of Gold's desk provided the (as yet absent) boss a view of his concealed computer monitor; atop a matching mahogany credenza, behind and to the throne's right lurked a laser printer as well as a row of books between ornate silver bookends—the credenza likely sheltering the CPU tower.

"Everything seemed fine this morning," Janice said, her manner now detached, business-like, "until I happened to glance at Mr. Gold's printer."

Nick asked, "How did that change things?"

Janice's face screwed up as she pointed toward the

printer tray, where Catherine could see a small pile of paper. Walking to the printer, pulling on latex gloves, Catherine asked, "Let's see what got your attention, Ms. Denard. . . ."

And, even as she pulled the sheaf of papers from the tray, Catherine could see what had disgusted Janice Denard.

CSI Willows was not squeamish.

Without a twinge, she had once walked into a room where waited a bloated corpse, undiscovered until the smell alerted a landlord; she had dealt with liquefied human remains, emotionlessly; she had handled disembodied arms, legs, limbs, torsos and heads without a flutter of her stomach.

But revulsion and rage flowed through her now, an immediate response that she had to force back, to retain and maintain her professionalism.

The top sheet was a pornographic picture of a girl about Lindsey's age, being violated by a male adult in his thirties. Catherine closed her eyes, then opened them to glance toward Janice. "You found these in the printer this morning?"

Janice managed a weak nod and backed away a half-step, as if something in Catherine's manner had frightened her.

Catherine placed the top sheet on the desk, with the image up, and Nick's face whitened; his eyes looked unblinkingly, unflinchingly at the image, then looked away.

"Nick," Catherine said, gently.

His gaze came to hers and he nodded a little, and she nodded back. They both had issues with this kind of crime, and they knew it . . . and they would both stay professional.

Catherine looked at the next image.

It was worse than the first, and on and on they went, nearly a dozen in all, every one featuring a minor, both boys and girls, every one obscene. When no one was looking (she hoped), she brushed the tears from her eyes with her sleeve, and somehow each sheet got laid out on the desk, and when she and her partner were done, each sheet was slipped into an individual transparent plastic evidence bag. Nick collected them all and held them face down in his hands.

Her eyes again met his and she smiled, just a little, to be supportive. He swallowed and nodded, but didn't seem able to summon anything close.

With the photos out of sight, Catherine and Nick turned their attention back to Janice Denard.

"Is this the kind of thing Mr. Gold might be interested in?" Catherine asked. "To your knowledge, I mean?"

"My God, no!" She seemed shocked that Catherine might even suggest such a thing. "There's no way," she continued, looking from one CSI to the other. "He's just . . . not like that."

"We can talk to him at nine," Nick said. "That's when he'll be in, you said."

Shocked, as if it had slipped her mind, she said, "He's out of town."

"Out of town!" O'Riley blurted. "Where?"

Her shrug was noncommittal, but her words were specific: "He flew to Los Angeles for a trade show that starts this morning. He left last Friday and isn't due back until the end of the week."

Catherine, trying to keep the incredulity from her voice, asked, "And you simply *forgot* that little detail?"

"No, no, no, of course not. . . . This, this *thing* that happened . . . and then you coming . . . I was taken by surprise, is all."

"If Mr. Gold wasn't coming in," Catherine said tersely, "why did you come in early to prep for him?"

"I didn't—I just came in at the time I usually do on Monday." She was shaking her head, growing more and more agitated. "If you knew Mr. Gold, you would never *dream*. . . ." Her voice trailed off.

Nick gestured with the pornographic sheets still in his hand. "You never know who some people really are."

Catherine gave him a quick look, then asked, "Why wouldn't we suspect Mr. Gold?"

"You just *wouldn't*. He's honest, he has integrity, he works hard. And he's dated a lot of women . . . mature women. I don't mean old, but women his own age."

O'Riley asked, "How old is Mr. Gold?"

"In his early forties, I guess. I can get you that information, if it's important.

Knowing that dating habits seldom had any real relevance to an interest in child porn, Catherine took the woman in another direction. "Who else has access to Mr. Gold's personal computer?"

Janice shook her head immediately. "No one."

Slowly, Catherine said, "No one has access to Mr. Gold's computer."

"That's right."

"You're his personal assistant."

The blonde risked a frown. "Do I have to tell you, a computer is *also* personal?"

"Some are more personal than others," Nick said dryly.

"Mr. Gold," Catherine said, letting each word out, one at a time, "is in LA and won't be back for a week . . . and yet you have no idea who could have printed out these pictures?"

The frown went away and a placating manner accompanied Denard's reply: "What I *meant* to say was, no one could have used Mr. Gold's PC to print those pictures. We each have our own private passwords, and there's no way anyone could use Mr. Gold's computer, unless he were careless with that password, which I assure you he was not."

Nick perked. "Was he *especially* careful about his password?"

Defensive now, Denard accused, "You make that sound suspicious! Are *you* careful about *your* password, Mr. Stone?"

"Stokes," Nick said.

Catherine could feel this interview starting to slip away from them, and she gave Nick a gently reproving glance, then said, "It is his printer, Ms. Denard."

"Our computers here are networked, linked together so that *any* of the work stations, or other offices, could have accessed Mr. Gold's printer."

"On purpose, you mean?" Catherine asked.

"Yes . . . but also by mistake! Just with a wrong keystroke."

Eyes narrowing, Catherine said, "So, we're looking at how many people, who've been in the building since the end of shift last Friday?"

"Nearly everyone. We work six days here most of

the time—Newcombe-Gold is rated number two ad agency in Las Vegas, you know."

Catherine asked, "How many employees?"

"With computer access?"

"Yes."

The woman didn't miss a beat; she knew her office. "Twenty-seven."

Trading dismayed glances with Nick, Catherine said, "Twenty-seven?"

"Plus Mr. Gold, of course, and Mr. Newcombe. Without computer access? There's five interns and half a dozen janitorial staff."

Turning to O'Riley, Catherine said, "We're going to need a search warrant for all the computers, floppies, CDs, everything."

O'Riley sighed, nodded, withdrew his cell phone and punched in numbers, stepping over to the corner of the office for some privacy.

Janice Denard's eyes were wide and she looked as white as Nick had on seeing the pictures. "Oh, no— please don't say you're—"

"This is a serious felony," Catherine said, cutting the woman off. Then to Nick, she said: "Call Tomas Nunez, would you? Tell him to get down here ASAP."

"On it," Nick said, hauling out his own cell phone and moving to the corner opposite O'Riley.

Tomas Nunez, the best of several computer gurus the department used part time, would come in to oversee the operation of taking the computers out of Newcombe-Gold. Catherine was about to seriously inconvenience this business, but there was no other way.

"A search warrant means you'll . . . search the building, right?" Denard asked weakly.

"A warrant means," Catherine replied, "that we'll take everything in, computers, maybe some of the other hardware, and most of the software, and our expert will work on it until we figure out the origin of this material. This isn't an employee logging on to some adult website on his coffee break, Ms. Denard—this is child pornography. A serious crime."

"Eighty percent of our graphics are computer generated!"

"We don't do this lightly. And we do regret the inconvenience."

O'Riley asked, "Is Mr. Newcombe in town?"

More flustered than angry, Janice glanced at her watch. "Yes, he should be here any minute now."

"Good." O'Riley returned to the cell phone, spoke a few words, then punched the STOP button and faced them. "Warrant'll be here in ten minutes. I got Judge Madsen to issue it."

Catherine, Nick and O'Riley all knew that crimes against children sent Judge Andrew Madsen completely around the bend and he, of all local judges, would act fastest to help them gain possession of the evidence.

"When exactly is Mr. Newcombe due in?" O'Riley asked.

As if on cue, a tall, lantern-jawed man appeared in the doorway, a laptop computer case strapped over his left shoulder. Perhaps fifty, he might have stepped from an ad for his expensively tailored gray suit. He had silver-gray hair and thin, dark eyebrows, and managed to look both confident and confused as he strode into Ruben Gold's office.

Ignoring O'Riley and the CSIs, he demanded of Denard, "What's going on here?"

"Mr. Newcombe," she said, taking a tentative step toward her boss. "I . . . I . . . found something . . . terrible, this morning, and I'm afraid. . . ."

O'Riley stepped between the man and woman, his badge coming up into Newcombe's face. "I'm Detective Sergeant O'Riley, Mr. Newcombe. You *are* Mr. Newcombe? These are crime scene investigators I called over—Catherine Willows and Nick Stokes."

"Crime scene . . ." Wheeling slowly, the polished Newcombe seemed finally to realize the CSIs were in the room. He repeated what he'd said, upon entering, but the words came out soft, even apologetic: "What's going on here?" Then, as an afterthought, he stuck out his hand and said, "Ian Newcombe, Sergeant, sorry."

O'Riley gave the man's hand a cursory shake and said, "Ms. Denard discovered something in Mr. Gold's printer this morning, and was exactly right in calling us."

"Something in a printer serious enough to call the police?" Newcombe said, his bewildered look travelling from O'Riley back to Janice.

Nick stepped forward and tossed one of the evidence bags onto the desk—image up. Newcombe eyed it from a distance, glanced at the officers, then—as if approaching a dangerous beast—took a few steps closer, moving past O'Riley, and finally braving to pick up the bag for a better look. . . .

"Oh . . . my . . . *God*. . . ."

"I take it," O'Riley said, matter of fact, "you've never seen these before?"

The adman dropped the bag onto the desk as if it were on fire, the laptop clunking against his hip as he involuntarily stepped back.

Nick spread the rest of the evidence bags out on the desk, like a terrible (if winning) hand of cards.

Newcombe glanced from picture to picture, his eyes never resting on one photo longer than a second, his mouth falling open in appalled shock, hands balling into fists then uncoiling and balling again.

"I have frankly never seen anything like this," he said, the calm in his voice obviously forced, his tone cold, almost mechanical. "One . . . hears of such things. These are . . . ," he searched for the word, ". . . revolting."

But O'Riley was still in charge, saying to the ad exec, "You have no idea how they could have gotten here?"

"None," Newcombe said. "I . . . I don't recognize any of these children, either . . . if that helps at all."

Catherine said, "So you're as surprised as Mr. Denard to find these photos in Mr. Gold's printer?"

"Absolutely. . . . How could that have happened?"

"That's what we have to find out," Nick said.

"But your company will be inconvenienced," Catherine said. "You can speak to your lawyers if you like, of course, but we'll have a warrant shortly and—"

He held up a hand in a "stop" motion. "Anything we can do to help, we'll do."

"I'm relieved to hear you say that, Mr. Newcombe, because we're going to have to confiscate every computer in this facility."

Newcombe's shock seemed to congeal on his face, then something new appeared in his eyes: alarm. *"What?"*

O'Riley's face was as expressionless as a block of granite. "Ms. Willows is correct. We're going to take along everything these criminalists consider to be evidence, so we can trace the source of the pornography."

"That's what I was trying to tell you, Mr. Newcombe," Janice said, appearing at the executive's side, looking up at him pitifully. "They're planning to shut us down."

The adman stood a little straighter. "Oh, they are, are they? Well, maybe I will call my attorneys, at that."

"You said you'd do anything to help," Catherine reminded him.

"Not shut down the source of income for thirty people," he said, eyes intense. "Not if I have anything to say about it."

Actually, Catherine thought, *twenty-nine,* but she said, "Sir," with a smile that at least pretended to be friendly, "that's just it: you don't. Have anything to say about it, I mean."

A uniformed officer walked in with a folded sheaf of papers and handed them to O'Riley.

"Thanks," the detective said, as the uniform turned and left the room. O'Riley gave the warrant a cursory read, then handed the papers to Newcombe.

The adman was on his cell phone before he was done with the first page.

"Is that your lawyer?" Catherine asked, helpfully.

"You can rest assured it is."

"That would be the attorney who handles all your business affairs?"

"Yes, and why is that of any concern to you?"

"It isn't—but it might be to you. This is a criminal matter and your attorney probably hasn't studied in that area since law school."

O'Riley got into it, saying to the exec: "But, hey—yammer at the guy all you want, if it'll make you feel better . . . and for, what? Five hundred bucks an hour? . . . He'll get back to you and consult with a real criminal attorney and then finally they'll tell you what I'm about to tell you . . . for free."

Newcombe looked pissed, but he said into the phone, "Just a moment, Wayne," then said to O'Riley, "And what legal advice can you share with me?"

O'Riley shrugged. "That you can't do shit."

The adman growled into the phone, "Wayne, I'll call you back from my office," and started to leave.

Catherine called out: "There's another thing your attorney can tell you, Mr. Newcombe!"

The executive halted in the doorway, looked over his shoulder at her, glaring.

"It's that if you *do* try to fight this," she said, "it could cause you far more harm than being shut down for a day or two."

Newcombe's eyes tightened, but there was no hostility in his tone as he said: "What kind of trouble?"

Catherine approached him, her manner calm, professional. "Let's explore the path that doesn't come with trouble. Let's say you don't stand in our way, we take your equipment, and find the kiddie porn source. Then, when the case makes the news—and trust me, it *will* make the news—we praise you and your agency in all the media for helping us ferret out this dangerous individual."

Newcombe cocked his head, skeptically.

"Or," Nick said, an edge in his voice, "not."

The executive came back into the room, put himself at the center of Catherine, O'Riley and Nick. "How long do you think we'll be shut down?"

Catherine said, "A few days, if we're lucky. You might want to call your insurance company—you may be able to file a lost time claim."

Newcombe nodded. "Our coverage may include something for this, at that. What else can we do to help you?"

O'Riley pulled out a pad. "Tell us about this trade show your partner's attending."

"The aaay miss buddy show?"

O'Riley squinted; it wasn't the most intelligent expression Catherine had ever seen on a face. "Pardon?" O'Riley asked.

The exec spelled it out: "The AAAA-MIS-BUDDY show."

The detective looked at the CSIs, his eyebrows raised in confusion; the spelling bee hadn't helped any of them, both Catherine and Nick shaking their heads.

Newcombe turned on a smile normally reserved for clients—its wattage lower than your average Strip marquee, but just barely.

"Sorry," he said, "too much time with ad people. The American Association of Advertising Agencies, AAAA, has a Member Information Services section, the MIS, and they are using the trade show in LA to introduce their Business Demographics and Data for You or BUDDY system."

O'Riley tried to write all that down, but it was clear he was struggling. So Nick asked, "And that's where Mr. Gold is now?"

"Yeah, since Friday."

Turning to Janice, Nick asked "You said he flew out, Ms. Denard—what airline?"

"Airline?" she asked, confused for a moment, then she said, "Oh, I'm sorry—Mr. Gold didn't use any airline: he flew himself."

Catherine nodded toward the silver airplane on the desk. "So he's a pilot?"

"Yes," Newcombe said. "As am I. The company owns the plane, but we both use it. At our own discretion."

Tomas Nunez strolled in.

The computer geek looked more like a refugee from a Southwestern biker gang than the best computer analyst in the state. Tall and rangy, his long, black hair slicked straight back, Nunez had a leathery brown, pockmarked face, a stringy black mustache, and deep-set eyes as brown as they were cold. He wore a black leather vest, black jeans and a black promo T-shirt for an album by Los Fabulosos Cadillacs.

Newcombe and Janice Denard eyed him like they thought he'd blown in to rob the place.

Nunez smiled, displaying even, white teeth, startlingly so against his dark complexion. "*Hola*, Catherine—Nick, you rang? Lucky for all of us I was close by—over at Mandalay Bay, catching breakfast."

Catherine brought him up to speed, including

showing him the pornographic printouts. He betrayed no emotion, which Catherine envied.

"You want all the computers processed?" he asked.

"Yes, Tomas—every last one."

He clapped once. "All right. Gonna need a trout with a Polaroid—maybe two."

Catherine nodded. Newcombe and Janice looked at each other as if Nunez's English was outer-space lingo. Catherine did not bother to explain that a "trout" was one of those uniformed officers who stood around at crime scenes, gawking more than helping, generally with their mouths hanging open—like a trout. One would be pressed into duty, taking photos of all the computers and where they sat, the wiring hooked to each one, and—if Nunez demanded it—pictures of devices they were hooked to, as well.

Before any of the computers could be processed, that photographic record had to be made.

"We're going to need more hands," Nick sighed, "and a Ryder truck."

O'Riley held up a hand for silence—he was already making the call.

Nunez approached Newcombe; the adman backed up half a step.

"Might as well start with yours," Nunez said.

Newcombe bristled and his hand tightened around the strap of his laptop bag. "Now, I'm sorry, but there I'm just going to have to draw the line. This is my personal computer from home!"

"Warrant specifies every computer on the premises," Nunez said. "That's a computer, these are the premises."

Newcombe tried to stare down the computer expert, and—though the tactic may have worked for Newcombe in the business world—with the likes of Nunez, the cause was a lost one. The geek just stared back deadpan, hand held out, until Newcombe finally laid the bag in it.

"Gracias," Nunez said. Turning to Nick, he said, "Nicky, can you get the pictures of this one—be real thorough, man—and pull it out while Catherine and I take care of the rest."

"No problem, Tomas."

"Gracias."

Officer Leary came in then, a Polaroid camera in his hands, his mouth yawning open, waiting for Nunez's hook.

"Hope you got a shitload of film," Nunez said.

Leary's expression turned confused, but the uniform had the good sense to tag after Nunez when the computer expert waltzed out of Gold's office and into Denard's.

Catherine followed and watched as Nunez had the officer take photos of the keyboard, the front of the computer tower, then the back to match the wiring and finally, Janice Denard's Zip drive and printer.

"Let's get crackin' on the others," Nunez said to Catherine. "I'll unhook hers, afterwards." He looked at Leary. "You got the idea now?"

Leary nodded. "No sweat."

"Not in this air conditioning," Nunez said. "Like Gary Gilmore said, let's do it."

Leary, Nunez and Catherine walked into the warren of cubicles, filled with workers now, and Nunez put his fingers in his mouth and whistled long and loud. Heads popped up from almost every station and, when he had their attention, Nunez raised his voice loud enough that Catherine figured they could probably hear him out in the parking lot.

"Las Vegas Metro P.D.," he called. "This building is now officially a crime scene. Please file out of the room and into the lobby without touching your computers. If I see so much as a keystroke, I'm breaking fingers."

Although several of the workers tried to ask what was going on, Nunez shushed them and herded them all into the lobby. Catherine watched carefully and no one had ducked back into a cubicle before marching out.

"That's it," Nunez said, in the lobby. "Thank you for your cooperation. Mr. Newcombe will be out shortly to explain to you what's going on."

When the last of the employees was in the hallway, Nunez turned to Catherine.

"Shall we get to work?"

"Tomas, my boss would admire your people skills."

Catherine joined Nick, who was still shooting photos in Gold's office.

"How are you doing, Nicky?"

He looked at her and forced a little smile. "Good. Good."

She touched his shoulder. "It's not easy for me, either. . . . Think I'll take a rain check on breakfast."

He nodded, his mouth twitched, and he got back to work.

2

EARLIER THAT SAME MORNING, THE THREE OTHER MEMBERS of the CSI graveyard shift had responded to a 419, i.e., a Dead Body call—representing another unpleasant discovery by a Las Vegas citizen.

From his usual spot in the front passenger seat, CSI supervisor Gil Grissom let out a small prayer-like sigh of relief as Warrick Brown heeled the black Tahoe onto the east shoulder of Las Vegas Boulevard. Grissom rarely drove, either to or from a crime scene; he was distracted, preoccupied, and while he was probably a perfectly fine driver, it disturbed him that he could arrive at a destination with no memory of ever having looked out the windshield along the way.

But at least as disturbing was Warrick's expeditious approach to driving. The young CSI had a low-key, even laidback manner at odds with a driving style that strongly suggested a manic streak lurked not far beneath the calm.

The dash-mounted blue strobe mixed in with the

flashing red lights of two parked prowl cars to paint the deathscape an eerie purple; it would still be a good three hours before the crack of dawn would do the same. This far north on the Strip, there were no wind-breaks and the drafts roared down off the mountains like angry spirits, perhaps heading over to haunt the sprawling ghost town across the road—the Las Vegas Motor Speedway, sitting as dark and dormant as a for-gotten mining town a century after the gold petered out. Mere weeks ago, tens of thousands of avid NASCAR fans had poured in and filled the place to the rafters for the Busch and Winston Cup races; now, however, the sprawling ghost town was inhabited, fit-tingly enough, by a skeleton crew, not due to come in for another five hours.

On this side of the road, almost due east, the federal prison camp, attached to Nellis Air Force base, could be made out by way of its illuminated perimeter, lights snaking a trail up and down the foothills almost a mile away from where Grissom stood. To the south of that, the Air Force base slept on, or at least no sign had pre-sented itself yet to indicate anyone on those premises had noticed the cop parade taking place just beyond their backyard.

That didn't mean the Fibbies wouldn't be poking their noses into a death so close to their doorstep—but for now, Grissom and his team had the scene to them-selves.

Jumping down from the back seat on shaky legs, a pale Sara Sidle glared at Grissom in the darkness. Though this was supposedly spring, a cold snap had steam pluming from their lips. Not saying a word, Sara turned toward the rear of the SUV where their gear was stowed.

"Up for driving on the way back?" Grissom asked, conversationally.

"Oooh yeah," she said, rolling her eyes.

Two prowl cars blocked the road on either side of the crime scene. The CSIs had already passed another patrol car at Craig Road, the first major intersection south of here, where an officer was diverting all northbound traffic west onto Craig. Grissom knew another officer would be stationed to the north at the mile-marker 58 interchange on Interstate 15, an officer whose job would be to divert the few cars heading toward Las Vegas Boulevard back onto the freeway and to the Craig Road exit to the south.

Besides the diagonally parked patrol cars, two more vehicles sat on the shoulder (Warrick had pulled the Tahoe in behind them). Immediately in front of the CSI vehicle was Captain Jim Brass's tired Taurus; beyond that was a dark-colored Toyota Corolla, which Grissom—tugging on latex gloves—couldn't see very well in the gloom. Bathed in purple light, Brass, a uniformed office and another man stood in the middle of the road near the front of the Corolla and Grissom strode toward them, as Sara and Warrick—crime-scene kits in hand—moved on up ahead.

The detective nodded to a citizen whose back was to Grissom—apparently the driver of the Corolla. Grissom was still out of earshot when the driver spoke again as Brass quietly listened, though his sad eyes spoke volumes.

As the CSI broke the circle and exchanged nods

with a uniformed officer, the detective was jotting something in his notebook.

When Brass looked up and saw the CSI boss, he said, "Mr. Benson, this is crime lab supervisor Grissom. Gil, this is David Benson."

The man extended his hand, but Grissom already had his latex gloves on, and shook his head while raising ghostly hands as if in surrender.

The witness looked innocuous enough—tall and thin with a reddish blond brush cut; he was nervous but not anxious. His ears stuck out a little, leaving plenty of room for the stems of his black plastic glasses, the lenses thin and possibly tinted a little, hard for Grissom to tell in the lights of the patrol cars and headlights.

Grissom dragged out the preliminary smile he bestowed on witnesses—it was generally as far as he'd go toward loosening them up—and said, "Mr. Benson, could you tell me what happened here?"

Benson, with an expression that said he'd just finished doing that with Brass, looked toward the detective for relief.

But Brass only said, "Please tell Dr. Grissom what you told me."

"All of it?"

Grissom flinched another smile, mildly impatient. "Just the highlights won't do, Mr. Benson. All of it, please."

Sighing, Benson looked down at the road for a moment, gathered himself, then his eyes met Grissom's in the swirling purple smear of lights from the vehicles. He pointed up the road, his hand trembling a little. "It started with me noticing a car, up there."

Grissom remained silent, but offered a nod of encouragement.

"Tell him what kind of car," Brass said.

Benson frowned in a mild mix of confusion and irritation. "Well, I already told you. Couldn't you have told him, as easy as asking me to, again?"

Brass sighed a small cloud, and said, "But I'm not the witness, Mr. Benson. You're the witness."

"Oh. I'm sorry. I just . . . nothing like this ever happened to me, before."

"Nothing like this happened to the victim before, either," Grissom said with an insincere smile. "So why don't you continue?"

"It was a white Chevy . . . Monte Carlo, I think."

"What was the car doing?"

"Doing?"

"What was it doing that attracted your attention? Was it weaving, was it speeding, was it going unusually slow . . ."

"Unusually slow! It's like I told Captain Brass, I wouldn't have noticed a thing, except the guy was kind of creeping along, hugging the shoulder. . . . Made me think maybe he was having car trouble, and might need help. But he could've been looking for something . . . like a turnoff, or something on the side of the road."

"Was he maintaining a steady slow speed?"

"I don't understand . . ."

"Did he slow down, then pick it back up again, then slow again, or—"

"Yes! Like that. And then, finally, he slowed all the way to a stop, and got out of his car."

"Were you right behind him?"

"No! He was way up ahead, and I slowed down my-self, when I was trying to tell if he needed help . . . but I kind of kept my distance, figuring I oughta do that for a while—I mean, there's all kinds of weirdos around. Somebody can seem to be in trouble, then you stop and get robbed or killed or something. It's a dangerous world to be a Good Samaritan in, don't you think?"

"It is indeed," Grissom granted. "So when he stopped, what did you do?"

"I stopped, too. I cut my lights. I . . . I can't exactly explain it, but I got a . . . creepy feeling. Like some-thing was wrong. I was just trying to get a handle on what was going on, you know?"

"Yes."

"So, anyway, like I said, I stopped too, killed my lights, and stayed back where he couldn't see me. I watched him get out, open the trunk, and pull out that . . . that *thing*."

With a shudder, the witness pointed up the road again, this time at something on the shoulder, a dark wrapped-up apparent corpse, near where Warrick and Sara were already at work, Sara snapping photos, the flash making tiny lightning in the night. Almost out of sight, beyond the parked cars, Warrick was bent down, probably searching for footprints. *It all comes down to shoe prints* was Warrick's byword, and Grissom could not disagree.

"And then?" Brass prompted.

Benson tucked his shaking hands into his pockets. "Then I watched him dump the . . . package, dump it on the side of the road, and I just knew right away that it was a body. I don't think I've ever been so scared—it was like all the blood left my body."

"What did you see that made you think it was a body?" Grissom asked.

"It wasn't the . . . the package itself, though the shape kinda suggested as much, but more how he acted. The guy moved kind of . . . funny, you know, on the way back to the car, like he was trying to wipe out his footprints or something . . . with the side of his shoe? Then the guy slammed the trunk lid, hustled back in the car and split. He wasn't goin' slow *then!*"

"And where were you while this was going on?" Grissom asked.

Benson turned and pointed toward the other side of the road. "You know where Hollywood Boulevard runs south of the track?"

"I do."

"I'd come across from the interstate."

"I thought that access was blocked at night," Grissom said. "Locked up."

The CSI knew that, while a public street, Hollywood Boulevard ran inside the fence line of Las Vegas Motor Speedway, and metal gates were in place to be dragged across, effectively shutting it down. The LVMS staff did that every night, or at least such was Grissom's understanding.

Brass answered the CSI's question. "Some days yes, some days no—mostly no."

Turning back to Benson, Grissom said, "If you don't mind my asking, what were you doing out here in the middle of the night?"

"Am I in trouble? Am I like a *suspect* or something?"

Grissom did his best to make his smile friendly. "Mr. Benson, the first witness is always the first suspect. That's why we have to ask you so many questions."

"But it's just routine," Brass interjected, giving Grissom a look.

"The deal is," Benson said, "I can't sleep."

"Just tonight?" Grissom asked. "Or is insomnia a problem for you?"

"It's a problem. I take medication. But if it doesn't work, I don't dare take more, I'll get sick. Sometimes I take a drive to help me relax. It's usually pretty quiet out here. And it's kind of . . . beautiful, in a funny kind of way, sort of like you're on another planet. It's sort of . . . What's the word I'm lookin' for?"

"Austere?" Grissom suggested.

"I don't know that word. But it sounds right."

"Where do you live, Mr. Benson?"

"Forty-six-forty-two Roby Grey Way."

Grissom knew that neighborhood—middle-class two-story homes not too far west of here, just off Craig.

The CSI asked, "If you thought the other driver might be having car trouble, why did you hang back when he stopped?"

"Like I said before, I know that in this city, everything is not always what it seems. You get to know that right away, in my business."

"And your business is?"

"I sell surveillance video equipment—I know the kinds of things that some people will pull. And I have a certain police-type, security-oriented way of looking at things. I remember reading literature where a gang faked car trouble and then when someone would stop to help them, the gang beat them up and robbed them. I didn't want to be on the end of that kind of thing."

"No one does," Grissom said. "Can you describe the man?"

The witness glanced at Brass—again, they'd been over this ground, obviously. Brass said, "It doesn't hurt to go through these details several times. I'll listen carefully, Mr. Benson, and jot anything new you might think of."

Benson nodded, drew a deep breath, and started in. "He was tall—probably taller than any of us. And he was Caucasian. You know—white?"

Grissom, considering that a rhetorical question, merely stared at the bespectacled Benson.

Who went on: "He was kind of skinny, I'd say— one-twenty-five, one-fifty maybe."

"What about his clothing?" Grissom asked.

Benson shook his head. "At night like this, about all I can say is . . . dark clothes. Really all I could tell from this distance."

"Was he in coat or jacket?"

"No. His arms were bare."

"Was it a T-shirt, or a shirt with sleeves?"

"I couldn't say."

"Hair color?"

Shrugging, Benson said, "Dark hair, I guess. Again, from this distance . . ."

Grissom nodded.

"I did ease forward," Benson added, "when he got back in the car, but all I got was a partial plate number. Will that do any good?"

Grissom's gaze went from Benson to Brass, who held up his notebook to show he already had it, and the CSI's eyes returned to and settled on the witness. "Nice job, Mr. Benson."

"Oh, and his right taillight was broken too."

"Good. Anything else distinctive about the car?"

"No. Not really. I wish I was of more help."

"You've been very helpful," Grissom said, sincerely. "We're fortunate to have a witness with your security background."

Benson broke out in a grin. "Well, thanks!"

Brass led the man back toward the Corolla.

Grissom stood shaking his head, as he watched the two men walk away. What was the old saying? "A good man is hard to find." A good woman, too, for that matter. . . .

But a good witness? Endlessly harder . . . yet, for once, Grissom seemed to be on the short list of the lucky in Vegas. Despite mild and understandable nerves, Benson appeared sure of what he'd seen and that could prove very helpful in court.

What would be even more helpful, though, was evidence; even a reliable eyewitness was a human being, after all, and Gil Grissom preferred not to count on human beings.

He moved up the road to check on Sara and Warrick. They were both standing over the bundle on the side of the road now, and—engine noise attracting his attention, as he walked to join his colleagues— Grissom turned to see Benson's Corolla making a U-turn and heading back south on Las Vegas Boulevard.

As he approached, the criminalist recognized the

sickly sweet stench of death, of decay; but even on the breeze, it didn't seem as overwhelming as one might expect, given its pungency.

Grissom looked from Sara to Warrick, finding no clues in their business-like expressions. He was putting on his wire-frame glasses as he said, "So. What have we got?"

"Well, it's definitely a body," Sara said, shining her flashlight down on a piece of carpeting about six feet in length and rolled three or four times around something; then, with duct tape, the whole bundle had been sealed once around the middle and around each end.

Sara gave Grissom a quick tour of the corpse, using the flashlight like an usher leading him to a theater seat. He could see at one end of the enchilada-like shape the dark hair of the top of a human head, and at the other bare feet, white but for heels blue with lividity.

"Smell is minimized," Sara said, "because this package is fairly well-wrapped . . . but that's not the whiff of somebody who died a few hours ago."

"Not hardly," Warrick said, with a quick lift of the eyebrows.

"Possibly a female," Grissom offered.

"From the small feet," Sara said, "I would say so, yeah. Could be a child, but not a young one—this body is over five feet tall."

Grissom nodded his curt approval of her assessment, then said, "All right. What else have we accomplished?"

"Photographed from every angle," Sara said.

Warrick added, "I've got some prints marked. I'll cast them as soon as we're done here." He pointed and

Grissom followed the gesture. "Piece of red plastic up on the road."

"Taillight, maybe?"

Warrick nodded. "Taillight, maybe."

Again Grissom nodded his satisfaction. "Could be a nice find. Our witness mentioned the dump vehicle had a broken tail."

"Dumper broke it, trying to unload the body?" Sara wondered aloud.

"Possibility."

Warrick squinted at Grissom. "You seeing it, Gris?"

"I'm seeing a possibility," he said, and told them.

A white Chevrolet Monte Carlo pulls to a stop in the northbound lane of Las Vegas Boulevard. It's dark and no one appears to be around. A driver in dark clothes climbs out of the car, looks around, sees nothing, then hurries around to the trunk, struggles with the rolled-up bundle inside and finally hefts it out. As he does, the bundle strikes the corner of the taillight, breaking out a small piece of plastic that falls unseen to the pavement.

Also unseen by the driver: Benson's Corolla, sitting up the road in the darkness, the surveillance-camera salesman surveiling every move the man makes.

The driver carries the rug and corpse to the side of the road, moves a few feet onto the dusty shoulder, his footprints clear in the dirt as he does, and he dumps the body to the ground. As he returns to the car, he sees his tracks and blots out some of the prints, but it's dark and he doesn't completely erase them all.

Then the driver slams the trunk lid, takes a quick look around and sees nothing; he climbs into his car and drives away.

Looking back down at the wrapped package, Grissom asked Sara, "You were about to unroll it?"

"Well, yeah," Sara said. Now she was squinting at her boss, detecting something in his voice. "Shouldn't we?"

"Let's do that back at the lab."

"You sure, Gris?" Warrick asked. "Once we remove this from the crime scene, we—"

"We've got photos, right?"

The two looked at each other, shrugged, then both nodded.

"Okay." He cast a smile on the younger CSIs, so they could tell he wasn't displeased. "I prefer to open this particular package in as clean an environment as we can get . . . and that means the lab."

"Not the side of a road," Warrick said, nodding, seeming vaguely irritated with himself that he hadn't come to the same conclusion.

Sara hadn't made the jump yet, it seemed, as she said, "You sure don't want to have a look now?"

He shook his head. "I bet you could never wait for Christmas morning. We'll do it at the lab."

Now Sara was nodding. A few moments later, the ambulance crew ambled up: two men, one short and thin, the other tall and thin, dressed in their blue uniforms; they took positions alongside the edge of the road and impatience came off them like heat over asphalt.

After a while, the short one asked, "How long you guys going to be?"

Grissom turned, looked at the man with a withering expression Medusa might have envied. "Well, the 'guys' and I—which is to say these criminalists—will be here as long as we need to be."

The short one shot him a defensive look, but swallowed nervously, saying nothing.

"But as long as you're here," Grissom said, suddenly cheerful, "you can help."

The tall one gulped and asked, "How?"

"Get us a clean sheet—the biggest one you've got. And a new body bag."

"Not the gurney?" the short one asked.

"Not yet," Grissom said. He held up one finger. "A sheet . . ." He held up another finger. ". . . and a new body bag. *New.*"

They shuffled off to their ambulance, and a couple of minutes later returned with a huge white sheet and, atop a gurney they'd hauled over, a body bag, which they brought to the edge of the road.

"Okay, gentlemen," Grissom said. "Let's lay out the sheet, and then oh so carefully rest our package on top of it."

Frowning, the short one asked, "We're taking the whole thing?"

"Yes. We'll load it up and take it back to the lab."

"Carpet and all?"

Grissom's expression was only technically a smile. "When one says 'whole thing,' that would indicate carpet and all, yes. Is there a problem?"

"That thing could really mess up our . . ." After trailing off, the short one glanced over at the body bag.

Grissom frowned. "That's not a new one, is it?"

"Well, it's the newest one we've got," the tall one said.

Despite what people might assume, body bags were not a one-time-use article. The truth was they simply cost too much. Grissom, however, had requested a pristine one because he didn't want to have to worry about any cross-contamination.

True, body bags were cleaned thoroughly after every grim use; but for his evidence to stand up in court, Grissom knew he needed a brand-new bag.

"Warrick," he said, at last.

"Papa needs a brand new bag?"

"I don't care what anybody says," Grissom said, flicking a little grin at Warrick. "*You're* the hardest-working man in show business . . . and you're going to prove it by heading over to Nellis and tell them what we need."

"And what we need is a brand-new body bag."

"Yes."

The Air Force base would have new bags. They had very little use for them here; but they had them on hand, just in case.

Sara gave Warrick a sunny if sarcasm-laced smile. "See—you get all the fun jobs."

"Greaaat," Warrick growled, like a depressed Tony the Tiger. "Haven't been on a scavenger hunt since grade school."

"Well, you do get to drive yourself," Grissom said, reminding him. "We'll stay here and work the scene."

Warrick grunted and strode over to the Tahoe.

Within an hour later, the piece of taillight plastic had been collected and bagged; dental stone was setting up in the footprints; and—with the ambulance crew hanging around and looking grumpy, but knowing enough now to stay away from Grissom—Warrick finally got back, a black body bag under his arm.

The purple of the red and blue of flashing lights had finally given way to the purple and pink smudging the horizon, courtesy of the morning sun, parting the darkness.

"What took so long?" Grissom asked.

"Hey, imagine the song I had to sing to sell them," Warrick said. "Starting with the guard at the entrance, then his supervisor, then the M.P.s, then the officer of the day, and the officer of the watch and God only knows how many more—I lost track. I'm lucky I'm not in the brig, or on my way to the Middle East."

"But is it a new bag?" Grissom asked, eagerly.

"Bran' spankin'. Doesn't take much to please you, does it, Gris?"

"I'm a simple soul," Grissom said, taking the body bag in his latex-gloved hands, while Warrick and Sara exchanged wide-eyed reactions to this remarkable statement.

Using the ambulance crew for assistance, the CSIs carefully laid the bundle inside the white sheet, wrapping it up as best they could; then they put the whole package into the body bag. The ambulance crew placed the body bag onto the gurney and rolled it back to their vehicle. Once loaded, they took off, the siren off now—no reason to rush with this patient.

While Warrick finished removing the casts of the partial footprints, Sara took more pictures, this time of the ground beneath where the carpet-wrapped body had been. Grissom spent the time surveying the area, looking for anything that might have come loose when they were moving the body. He found nothing, but that didn't worry him. He had evidence, lots of it, waiting back at the lab . . .

. . . and, for once, the killer had even been kind enough to gift-wrap it.

Dr. Al Robbins was waiting for them in the morgue. A good twenty to twenty-five degrees cooler than the rest of the labs, the morgue always gave Grissom both a feeling of calm and of purpose. Something about the change in temperature made the room seem more peaceful to him, the very crispness of the air inherently reassuring. The atmosphere seemed somehow . . . scientific. Here, Dr. Gil Grissom felt insulated from the chaos that brought him his "patients": the victims who needed him. This was the last place where Grissom saw most victims, in the flesh at least, so it became a place that filled him with a deep sense of purpose. A morgue was a kind of church to Grissom, the autopsy tray a sort of altar; but these victims were not to be worshipped, nor were they to be sacrificed. They had come here, albeit against their will, to ask him to do right by them.

To find justice for them.

And their killers.

The gurney bearing the body bag containing the carpet-wrapped corpse had been drawn up next to the metal table over which Doc Robbins spent most of his time. Grissom, Warrick and Sara had all pulled on blue lab coats and latex gloves. Robbins stood leaning against the table in his usual surgical scrubs, his metal crutch propped in a nearby corner.

"And what have you brought me today?" the coroner asked, his eyes on the body bag.

With the slightest twinkle of humor, Grissom asked, "Why, you didn't look inside?"

Robbins smiled. "Nope—just finished some reports and got in here myself. I found this waiting for me. I figured you wouldn't be too far behind."

"We don't know what it is ourselves, for sure," Grissom admitted, "other than a body that didn't die today." And then he proceeded to fill Doc Robbins in.

"So you've brought the crime scene to me, for a change," Robbins said, opening his eyes wide.

"A big part of it," Grissom said.

"I have to admit I find that somewhat . . . exciting."

"Why?"

"Why do you think our resident lab rat, Greg, is so eager to get out in the field? To be in on the discovery. To be part of the process from the beginning. The chance to be Sherlock Holmes, and not Doctor Watson. To have the feeling that you CSIs have when you find that crucial piece of evidence, on the scene."

Grissom shrugged a little. "You often find the crucial piece of evidence, right on the corpse. Or in it."

"True. But there's something about a crime scene that's inherently more exciting than the lab."

"I disagree. I find them equally stimulating."

Neither Grissom nor Robbins saw Warrick and Sara exchanging rolling-eyed glances at this exchange.

"Well," Robbins said. "Let's have a look."

Grissom stepped over to the bag and unzipped it. All that was visible through the opening was the white sheet. He spread the sides of the bag and

Warrick pitched in to help him slide the bag down over the sheet; then carefully, Grissom peeled back the sheet and revealed the carpeting, the package still sealed with duct tape.

"I don't suppose Cleopatra's in here," Robbins said.

"Let's see," Grissom said.

3

In Janice Denard's office, computer whiz Tomas Nunez sat at the desk while the assistant herself and Catherine Willows occupied two chairs against the wall. Nick Stokes hovered just behind Nunez, who was on his cell phone.

"Round up the whole crew," Nunez said into the phone. "Yeah, Webster and Wolf too—everybody but Bill Gates. This is gonna be a big one, my brother. Lemme tell when you get here—time is precious."

Listening again, Nunez spun toward Nick and seemed to glower at him, but it was intended for the party on the other end of the line. "No way!" the computer expert said, his voice louder, edgier. "That won't do at all. I need you all here an hour ago. Two words: kiddie porn."

This time the response seemed to please Nunez more and he almost smiled. "I knew you could make it happen." He ended the call and grinned up at Nick. "Cavalry's on the way. . . . Now, where's that sergeant of yours?"

"O'Riley's in the lobby with Mr. Newcombe," Catherine said.

A few minutes ago, the detective and Ian Newcombe had gone out to the lobby so the agency's co-owner could do his best to explain the situation to his staff. Janice Denard had stayed behind, and still seemed shaken. Catherine reached over and patted the woman's hand.

"I know you feel invaded," Catherine said. "Even violated. But that's part of what this is about—someone who violated this agency's trust. Someone working in this building who used your company's computers to do something that doesn't have anything to do with advertising."

"I know," Denard said, but the words didn't exactly ring with cognizance.

Of all the CSIs he might have been teamed with on this call, Nick was relieved, even glad, to have Catherine Willows at his side. When it came to crimes against children, Catherine had a definite mean streak . . . as did most cops, truth be told . . . but with her daughter Lindsey on her mind Catherine would, Nick knew, give every ounce of her skills, talent and energy to get a conviction on this one.

As would Nick.

The abuse Nick Stokes had suffered as a child was something he had dealt with. He knew the experience had played a role in his choosing law enforcement as a career; he knew, too, that he had a craving, even a need for justice exceeding the norm. Nonetheless, he prided himself on his professionalism and tried not to carry any remnants of the victim-getting-even syndrome into his work.

He was well aware, and in certain moments even relished, the opinion shared among many of his co-workers that, for all his sunny disposition, he was hardnosed and a workaholic; he knew, if they didn't, that he also strove to be fair and objective.

Still, there could be no question that his history made these cases more personal to him than the average crime, that such a case increased his thirst for justice to the level of crusade. That whoever was behind these wretched photos would not be allowed to walk. No way.

"What's next?" Nick asked. "I've never worked anything of this magnitude with computers."

"Oh, you're gonna love it," Nunez said dryly, and ran a hand over his face. He was half-standing, half-sitting on the edge of the desk. Then, after considering Nick's question for a few moments, he glanced over at Denard and gave her a quick smile that to Nick was not terribly convincing. Rather contrived, in fact.

"Despite what we've told your boss," Nunez said to the woman, "we'll do our level best to try not to shut down your business any longer than is absolutely necessary—that's why, just now, I called in all the troops. The more hands I have available to me, the better off you folks will be."

"Thank you for that," Denard said, earnestly.

"So," Nunez sighed, continuing, "the first thing we'll do is load all this stuff up, get it back to the lab and, fast as we can, start imaging it."

Denard frowned. "Imaging?"

"That's computer-nerd-speak for copying," Nunez

explained. "We'll copy all the hard drives and all the media in the building—floppies, CDs, DVDs, zip disks, everything. You use tape backup?"

"Yes."

"We'll need that too."

"You're . . . you're stripping us bare."

This choice of phrase seemed at once apt and ill-chosen to Nick.

"Yes we are, ma'am," Nunez said. "We'll get all of that stuff imaged, soon as we can, and then we'll give you copies too, so you can get your business up and running again."

"How can we do that without computers?"

"You may have to rent or lease some, for what should be a matter of days. That's strictly a business decision for you people to make."

"I'm not the boss of this place!"

"Nor am I. But I am the boss of the computers and all media 'of this place.' That's my job, and it's the law. No offense is meant, and I certainly don't relish causing a hardship to your business. Do you understand?"

The color seemed to have drained from Denard's face and Nick wondered if she was about to faint. "You'll give us copies. . . . What about the originals?"

Nunez folded his arms. "Those will be locked up in the police evidence room until this matter is resolved. When I start searching your equipment for the source of the illegal material, *I'll* be searching copies, too. The originals will be perfectly safe. Other than copying them, your property won't have any processing done—nothing will happen to it. It will be completely safe in our evidence lockup."

Denard was shaking her head now, disconsolate again, much as they had found her when they first arrived. Catherine tried a few more soothing words, but she didn't have much luck with the woman, and soon gave it up.

"Oh-kay," Nunez said, standing, turning his gaze from Denard to Nick. He clapped, once. "Let's start getting this equipment loaded up—the truck here yet?"

"I'll check," Nick said, moving toward the office door.

He wove through the maze of cubicles, making his way past the conference room to enter the long corridor that led back to the lobby; funny—the floor had been deserted when they'd entered, then was filled with workers starting their day, and now, not long after, was deserted again. Something eerie about it. It was as if the CSIs had the power to . . .

But Nick stopped the thought cold.

It wasn't the CSIs who had the power to stop the world, or even the police in general—it was crime. Criminals. The job of the police, and the CSIs, was to see to it that its reign was a brief one. . . .

Barely halfway down the hall, he could hear Ian Newcombe's voice carrying from the lobby, where the ad agency partner continued to address his personnel.

"I know it's irritating," he was saying, "and frustrating, but these police and crime scene people have a job to do, and we have to let them . . . and do anything we can to assist them."

"Are we in any danger?" a woman asked, toward the front.

"Physical danger? No. Not at all."

"Mr. Newcombe, may I ask a question?" a very professional-looking woman in front asked.

"Certainly," the executive said.

"Are we still getting paid?"

A tiny amount of nervous laughter rippled, but the faces were mostly grave.

"Yes," Newcombe said, and the wave of relief was palpable . . . and short-lived. Because the exec went on to say: "At least for the time being. We don't know how long this is going to go on . . . how long the authorities will take with this matter. Our computers are being seized. All of our software."

A ripple of discontent replaced the relief.

Newcombe raised a hand and silenced it. "We don't know the ramifications yet, but for now—for the short-term, yes. And please understand, it's to my selfish personal benefit to keep the best team in Vegas advertising on the payroll."

Relief again. Nick did not envy these employees their emotional roller coaster.

"We'll let you know when we're up and running again," Newcombe said, blandly summing up. He turned to O'Riley, and put him on the spot: "Detective, do you have any idea how long that will be?"

O'Riley shrugged; he was a good guy, but not Nick's pick for handling p.r. "I'll talk to the experts and get a better idea. But I can't tell you now."

Another negative roll of the emotional roller coaster, and Nick had had all he could take of it. He walked to the front door and stuck his head out to see a Ryder truck backing into the parking space next to the black Tahoe.

When the truck stopped, Nick watched the driver climb down and come around to the back of the vehicle where he opened the rear overhead door. Just as he did, a sky-blue Dodge van pulled into the lot and parked on the far side. Four men got out and strolled across the parking lot, making a total of five new people coming in, all of whom Nick assumed were answering Nunez's bat signal. One of the five, the driver of the Ryder, was a uniformed officer Nick recognized from swing shift—a tall blond guy named Giles. Another one, a passenger in the van, was an African-American FBI computer investigator, and now a connection finally made itself in Nick's mind: the guy's name was Carroll! They had worked one job together, first year Nick joined LVMPD CSI, albeit briefly, cop ships passing in the night.

Carroll wore jeans and a navy blue T-shirt with a large yellow FBI across the chest. Nick didn't know the other three, all of whom were dressed in T-shirts and jeans as well. But from recognizing the first two, he figured Nunez had already started calling in favors to get all the imaging done ASAP . . . whether that meant a week or just under a year, Nick had no idea.

"You the CSI on this?" Giles asked as he led the others inside.

"Nick Stokes," he said, nodding to the others. They paused and shook hands, all around; Nick was not, at the moment, in latex gloves. "There's two of us here— you'll meet Catherine Willows, soon. She's prettier than I am."

"Wouldn't be tough," Giles said good-naturedly. "Where's our guy Nunez?"

"I'll take you to him. You're going to be passing through some very unhappy campers."

None of them looked surprised.

The employees were still shuffling around in the lobby, most of them watching Nick and his squadron of computer investigators as they marched through. O'Riley waved Nick over and the tech group huddled just outside the corridor while the CSI and the detective had their own two-man huddle.

O'Riley said, "I'm callin' in some backup to help me interview these employees. If I don't, it'll take all day and they're already starting to look like a mob."

It occurred to Nick that O'Riley would make an excellent Frankenstein's monster for these angry villagers, but he nonetheless had to dampen the detective's notion, at least a little.

"That's a good idea," Nick said, "but we're gonna have to fingerprint them all before they go. And there's just me and Catherine."

O'Riley nodded. "How long you been on shift, anyway? Since last week?"

"It's going to be a full double shift."

"With all that overtime," O'Riley said, "I'll know who to come to for a loan. Mobley's gonna love you."

O'Riley meant Sheriff Mobley, whose hobby was cracking down on overtime; the police and of course the CSIs were under the sheriff's jurisdiction in Vegas.

Before long, Nick had escorted the makeshift computer squad to Janice Denard's office. When they gathered clumsily at the door, Nunez looked up and grinned. "Hey—the compu-posse!"

They trooped in and Nick went to Catherine's side.

Her eyes were wide; she hadn't expected so large a crew.

"You all know each other?" Nunez asked as he rose from Janice's desk and came around.

"I know Giles and Carroll," Nick said.

"You'll know everybody before we're through. Better than you want."

The computer expert made intros all around, starting with Webster, a tall, thin state trooper who seemed unable to stand still. The other two, Nunez explained, were freelancer buddies of his: Wolf, a short muscular guy whose name suited him; and Moes, a slightly overweight bemused middle-aged man who among the group looked closest to a stereotypical computer geek.

Nick and Catherine watched and listened as Nunez explained the situation to his volunteer team; neither CSI had any additions or corrections, and were impressed with Nunez's summary, since the man had followed them onto the scene.

He closed by saying, "It's Monday—best-case scenario, I want this company back open for business by Wednesday."

"What's the worst-case scenario?" Wolf asked.

"Thursday. . . . We can't punish this business for the perversity of one employee. That means we've got plenty of work to do and not much time to do it in, so let's get started."

Catherine stepped forward and offered a businesslike smile. "I'd like to thank you for helping out. And while you get on it, Nick and I'll start fingerprinting the employees."

Somewhat forgotten in her chair off against the

wall, Janice Denard piped up, in voice tinged with both outrage and resignation, "You can *do* that?"

Nick turned to her and said, pleasantly, "At this stage, it will be voluntary; but it's a good way to get yourself exonerated right away."

"I'm afraid I don't follow you."

Nick shrugged. "Sooner or later we'll find out which keyboard sent that print order to your boss's machine. When we do isolate the work station, we'll dust the keyboard for fingerprints. We *will* match those prints to someone, most likely someone who works in this facility . . . and then we'll be a lot closer to finding out who's guilty and who's innocent."

Denard said, "Well, you might let me pave the way by volunteering to go first."

Catherine said, "That's a nice gesture. We appreciate it. Anything you can do to keep the feathers unruffled around here would be helpful."

Denard managed a brave nod. "I'll try."

As Nick and Catherine set up fingerprinting shop, Tomas Nunez supervised the dismantling of Newcombe-Gold. This would be the most time-consuming part of the effort and, even with the extra help, would take hours. Nunez had already directed Leary to get a head start photographing each computer, all the peripherals and the wiring in the back, but even so, the uniformed officer still had plenty of pictures left to shoot when the team arrived.

Carroll and state patrolman Webster pitched in to help Leary. The plan was that when the photos were finally done, Nunez would personally disconnect each item, tag it, and hand it to one of his team, who would carry it out to the truck where Giles would catalogue and load each piece by hand. Catherine was just finishing fingerprinting Janice Denard, handing her a paper towel to wipe her hands, when O'Riley strolled into the room.

"I have three guys helping me now," O'Riley said. "We're maybe halfway through doing these preliminary interviews."

Catherine asked, "Have your questions alerted them to what's going on?"

"No. Of course they already know it had something to do with computers, and probably figured out we're not tryin' to figure out who's playin' computer solitaire on office time. And anyway, this thing isn't likely to stay hidden."

Denard said, "Well, *I* won't spread it around!"

Catherine smiled at the woman. "I'm sure you won't. But Sergeant O'Riley is right—it's unlikely to remain our little secret." She turned back to the detective. "Can you start sending them our way, for fingerprinting?"

"I'm glad to hear you say that," O'Riley said. The big man plopped into a chair, sighing, clearly exhausted. "Sooner we get these pissed-off people outa here, the happier I'll be. But telling 'em they got to stand around a while longer, while you get 'em fingerprinted, isn't going to make them love us more. How about one of you guys delivers that cheery news?"

Letting out a mirthless laugh, Catherine said, "I'm it." Then, clapping the detective on the shoulder, she added, "You can be my backup. Case somebody tries to kill me."

O'Riley gave her a look.

"It's not just a job, Sarge—it's an adventure."

Shaking his head, the detective hauled himself to his feet and followed her out.

While Catherine went to the lobby, Nick asked Janice Denard for a master employee list.

Nick explained, "We need to track who we have and haven't spoken to."

Denard rose to her feet; her eyebrows rose, too. "Take me a little while without the computer."

"I hear that," he said, giving her the sympathy she clearly craved.

In the lobby, Catherine was confronting the grumbling crowd, while off to various sides of the lobby, three detectives were pausing in the midst of interviews. After introducing herself, she said, "As you've gathered, we're looking for a suspect in a serious crime."

"*What* crime?" a voice yelled, echoing.

With a tight smile and a shake of the head, Catherine said, "I'm afraid I'm not at liberty to talk about it at this point; but here's the deal—in order to eliminate each of you as suspects as quickly as possible, we would like you to voluntarily submit to being fingerprinted."

"How about—*no*," a red-faced man said near the front of the crowd.

From behind him, another man suggested, "How about *hell* no!"

Catherine shrugged and remained low-key, even light. "There's another option. We can get court orders for each and every one of you, and that could take quite some time considering the number of people who work here. Then we'll just wait until the court orders arrive. Another possibility is releasing you now, and then you can come into the crime lab for finger-printing. Maybe you think that would make an inter-esting day trip."

"You don't have to be sarcastic," a woman snapped. "We're just trying to do our jobs."

"I know the feeling," Catherine said.

This seemed to make the point as well as anything.

"I'm going to ask a show of hands," Catherine went on. "Who is willing to be fingerprinted, without a court order?"

Gradually, all of the employees raised their hands, as if in half-hearted surrender.

They were in that posture when Nick came in car-rying their print kits and the employee list he had got-ten from Denard.

Nick said to Catherine, quietly, "Let's not drag them into the crime scene."

Catherine, nodding that this was a good idea, pointed toward the receptionist's desk and he nodded. Going down the list, they printed twenty-two employ-ees, while O'Riley and the three other detectives com-pleted their preliminary interviews. All the while, the employees and CSIs watched Nunez's guys hauling the very guts of their business outside to the waiting truck.

When Nick and Catherine finally finished up, they cornered Janice Denard one last time, in her office. Neither Catherine nor Nick confronted her about her lack of "paving the way" with the employees, re the fingerprinting. But the personal assistant clearly read displeasure on their faces, just the same.

"What's the problem?" Denard asked.

"I thought," Catherine said, "you told us twenty-seven people had computer access."

"That's right."

"We've got prints for twenty-two."

Nick said, "Mr. Gold is out of town—where are the other four?"

"Who are they?" Denard asked. "You must have their names, you cross-checked—"

Nodding, Nick read from the list, "Jermaine Allred, Ben Jackson, Gary Randle, and Roxanne Scott."

With a one-shoulder shrug, Denard said, "Well, for starters, Roxanne Scott is my counterpart."

"Counterpart, how?" Catherine asked.

"Ms. Scott is Mr. Newcombe's personal assistant and the assistant office manager. She just started her vacation today."

Catherine was frowning, partly in confusion. "Mr. Gold's gone, and Roxanne is gone? One partner and the other partner's personal assistant? Isn't that unusual? Doesn't that put the business at a disadvantage?"

"Not as much as having our computers hauled out of here," Denard said, somewhat acidly. Then, gathering herself, she calmly explained, "The two partners have different responsibilities, which I would say is typical, not at all odd."

"Go on."

"Mr. Gold works on the client side, Mr. Newcombe on the fiduciary side. With this arrangement, they don't both have to be here all the time, and they can nonetheless have an understanding of what the other is up to, which is key, since major company decisions are still made jointly."

"But Roxanne was here Saturday?" Catherine asked.

"Yes—her vacation started when she went home that day."

"Do you know where she is?"

Denard smiled, and it seemed vaguely strained. Was there, Nick wondered, a hint of jealousy in that near smirk?

"Roxanne and her beau," Denard said, somewhat archly, "went to Tahiti for the week. Frankly, I wish I could say the same. . . ."

"All right," Catherine said, finally processing all of that, sighing. "How about the other three?"

"Give me a few minutes to check on the others, will you? Without my computer—"

"Yes," Catherine said, a little sharply. "It will be difficult."

"Well it will."

And Janice Denard went briskly from the office.

Nick considered, briefly, making a cat growl, but thought better of it.

While the two CSIs waited for Denard to track down the three absent employees, they packed up their gear and walked through the empty office. The place really was like a big haunted house, empty even of its ghosts, all the employees having slowly filtered out to go home, as their fingerprinting obligation was fulfilled.

Now the place reminded Nick of some end-of-the-world movie, where vampires or zombies or mutants awaited around every corner. Like the empty streets of those B-movies of his adolescence, the Newcombe-Gold offices—stripped only of their computer equipment—were at once weirdly normal and strangely wrong, as if the human race had vanished from the planet overnight, though Nick was relatively sure no zombie waited around the next corner. Then he turned it and almost ran into O'Riley.

Nick jumped and the stocky detective gave him a quizzical look.

"What?" the detective asked.

Catherine was looking at Nick, amused.

"Sorry, Sarge, you just startled me," Nick said.

Wryly, Catherine noted, "He sometimes has that effect on people."

O'Riley made a little face—repartee was not his long suit—and fell in step with them and the trio made their way to the front door where Tomas Nunez watched the last of the computer equipment being loaded into the truck. Twenty-nine computers, thirty counting Newcombe's laptop, and all the zip disks, CDs, floppies and tape backups that Nunez could find, were piled into the back of the Ryder. It was a haul that came close to filling the rental truck.

"How goes it?" Nick asked.

"That's the load," Nunez said. He heaved a huge sigh; there'd been lots of sighing, today. "Now comes the hard part—we take all this stuff back to the lab and dig in. Wherever the perp has the stuff hidden, we'll find it."

"Good to hear," Catherine said, exhaustion in her voice.

Janice Denard walked out to join them in the parking lot. "I have the rest of the information you requested."

"Yes?" Catherine said.

"Ben Jackson left Friday to go out of town, and took a vacation day, today, for his return flight."

Squinting in sunlight, Catherine asked, "You know where he went?"

Denard held out two open, empty hands. "I think maybe he said something about Idaho—that's where he's from."

"And the others?"

"Jermaine Allred called in sick this morning."

"He didn't talk to you?"

She shook her head. "By the time he called, I was with you. Our receptionist, Debbie Westin, took the call."

"Jermaine told Debbie," Denard was saying, "he had the flu and expected to be in tomorrow."

Catherine nodded. "And the last one?"

"Gary Randle," Denard said. "He had a meeting with a client this morning."

Looking at his watch, Nick said, "He's not back? It's past three."

Denard shrugged. "Meeting could have run long— typical in the ad game. He could have gone for a late lunch, either with the client or by himself, or he could be on his way back."

"He doesn't have to check in?"

Another shrug. "Mr. Randle has been with the firm quite a long time—one of the top people. He has a certain amount of freedom, not unlike Mr. Newcombe or Mr. Gold."

"Is he a partner?" Catherine asked.

"No, but he has been a steady earner for the firm

for many years. No one questions the hours of a top earner."

"I can see that."

"You're welcome to wait," Janice said. "I'm sure he'll be in sometime this afternoon." Nick looked at Catherine, and Catherine looked at Nick.

They were both coming up hard on the end of a double shift, and had to be back in tonight. At this point, all Nick wanted to do was catch a sandwich and grab some snooze time; he hoped Catherine felt the same way.

Her expression said she did.

"I don't think we'll wait," Catherine said.

Nick hoped his sigh of relief went unnoticed.

Denard asked, "Are you posting an officer here?"

That was O'Riley's bailiwick, and he responded: "No. We've taken the evidence with us. You're free to go on about your regular business."

Denard just looked at him.

Then she said, "We'll be running a skeleton staff— even Mr. Newcombe has gone. I'll be here, and some of the janitorial staff."

Catherine asked, "These last three employees, can you give us their home addresses and phone numbers, please? We're at the end of our shift. We'll give them a call as soon as we can."

Denard handed Catherine a sheet of paper. Looking over her shoulder, Nick saw the vitals for the three missing employees.

"Nice," Nick said to her. "ESP?"

Smiling a little, Denard said, "You learn to anticipate. Comes with the job."

"Thank you," Catherine said. "This has been a

rough day for all of us. . . . I promise you, we'll follow this up as soon as we can."

The blonde's smile faded and Nick was shocked to see that tears were welling in the blue eyes. "This is a good place to work, good people, a good company—how could this happen?"

Nick wished he knew what to tell her, but he didn't. "It can happen anywhere," he said, a feeling of cold confidence running through him. "But whoever did this won't do it again—not here."

Catherine offered her hand and Denard took it, shook it, and the two CSIs headed for the Tahoe.

"I changed my mind," Catherine said.

"How so?" Nick said.

"I do want breakfast. You still willing to buy?"

"Sure. Sky's the limit. Denny's?"

4

IN THE MORGUE, WARRICK BROWN HELPED GRISSOM LOWER the carpeted package to the floor, after which Sara took more photos.

Warrick got what Doc Robbins was talking about, with his Sherlock Holmes speech, because the lanky CSI felt the same way. Every crime scene brought opportunities to outthink a bad guy, to outsmart a criminal. Justice was the goal, and you could express that in various high-flown ways; but the truth of the CSI game was that it *was*, in part, a game.

Though he'd never spoken these thoughts and feelings aloud, not even to another criminalist (and certainly not to Grissom), the rush Warrick felt when he chased down that crucial piece of evidence, putting some perp behind bars, was not unlike the euphoria he'd felt riding a hot streak, back in the days when gambling ruled his life. "As with every grand opening," Grissom said dryly, "start by cutting the tape."

After withdrawing a utility knife from his pocket, Warrick cut the three strands of duct tape. The enchilada-shaped bundle loosened and the sickly sweet scent of decay rose like foul if invisible smoke.

Sara and Warrick took a time-out to apply some vaporizing ointment around their nostrils, to cut the smell. Doc Robbins seemed immune at this point, and nobody even bothered to pass the jar of Vick's toward Grissom—Warrick knew Gris's attitude was that this was science, and smells told you things, and were just generally part of the deal.

Soon, Warrick, Grissom and Sara were each slowly peeling off a strand of tape, placing them in individual evidence bags for later examination. God only knew what kind of fibers or other evidence might be embedded in the adhesive and there might even be, if they got really lucky, a fingerprint somewhere. Ironically, the tape and carpeting would probably tell them more about the killer than the victim's body.

Warrick had to fight the urge to just unroll the damn thing, and quickly—an urge he knew Sara shared and probably, though the man would never admit it, Grissom, too—and see what grisly present the killer had left rolled inside the piece of carpeting. Doing that, however, could destroy valuable evidence; and that knowledge alone prompted Warrick to calm himself and take his time.

They unrolled the bulky bundle once, exposing a sixteen-inch-wide piece of carpeting. This was the time-consuming, tedious work that TV cops always seemed to get done during a commercial break. In reality, the process could take anywhere from one to several hours, depending on what they ran into.

When Warrick looked at the exposed piece, then at

what remained of the roll, he knew damn well they were going to accumulate some serious overtime on Cleopatra.

Sara took more photos as Grissom and Warrick went over the piece with their mini Maglites and tweezers. Robbins's part would come soon enough, but he hovered behind them, his gloved hands folded Buddha-like over his belly as he watched their every move, as if expecting them to yank the killer bodily out of the remnant.

Once they had gone over the section carefully, Warrick put a new bag in his hand-held vacuum and went over the section. When this process was finished, these bags would be sent to Trace for chemical analysis of their contents.

Before long they were unrolling a second section. Sara took pictures of the exposed piece from four different angles, then the three of them got down on their hands and knees, and went over the fabric practically fiber by fiber, just as they had the last one.

Warrick put another bag in the hand-held vacuum and went over this section. Finding nothing, they unrolled another sixteen-inch swath, and then another, and another. . . .

By the time they exposed the first piece of the corpse's flesh, Warrick's stomach was growling and they had piled up over two dozen evidence bags with hair, fibers, a penny and material that appeared to be crushed leaves.

Another hour of intensive work passed before they had the body free. It lay on the floor at their feet, the three of them looking down at it. The stench challenged the Vick's Vapo-Rub around Warrick's nostrils, and whether his growling stomach craved food or not, Warrick Brown just wasn't interested in eating, right now. . . .

"As we thought, female," Sara said. "Mid-to-late twenties?"

"That's how I call it," Warrick said, and Grissom nodded his agreement; then Warrick and his boss lifted the body onto the coroner's metal table. Utterly free, now, of her casing of carpet, Cleopatra emitted a sick perfume that seemed to engulf the whole room. Grissom sniffed at the air, like a dog seeking just the right spot.

Warrick wondered if Gris could actually estimate stage of decay by the degree of smell; but, that being a talent he had no wish to develop, Warrick did not seize the opportunity to ask.

Robbins bent over his new patient. "Some decomposition. She's been dead for a while."

Nude, the woman had matted black curly hair cut into a low-maintenance pageboy. Her face was still basically intact, although both jaws seemed to have been broken post-mortem, and were now offset by at least three inches, the flesh around her mouth having begun to tear away.

Her eyes were closed; her face, composed and peaceful. But a bizarre aspect struck them all: she wore too much makeup, almost clownishly so—crimson lipstick, an abundance of rouge, mascara nearly dripping from her eyelashes. Applied way too heavily, and carelessly, and perhaps hastily.

Was the makeup post-mortem, too? It seemed . . . fresh.

"Area around her right eye," Sara said, clinically, "swollen . . . heavy makeup layered over the welt can't disguise the fact she's been punched in the face."

"Good," Grissom said, as if to a student.

But then, they were all students of Grissom's.

"She was beautiful once," Grissom said.

Sara looked up, almost shocked. "That's not very . . . scientific."

"Beauty is a subjective thing," Grissom admitted, staring down at the face. Was that sadness in his eyes? "But by the standards of our culture . . . even with the damage, the camouflaging, perhaps ritualistic make-up . . . this was a beautiful young woman."

Warrick could only agree. The woman's olive skin had gone drab and gray, but in her long straight nose and wide full lips, the shadow of the beauty that had been seemed obvious to Warrick.

Gently thumbing open her eyelids, Robbins revealed large, lifeless brown eyes that Warrick imagined might well have sparkled with life . . . before her death.

"Petechial hemorrhaging," Grissom said.

Robbins nodded, studying his patient. "Sign of asphyxia."

"The welt tells us she was punched before she died—question is, how long?"

Robbins shrugged facially. "We'll know when I've finished the autopsy."

Her skin was a mottled gray, blue and white mess that would indeed tell them a long, detailed story about her death, once Robbins completed his work. Her torso and limbs seemed to be in relatively good shape, but for a dark necklace of torn flesh that suggested the cause of death—strangulation—and something, in its own way, even more disturbing. A vicious tearing of the flesh around her vagina, coupled with the broken jaws, gave Warrick an unsettling notion of what this body had endured after the murder.

Sara's eyes were tight, but if the horror before them, and all it suggested, had shaken her, she was not letting it show. Clinical, professional, she was the first to say it.

"Necrophilia?"

Grissom nodded.

Sara bent to study the victim's face—specifically, the broken jaws causing the bottom half to be offset; this, with the swollen eye and garish makeup, gave Cleo a slightly surreal appearance.

"My turn," Sara said. "For an unscientific observation."

"What?" Grissom asked.

"Something familiar about her," Sara said, cocking her head a little. "It's hard to look past the makeup and the distortions caused by beating and death, but . . . I'd swear I know this woman from somewhere."

Warrick and Grissom both took a closer look too; they had been looking at a corpse, and now they looked at the person, trying to see through the destruction and obscene face paint.

"Yeeaaah," Warrick said. "I do feel like I've seen her somewhere before. Damn! What is it that's so familiar about her?"

Gil Grissom felt a cold burn settle in his stomach; he recognized this woman.

"Meet Candace Lewis," Grissom said.

The two young CSIs looked at him with wide eyes. Then they looked down at the autopsy tray.

Warrick was first to find his voice. "Oh, shit. . . ."

Sara was studying the face through narrowed eyes. "You think this is Mayor Harrison's personal assistant? I don't know about that. . . ." But Sara kept looking, then finally she said, "No," but it wasn't a disagreement. "No, no, you're right. Yeah, I see it, guys. It *is* her."

This, Grissom thought, *was all they needed right now. . . .*

In the three weeks since Candace Lewis's disappearance, the young woman—previously all but unknown to the media—had garnered more Vegas coverage than Danny Gans, Clint Holmes and Siegfried & Roy combined.

The twenty-eight-year-old brunette, personal assistant of Mayor Darryl Harrison, had attended a political dinner not long after the first of the month; and then, on her way home that evening, she had fallen off the planet.

Her car, a three-year-old Lexus, had been found in the driveway of her townhouse within a gated community near the intersection of Green Valley and Wigwam Parkways. Fingerprints in the car matched Candace's and Mayor Harrison's prints were found on the passenger doorhandle and seatbelt; but no one else's prints were found anywhere in or on the vehicle.

Given the arid nature of Vegas, Grissom hadn't been that surprised that no other prints had been found. Fingerprints exposed to the weather didn't last long here; and even those protected by being inside the car and under a carport didn't have a terribly long lifespan.

For his part, Mayor Harrison explained his fingerprints in Candace's car by saying, "On the day she disappeared, we went to lunch together . . . and that was the only time I ever rode in her car."

The mayor's story had been backed up by Jill Ganine, a KLAS reporter with a nose for news and the teeth to hang onto a story. She arrived at CSI HQ with a videotape shot by her cameraman that showed Mayor Harrison climbing out of Candace's Lexus on the day in question. But almost from the moment the tape had aired, tongues had wagged around the city that the "lunch" was actually a euphemism for something else altogether. So, whether the tape had exonerated Harrison, or merely suggested a motive for him, was still an open question. To Gil Grissom, anyway.

Most of the media though—KLAS and Jill Ganine excepted, their take on the story having been established at the outset—did not have Grissom's open mind or need for proof.

Mayor Harrison had been vilified for the alleged affair, particularly in the newspapers; and of course the political and sexual aspects of the case, added to the glitzy Vegas backdrop, caught the attention of the national media. In a matter of a few weeks, a promising political career—the result of years of hard work and meticulous grooming—had been reduced to a talkshow joke.

"How deep are we standing in it?" Warrick asked.

"I don't think science has come up with that measuring tool as yet," Grissom said, mock-pleasant.

Sara said, "So it's a media crime. How does that affect us? Can't we just fly in under the radar? Doesn't it help that we're night shift?"

"Well, let's take it point by point," Grissom said.

He held up one finger.

"Until just now," he said, "Candace Lewis was a missing person, and a probable kidnapping, with the investigation under the jurisdiction of the FBI; and now she'll be ours again."

"Isn't that a good thing?" Sara asked.

He answered by holding up a second finger.

And saying, "Let's not forget that we picked up the body at the doorstep of a federal installation, in a high-profile political case. So, maybe the FBI isn't out of our hair just yet."

"Not a good thing," Sara admitted.

Grissom ticked off a third finger. "The late Ms. Lewis is the personal assistant to the mayor and, rumor has it, his lover."

A fourth finger came up.

"Not to mention," he continued, "that Mayor Harrison's chief political rival right now happens to be the man likely to run against him in the upcoming election. . . ."

"Unnnggggh," Sara said.

Warrick had the glazed expression of a caught carp. ". . . Our boss."

"Our boss," Grissom said amiably. "Sheriff Brian Mobley."

Captain Jim Brass chose this moment to come walking into the morgue, and noticed Grissom's up-raised hand with four fingers raised. With a smirky little smile, the detective said, "What you cipherin' there, Jethro?"

The pop culture reference didn't penetrate Grissom's concentration, and he motioned with that up-raised hand, in a presentational manner, to the body. Brass's eyes followed the CSI's gesture.

"If I may," Grissom said, "Jim Brass—meet Candace Lewis."

"Holy shit," Brass said, his normally sleepy eyes wide awake, whites showing all around. "Does the press know?"

Shaking his head, Grissom said, "We just now I.D.ed her. We won't make an official identification until we check her prints."

Brass was at the edge of the tray, looking down at the garishly made-up corpse. "Oh, that's her, all right. Hell." He cast his mournful gaze on Grissom. "You and I better go see Mobley, my friend—this is gonna get *real* ugly."

Grissom grimaced, not relishing the notion. "Do I need to go? Isn't that more . . . administrative?"

The cliché most people fell back on to describe Grissom and Sheriff Mobley was oil and water; the CSI supervisor himself viewed their relationship as more along the lines of gasoline and a lit match. It wasn't so much that Grissom didn't like Mobley—he didn't really have enough regard for the man for that to be an issue.

Despite all the blustering about law and order during his campaign, Brian Mobley was a politician first and a sheriff second; and Grissom disliked politics intensely. The constant battles over the CSI budget had been so bitter that Grissom had even considered resigning the supervisor's post so he could concentrate on the science; but in the end, he'd stayed on when he realized that if he didn't fight the budgetary constraints, no one would.

Only the high success ratio of arrests-to-convictions—they were rated number two crime lab in the nation—had helped convince Mobley (and other politicians) to keep the money flowing. With tourism the primary industry, keeping Vegas safe was a priority; this, added to the CSI success rate, enabled the lab to tap into the top technology in the field. But it also meant Gil Grissom had to deal with Brian Mobley far more often than he cared to.

"We're both going to have to deal with Mobley," Brass was saying, "throughout this mess—so I'd advise you to come. I can't force you."

"Let's get it over with, then," Grissom said. Turning to Sara and Warrick, he said, "Start working the evidence—I'll be back when I can."

"Fingerprinting first?" Warrick asked.

"Yes—and let me know for sure this is Candace. I know, I know . . . it's her. But let me know when it's *officially* her. For one thing, we'll have a family to notify."

A sober moment followed this observation.

Then Grissom said, "DNA can wait. All right?"

"All right," Sara said.

Warrick merely nodded, already gathering the evidence bags.

Stepping up to the tray, Robbins said to Grissom, "I'll page you if I get something significant during the autopsy."

"Thanks, Doc," the CSI supervisor said.

Then Brass and Grissom were walking down the hall, the former calling Mobley's cell phone.

"Brian," Brass said, "take my word for it, it's important. And it's not something you want broadcast over an unsecure line. . . . Okay. Fifteen minutes is fine. . . . No, Grissom's office. . . . That's right, Grissom's office."

Career politician though he was, Sheriff Brian Mobley was also a man of his word, and the kind of man who took matters of time seriously, one of the few things Grissom liked about him. Accordingly, Mobley walked into Grissom's office exactly fifteen minutes later.

Grissom felt at home in his office, much the way an animal might in its den or nest. He was wholly unaware that to others his office seemed uncharacteristically cluttered, even chaotic, for such a serious man of science, much less an individual charged with the duties of a manager.

Gray metal shelves lined the walls to the right and left of the door, home to two-headed pigs, various arcane experiments, books and periodicals from various centuries. His desk perched in the middle of the room, arrayed (or perhaps disarrayed) with piles of paper, a phone and an art deco lamp. More shelves, cubbyholes and other equipment consumed the back wall. The front section of the large room housed a small work area with a modest quantity of lab equipment.

When Mobley entered, Grissom was seated behind his desk, while Brass stood off to one side, careful not to lean against any of the jarred samples on the shelves. Whether the detective did this out of respect for Grissom's quarters, or out of fear that something might grab him, Grissom could not venture a guess.

Mobley positioned himself in front of the desk, fac-

ing Brass. The sheriff's aide and campaign manager—
Ed Anthony, a short, pudgy individual for whom the
term "toady" might well have been coined—tagged
along in the sheriff's wake like a remora hanging on
for dear life.

"I don't like having my chain pulled, Jim," Mobley
said tightly. "I have a lot on my plate right now."

Twinkies and Big Macs, most likely, Grissom thought.

At Mobley's side, Anthony said, witheringly, "The
sheriff doesn't have time for any of your fun and
games, Captain." The aide had a flat face except for a
sharp-beaked nose, thinning dark hair and shiny
blackbird eyes.

"Just what is so goddamned important?" Mobley
demanded, continuing to ignore his host behind the
desk.

Without a word, Brass took a photo from his inside
sportscoat pocket and handed it to Mobley, as if serv-
ing a summons.

The sheriff studied the picture—a Polaroid Sara had
shot of their Cleopatra, on the morgue tray—while
Anthony peeked around his boss's shoulder for a
glimpse.

But neither seemed to recognize the woman whose
face had graced the front page of both the *Sun* and the
Review-Journal for the better part of the last twenty days.
Of course, Grissom thought, *she didn't look* exactly *like this,
when she was alive, and applying her own makeup. . . .*

Brass waited for several long moments and, finally,
when Mobley looked up in wordless confusion, Brass
said, "Straight from the morgue, Sheriff. . . . Candace
Lewis."

"Oh my God," Mobley said hollowly, glancing back at the face.

Anthony seemed hypnotized by the picture; his eyes were huge. "Hell. . . ."

Nodding, Brass said, "That pretty much sums it up."

The aide took a sudden step forward. "And what's the meaning of summoning the sheriff to CSI about this?" Anthony demanded.

Brass answered, but directed it to Mobley: "To give you a heads up, Sheriff, and a head start. I thought this better dealt with on our turf." To both of them, Brass said, "The press will have this before the end of business, today . . . much sooner, probably . . . and you're going to have to respond in some way."

Mobley nodded. "Thanks, Jim," he said softly, sincerely. "We'll start working on a statement right away."

"Brian," Brass said, his voice remarkably gentle considering all the contention that had existed between these two, "you do know that you'll have to recuse yourself from the case. You might want to do that right now, at the outset."

Anthony took a step forward and stopped when he realized he had nowhere else to go, an angry terrier on a short leash. "Why the hell should he recuse himself? It's a major case, under his aegis!"

Moments before, the campaign manager had wanted to know why they were bothering the sheriff with this triviality.

"*Why?*" Brass snapped. "Jesus, man, what the hell kind of advisor are you? Why would you even need to ask that question? He's running against Harrison for mayor!"

"We haven't announced as yet," Anthony said, defensive.

Brass shot the little man a look that should have shut him up.

Instead, puffing up, the aide said, "That's *exactly* why he should stay on the case, and spearhead the investigation! The sheriff can demonstrate that he's the one man in Las Vegas who can keep the city safe."

To his credit, Mobley was having none of it; he was, in fact, shaking his head and patting the air, trying to slow down his overly aggressive aide.

"Why, you can't *buy* this kind of publicity!" Anthony crowed.

Speaking for the first time since Mobley entered, Grissom said, "And you wouldn't want to."

All eyes turned toward the criminalist, as he rose and stepped from around the desk; he edged past the mayor and stood at Brass's side.

"With all due respect, Mr. Anthony," Grissom said, "your advice to your candidate couldn't be more inappropriate."

The political hack seemed to notice for the first time Grissom's presence in his own office. "I . . . *know* . . . you," he rumbled. "You've caused us trouble before!"

Grissom's smile was tiny, if large with condescension. "There are two reasons why your plan won't work."

"Which are?"

"Number one: your client, the sheriff." Grissom nodded toward Mobley, who also seemed only to have recently noticed the CSI's presence. "He has something to gain by this woman's death—the embarrassment and perhaps downfall of his opponent in the mayoral race—so there's no way he can work the case."

Anthony said, "I said we haven't announced yet, and anyway, we can find a work-around. . . ."

Grissom's eyes met Mobley's; Mobley's met Grissom's.

"Be quiet, Ed," the sheriff said, resigned, clearly accepting what Grissom had already said and probably knowing what was coming next.

"And two," the CSI supervisor said, "because the sheriff has something to gain, that also makes him a suspect."

Anthony started to puff up again, but Mobley held up a hand, like a traffic cop. "The man's right, Ed."

"A suspect!" the aide snorted. Then he blustered: "The sheriff can't be a suspect. . . . You can't be a suspect, Sheriff. . . ."

Mobley faced his campaign manager. "Ed, here are your options: either shut the hell up, or go wait in the car."

Stunned, Anthony took a step backward.

The sheriff's attention turned completely to Grissom. "Gil, you and Jim will have complete autonomy in this investigation. Every asset of the LVMPD is at your disposal." He turned to Brass. "I can put that in writing, if you consider it advisable."

A syllable that might have been "no" escaped from Anthony.

Brass said, "Since that's not our standard procedure, I don't believe it's necessary. But if you anticipate elements within the department who might want to work against you . . . well, then maybe you should repeat what you just said to us, in your public statement."

Eyes narrowed, Mobley nodded. "I like that."

Bored with politics, Grissom said, "We need to talk DNA."

"You've got DNA already?" Mobley asked, surprised.

"Not yet." Grissom held out a swab. "But wouldn't you like to be eliminated as a suspect as soon as possible?"

Mobley opened his mouth, perhaps to comply, but Grissom seized the moment and took the swab.

The CSI bestowed the sheriff a small smile. "Thank you, Brian."

Anthony, apparently not able to contain himself further, stepped forward. "This really is disgraceful, Dr. Grissom. Your behavior—"

Grissom used another swab on the open mouth of the startled aide.

Pleasantly, the CSI said, "You're a suspect, too, Mr. Anthony. You also stand to gain from this woman's death. And I'm sure you're eager to be cleared, as soon as possible."

Speechless for a change, Anthony stood there, staring in dismayed wonder at the criminalist.

Mobley's attitude, however, remained professional. His face moving from Brass to Grissom and back, he said, "We've had our differences, gentlemen. But I appreciate what you're trying to do. All I ask is that you catch whoever did this thing."

Dealing with the swabs, Grissom beamed and said, "We're processing evidence as we speak."

Diplomatically, Brass said, "Sheriff, we already have some leads—we're on top of it."

Mobley seemed to stare into nothing for several moments; he sighed, tasted his tongue, then asked, quietly, "Did either of you know the Lewis girl? Ever meet her?"

Brass shook his head; Grissom, too. Anthony lurked on the periphery, hanging back now—since the swabbing, he seemed a little afraid.

Meanwhile, Mobley joined the sad choreography of shaking heads. "Hell of a nice kid. Bright. Going places. I really liked her, even if she was working for Harrison."

Anthony, his voice different, said, "For a while there, we were dealing with Candace . . . Ms. Lewis . . . more often, more directly, than the mayor."

Mobley shifted on his feet; his tone shifted, too. "Jim . . . Gil . . . Even though my candidacy hasn't been announced, I'm not gonna lie to you—I want to be mayor. With the exception of my family, my career is the most important thing in my life, and this is the biggest career move I've ever contemplated. . . . But I do not relish becoming mayor thanks to the misfortune of another. Not Candace Lewis, not Darryl Harrison. I want this badly . . . but not like this. Never like this."

Grissom had to admire the dignity of that.

Brass seemed a little embarrassed by Mobley's earnestness. He said, "I've only met the mayor once or twice, Brian—what can you tell me about him?"

The sheriff thought about that for a moment. Then a little smile blossomed and he even summoned a rueful laugh. "Maybe I'm not the one you should be asking."

"But I am asking," Brass insisted.

Grissom watched the interplay with interest: he didn't know if Brass was fishing for something, or was maybe taking the opportunity to make Mobley squirm.

Finally, after a long sigh, Mobley said, "I will tell you this: Darryl Harrison's a good man. We have different political views, but have I nothing to say about him, negatively, on a personal level." He shrugged. "I just don't happen to think he's the right man to lead Las Vegas for the next four years."

"Then he's honest?" Brass asked.

"Far as I know," Mobley replied, with a nod.

"No skeletons in the closet?"

The sheriff grunted a mirthless laugh. "Why don't you just ask it, Jim—*was he sleeping with her?*"

Brass's smile was there, then gone. Grissom wondered if he'd really seen it or just thought he had.

"Well—was he?" the detective asked.

"I don't know. And I don't have to tell you, we didn't conduct the investigation into the disappearance. That was the FBI. And if the federal boys found any evidence of Harrison and the girl having an affair, they didn't share it with me."

"The tabloids say they were."

"How seriously do you take that?"

A beat, and then Brass asked, "No plans to hint at it in the campaign?"

"I can't say we didn't discuss it," Mobley said. "Frankly, it was Ed here who was pushing for it, and you can ask him yourself—I told him there was no way I wanted to go there."

They all glanced at Anthony, who confirmed his boss's story with a nod. *But then, he would, wouldn't he?* Grissom thought.

Brass said, "I'm aware your official press position's been that you won't discuss it."

Mobley nodded insistently. "That's right. Exactly right."

"Obviously, this is no time to change that policy."

"Obviously." Looking from the detective to the CSI, Mobley asked, "Is that all you want to know?"

In his patented angelic manner, Grissom posed an apparent non sequitur: "Do you have carpeting in your home, Brian?"

The sheriff blinked. "Well, sure. Some. Living room, bedroom."

"How new is it?"

Mobley shrugged. "Well, hell . . . I don't know."

"We'll need to take a sample," Grissom said.

Finally realizing what Grissom was doing, Mobley sighed. "Send somebody out whenever you want. Could you wait until I've spoken with my family about this?"

Grissom's cell phone rang and Anthony jumped; the conversation froze while the CSI plucked it off his belt and hit the button. "Grissom."

"Sara, Gil. We checked City Hall records . . . from when Candace Lewis started work? Fingerprints are a match."

"Thanks," Grissom said and ended the call.

Turning to the sheriff, he said, "Fingerprints confirm the body's definitely Candace Lewis. You better start working on that statement, Brian—the press is going to have this before long."

Not asking if they were done this time, Mobley turned to leave and practically tripped over Anthony, who hustled to get out of the office ahead of his boss.

And when the politician and his toady were gone, Brass laughed nastily and said, "That's why I love working for that man—he's always so inspiring."

"Tell you the truth, Jim," Grissom said, "I thought the sheriff behaved rather well."

"Yeah. Well. I guess you're right. But that guy Anthony is a piece of work."

Feeling that comment required no confirmation, Grissom said, "I'm going back to check on how our side's doing. Interested?"

"Right behind you."

Doc Robbins was still in the middle of the autopsy, and Warrick and Sara were in the midst of processing various elements recovered from the carpet. They seemed not to be in need of help, so Grissom and Brass returned to the former's office where he turned on the TV on a small stand in the corner, and waited. He knew it wouldn't be long and he was right.

Less than an hour later—a time period during which Grissom humored Brass by discussing with him various political ramifications of the situation, none of which interested the CSI except in terms of enumerating suspects—the Candace Lewis story took over the airwaves.

Local anchorman Bernie Gonzalez's slicked-back black hair and expensive suit filled the screen as the local news interrupted a soap opera, so Mobley could give his press conference about their real-life soap opera. Grissom wondered if the interruption was merely for the Vegas audience or if it had gone national.

The picture shifted to City Hall where Mobley stood behind a lectern out front near Stewart Avenue. The sun beat down from almost straight overhead and a gaggle of reporters formed a semicircle in front of Mobley.

"I have a short statement to make," Mobley said, unfolding a single sheet of white paper and spreading it out onto the lectern. "And then I'll take a few questions."

The reporters shuffled a little, but didn't interrupt.

"Most of you already know that the body found on North Las Vegas Boulevard this morning was that of Candace Lewis, the missing personal assistant of Mayor Darryl Harrison. The sheriff's department—as well as my family and myself—wish to extend our deepest condolences to the Lewis family. I would like to assure them, in fact to promise them, that the LVMPD will do its very best to bring her murderer to justice. Questions?"

"Will you be heading the investigation?" one of the reporters yelled.

"No."

Before a follow-up could be addressed to the sheriff, another reporter blurted, "Are you planning to run for mayor?"

"That subject is not appropriate to this press conference. But I will say that my candidacy for that office is under serious consideration."

"And is that why you're not going to be involved in the investigation? Conflict of interest?"

"Until now," the sheriff said, off-script now and choosing his words carefully, "this has been a federal missing persons investigation. Now that it's a homicide, the LVMPD will take charge. I don't run homicide investigations: as you know, I oversee both the police and sheriff's departments, here. Those are my responsibilities."

"Then who *will* be running the investigation?"

"Two of our finest law enforcement professionals. And they are the ones to whom you should direct your future questions: Captain Jim Brass and CSI supervisor Gil Grissom. Thank you."

Watching in Grissom's office, Brass turned to the CSI, who shot him a glare and said, "*You* handle the media. I don't *do* media."

"You don't do it well," Brass admitted sourly.

Then both of them turned their eyes back on the screen, where the media throng was still shouting questions. But Mobley was in the process of disappearing back inside City Hall, leaving the reporters wondering what hit them.

But Grissom knew very well what had hit him and Brass: Mobley had just dumped this political hot potato into their collective lap. Aiming the remote at the TV and clicking off the power, he wondered if the day could get any worse.

About five minutes later, after Brass had shuffled glumly out, it did.

An oily voice said in a much too friendly manner, "Gil Grissom. Still offering twenty-four-hour service, I see—how can you stand these hours?"

Grissom swiveled in his chair toward the door,

where—leaning against the frame, his blond hair slicked back straight like a snake trying to molt—resided a smiling Rick Culpepper.

Culpepper wore a well-tailored gray suit and a dark gray tie on a very light gray shirt. His arms were folded and his manner was casual in an all-too-studied manner. After all, the last time this "friendly" caller and Gil Grissom had met up, the two had been so at odds over a disputed prisoner, the FBI man had started to draw a weapon on the CSI.

The two law enforcement agents had crossed paths more than once; to Grissom, Culpepper represented the justice system at its most amoral. If Grissom could have picked one person not to see today, it well might have been Rick Culpepper.

"May I help you?" Grissom asked, in a voice usually reserved for suspected shoplifters.

The FBI agent eased into the room, helped himself to a chair, leaned back, crossed a leg, smiled with a million teeth. "Heard you found a body at Nellis this morning."

"No."

Eyebrows raised. "You didn't find a body at Nellis Air Force Base?"

"We found a body *outside* the Air Force base."

"Ah. Right. You're always precise. Admire that in you, buddy."

"Thank you."

"I also heard that the victim is the subject of an investigation of ours."

Grissom couldn't help himself. "That missing person that you didn't find? Yes."

Culpepper folded his arms, smiled big. Then he said, "Yeah, well, we're going to want to be kept in the loop, where your investigation's concerned."

"Are you? What is it people in hell want, again?"

"Hey, buddy, there's no need to be snotty—you don't still hold a grudge! You were working one case, I was working another—sometimes there's conflicts of interest, even between friends . . . if you gather my meaning."

Grissom said nothing.

"After all, we're on the same team, just different squads. All after the same thing, right? Justice."

Culpepper could crawl under Grissom's skin like few other people on this earth. But the CSI's voice remained calm. "We're after the truth about crimes, and justice can flow from that. But, Culpepper, I have no idea what you're after—except maybe a corner office with a view."

Culpepper rose, as if in slow motion, and smoothed out his suit; he glanced at the surrounding clutter. "Not everybody can have an office like this. . . . Just keep us apprised, buddy. Okay?"

"Sure," Grissom said, hoping it would speed the agent on his way.

"See," Culpepper said from the doorway, unable to leave without having the last word. "We are on the same team."

And by way of goodbye, he fired a finger gun at Grissom and winked.

When the agent had gone, Grissom decided that he would indeed inform Culpepper of their progress— just as soon as the killer was arrested, tried, convicted, sentenced and safely behind bars awaiting lethal injection. Even then, Grissom thought, Culpepper would still look for a way to turn the case to his advantage.

Grissom bent over some paperwork and forced himself to concentrate; he would not allow the federal agent to get to him. But his head popped up when someone knocked on the jamb. He was ready to snap at Culpepper if the FBI agent had returned, only it was Greg Sanders framed in the doorway, a small stack of printouts in hand.

The slender young DNA expert with the spiky hair and longish sideburns smiled nervously his sharp, brown eyes darting around. Greg always seemed to be one espresso over the line.

Grissom willed calm into his voice, making sure the Culpepper irritation didn't bleed in. "Yes, Greg?" He knew he intimidated Greg and the kid was nervous enough, already.

"Test results on your Air Force base vic."

Pleasantly surprised, Grissom said, "That was fast."

Sanders shrugged. "We had DNA from her hairbrush we got from the Lewis woman's apartment, back when she disappeared. Having the body made it easy—I didn't have to wait while we replicated over and over from one cell."

"I know how DNA is processed, Greg. And?"

Greg looked lost. "And what?"

As usual, Greg's attention deficit disorder seemed to have kicked in, the tech so wrapped up in what he *hadn't* had to do that he'd forgotten the reason for his visit . . . which was what he *had* gotten done.

Letting out a sigh Grissom asked, "And what *did* you find, Greg?"

"Oh!" Greg said, snapping out of it. "The DNA matched. The body in the morgue is definitely Candace Lewis."

"Thanks, Greg."

"Hey. My pleasure. Any time. No problem."

"The report, Greg."

"Sure." Greg handed him the report, twitched three or four awkward smiles, and left.

Grissom absently fingered through pages that all added up to just one thing: what had been a high-profile missing persons case had turned into an even higher-profile homicide, and the two best suspects?

The mayor of the city and the sheriff who kept the peace.

The CSI allowed himself a small, personal smile. It was a good thing he believed so firmly in following the evidence, because if he followed hunches—like his friend Brass—Gil Grissom would've had a really bad feeling about where this case was headed.

5

After some sack time and a few mindless hours of ESPN, Nick Stokes felt like a new man. He could tell that Catherine was in a much better mood now, too—sleep and a little quality time with her daughter always seemed to work wonders.

With Grissom's permission, Nick and Catherine were starting their shift midway—three A.M.—which would allow them to work into daylight hours, and be along for interviews with witnesses and suspects. Also, it would put them only halfway through shift when Nunez and his computer cronies showed up to go to work at seven.

The two CSIs joined Nunez's compu-posse then in the large, air-conditioned, garage-like room at the rear of the complex.

The Ryder truck sat parked in the middle of the room with Nunez's team taking the computers out one at a time and placing them on banquet-style tables assembled around the truck. The scene looked vaguely like a swap meet. That vibe quickly faded, however, as the experts got to work: each hard drive was imaged twice, with one copy being put in the computer to be returned to Newcombe-Gold and the other marked for Nunez to search. Each of the originals was tagged and sent to the evidence room.

"Evidence room" was something of a misnomer ever since the LVMPD had been forced to add a building to the CSI complex in order to accommodate the overflow from all the department's investigations. The small, one-story, concrete building out back had a dozen rooms on the first floor and almost that many more in the even more heavily guarded basement.

This overwhelming backlog of evidence had built up fast because of the slow grind of the wheels of justice—not just the court system, but bureaucratic security measures. Each piece of evidence was now affixed with a scan tag, so that when Nick went there for evidence it felt like going to Sam's Club. Scan the number, take your prize with you. One room held computer equipment, others housed stereo equipment, tires and so on, while the really dangerous stuff, the drugs and guns, were stored within the bunker-like security of the basement. Access to this part of the building was only slightly harder than getting into the control room of a nuclear missile silo.

Nick observed Carroll and Giles and the others poring over the computers, then he turned to watch their boss. Seeing the biker-like Tomas Nunez delicately tapping the keyboard of his laptop was like watching Lurch play the harpsichord for the Addams Family. The rangy Hispanic computer expert had jacked

Ruben Gold's hard drive into his massive forensic computer and was using a program called ILOOK.

Developed by a Britisher named Elliot Spencer, ILOOK was the best computer forensic software this side of the National Security Agency, and Nick was pretty sure the NSA wasn't going to share its techno-wealth with the LVMPD. Nick leaned over Nunez's shoulder, Catherine next to him, as the expert punched keys, currently running through print orders searching for the work station that had ordered Gold's printer to run off the pornographic images.

"You know," Nunez said idly, "in 1995 only five percent of all crime involved computers. Now the figures are more like eighty-five percent." He went silent as he studied his monitor.

Catherine glanced at Nick, obviously surprised by these stats.

Nick didn't doubt Nunez; on the other hand, the computer expert might be viewing crime through his end of the CPU. "Anything yet?" he asked.

Nunez touched a line on the screen. "Yeah. Already something crucial: the print order was *not* generated from Gold's computer."

Catherine and Nick again traded glances, and the former asked, "But do we know where the order did come from?"

Nunez looked hard at his monitor, then said, "That would be a big bingo—work station number eighteen."

"Whose station is that?" Catherine asked.

Nick looked at the printout Janice Denard had

given them that showed who occupied which work station. "Ben Jackson."

Catherine sighed, rolled her eyes. "It *would* be one of the handful we didn't fingerprint."

"*Yet,*" Nick remind her. Something didn't feel right, and he asked, "Didn't Janice Denard tell us that Jackson was gone all weekend?"

"Yeah." Catherine looked at her watch. "Let's go see if he came to work early today, now that he's back in town. Maybe he'd like to show us snapshots from his trip."

The edge in Catherine's voice troubled Nick. "Let's not get ahead of ourselves," he said, getting out his cell phone. "I'll fill O'Riley in. See if he can meet us over at Newcombe-Gold."

Turning to Nunez, Catherine said, "You'll call if you find anything?"

"In a cyber second."

Twenty-one minutes later, Nick Stokes was wheeling the Tahoe into the Newcombe-Gold parking lot, where on this sunny morning only a handful of cars were parked. The CSIs were getting their silver crime-scene kits out of the back of the van when Sergeant O'Riley pulled his Taurus into a slot next to them.

O'Riley ambled over. He had dark circles under his eyes and looked a little like the zombie Nick had almost mistaken him for, the other day.

"No fair," the detective said. "You guys caught some sleep."

Nick grinned. "Three hours'll do wonders."

Catherine made a wry face. "At Nicky's age, it will."

"Aw," O'Riley said to her, "you're beautiful at any age."

"I'm going to take that as a compliment."

They started toward the building, O'Riley saying, "Sounds like our computer geeks are making some progress."

Nick said, "Sounds like."

The agency's front door was unlocked. The attractive brunette receptionist was working and it took only a minute or so for Janice Denard to answer the summons. The two CSIs and the detective moved with Denard away from the reception desk, for some privacy.

The office manager had replaced yesterday's polka-dot dress with snug-fitting blue jeans and a long-sleeve red silk blouse with the top two buttons undone.

"Casual day?" Catherine asked lightly.

Janice sort of smiled. "Casual *every* day, thanks to you people."

That may have come out harsher than Denard intended, but Catherine didn't react. Oddly, it was Nick who found himself working hard to swallow an angry retort.

It was just that the woman's reaction was all too typical. People wanted protection, wanted law enforcement to keep all the badness in the world away . . . but without disturbing anything, without disruption.

Such an attitude played into why, the longer they were on the job, so many officers grew cynical. For his part, Nick tried hard to keep any cynicism in check—spending so much time in the lab, hitting the science end, helped. Still, Nick knew the Denard woman was doing her best to cooperate, balanced against her need and desire to keep making her living.

Funny—it wasn't that Nick was in a bad mood, really. Neither was Catherine. Nor did they seem particularly on edge, but . . .

. . . something about the nature of this case was working on them, and not in a good way. He would try to keep tabs on himself . . . and Catherine. Grissom's voice seemed to whisper in his ear: *Not subjective, Nick—objective.*

Catherine was bringing Denard up to speed, closing with, "Is Ben Jackson in yet? We need to talk to him."

"Oh, my God," Janice said, a hand coming up in front of her mouth. "Not Ben!"

"Let's not get ahead of ourselves," Catherine said pleasantly. "It was Ben's work station that ordered the print job, but that doesn't necessarily mean he's the one who did this."

Straightening, obviously trying to calm herself, Denard said, "Well, I hope it isn't Ben. It doesn't seem that it could possibly *be* Ben. . . ."

O'Riley asked, "Who is he around here?"

"Well he's a sweetheart," Denard said. "Just a real sweetheart!"

Nick smiled a little. "Maybe you could be a little more specific."

"Yes. Sorry." Denard seemed mildly flustered; but then she composed herself and went on: "Ben's a young man who joined the firm just last summer—after he graduated from college."

"Is he in today?" Catherine again.

Janice nodded toward the doorway to the corridor of offices. "I'm pretty sure I saw him get here, oh, a little while ago. Half an hour maybe? He, Jermaine, and Mr. Randle, and maybe Mr. Newcombe are the only ones who'll be coming in today. Doing what they can, mostly on the phones. The rest of our staff won't return until we call them back."

O'Riley asked, "Are Mr. Allred and Mr. Randle here yet?"

Denard nodded, qualifying it: "Jermaine for sure. I told him the computer towers were gone and that the place was shut down. Naturally, he wanted to know why."

"What did you tell him?"

"Just that it was part of an investigation. I'm afraid I . . . I lied to him."

O'Riley arched both brows. "How so?"

"I . . . I told I didn't know what the investigation was about. He seems annoyed, I have to say."

"Just annoyed?" Catherine asked. "Not surprised?"

"Surprised, too. Then he said he might as well just go home, but I stopped him. I told him I thought you people would probably be back today, to talk to him and the others. Actually, I asked all three of them to stick around."

"Was anyone upset by that?" the detective asked.

"Not really. Jermaine said he had some drawing to do and he didn't need the computer anyway—not all of our graphics are computer-generated—so he went to his work station."

Nick said, "Let's go back to Ben Jackson for a moment."

"What about Ben?"

"You're positive he wasn't here over the week-end?"

"I'm positive as far as my personal knowledge goes . . . but if you'd like, I'll check the sign-in book. . . . Come with me."

Heels clicking, Denard led them back to the reception-ist's desk. She made a request and the woman withdrew a large black three-ring binder from her center desk drawer desk.

Denard rested the big book on the counter and rif-fled through the pages to last Saturday. Methodically, she ran a finger down the lines. "No. . . . No, there's no sign of Ben's name. He wasn't here this weekend."

They strolled away from the desk again, Catherine saying, "Well, isn't there any way he could have come in without *signing* in?" They stopped and formed a lit-tle semicircle. Denard shrugged.

"I suppose, but people get *paid* by this book . . . so they always sign in when they come to work. Besides, Ben was out of town."

Nick said, "Or was supposed to be out of town."

Denard frowned. "Why would I disbelieve him? Why would you?"

Catherine said, "As far as signing in . . . maybe he didn't come in for work. . . . Maybe he came to do something else. Something recreational. . . ."

Picking up on this, O'Riley asked, "Is there any way Jackson could have been here without anyone seeing him?"

Denard had started shaking her head halfway through the question. "Doubtful—too many people around. Yes, people come in and out, but there's always someone around during the day."

"Back ways into the building?"

"Of course—but all but two are fire exits with alarms."

Nick said, "Two doors is one more door than you need."

O'Riley pressed. "Could Jackson have gotten in at night when no one was around?"

Again Denard shook her head. "He doesn't have a key."

"Who *does* have keys?"

Denard list's was short: "Mr. Newcombe, Mr. Gold, Roxanne Scott and myself—that's it."

Nick considered that for a moment. "Someone could 'borrow' one of those keys, and make a copy. . . ."

Denard's expression was skeptical. "Isn't that a lot of trouble to go to, just to use a work computer, after hours?"

But Catherine and Nick exchanged looks that said each had had the same thought: someone dealing in kiddie porn over the net might well want to keep that material off his home computer. Using a work computer might muddy the waters, nicely, should the police be alerted . . . like now.

O'Riley was still at it: "You're sure you didn't see Jackson on Saturday?"

Denard was admirably patient. "No, I didn't, but then, I left early. It was Roxanne who locked up."

"Roxanne," Catherine said, "who's currently on vacation."

"Yes."

Gesturing toward the reception desk, Nick asked, "Can we get a photocopy of the Saturday sign-in page, from the binder, please?"

"Certainly. I'll be right back."

Catherine said, "We might as well go with you. We'll want to speak to Ben and have a look at his work station."

"Whatever you need," Denard said, but a weariness had crept into the woman's voice.

They followed her down the long corridor, falling in line behind her, single file; then they were in the work area, where she escorted the safari around a wall of cubicles and down a path to another hive of partitions. Denard stopped at the third cubicle down.

"Ben's work station," Denard announced.

"But no Ben," Nick said.

Denard checked her watch, shrugged with her eyebrows. "He might be in the break room or in the washroom. Might even have stepped out for a moment."

"Stepped out?" Catherine asked, with a little frown.

"Advertising is a high-stress business," Denard explained. "You'd be amazed how many of our employees smoke. Since there's no smoking in the building, they have to go out back. We have a small area out there to accommodate them."

O'Riley wanted to take a look at that, and Denard gave him instructions; then the burr-headed detective lumbered off.

As Catherine set down her crime scene case and prepared to go to work, Nick took a quick look at the cubicle, which seemed at first just another of these anonymous interchangeable compartments. Then he looked closer and noted the touches Ben Jackson had added to make the place his own.

Thumb-tacked to one of the cloth walls was a pennant from Iowa State University—CYCLONES! A five-by-seven frame on his desk displayed a photo of a beaming blue-eyed blonde woman in her early twenties—Jackson's girlfriend or wife, presumably. Ten mini-bobble heads stood in a line atop Jackson's computer monitor: baseball players, a few of which were caricatured well enough for Nick to recognize.

Catherine held up the framed photo in a latex-gloved hand. "Who's this?"

Denard, who'd been hovering nervously in the nearby hallway, glanced around surreptitiously, then said, sotto voce, "Ben's wife, Laura. They've only been married a few months. That's part of why I can't believe it was him."

"Ms. Denard," Catherine said, "we do not assume it's Ben. Please—no jumping to conclusions."

When Nunez and crew, with the help of uniformed officers, removed the computer towers, the monitors and keyboards had been left behind. But Nunez had prepared a list of serial numbers with the names of the Newcombe-Gold employees at a given work station. Right now Catherine was checking the keyboard's serial number, making sure this was indeed Jackson's keyboard—which could have been switched, after all.

"This is Jackson's keyboard," she said, bumping into Nick for the third time.

"There's not room for two of us in here," Nick said.

"While you do this, why don't I go with Ms. Denard, to copy the sign-in book page?"

"Why don't you?" Catherine said. She was poised at the computer keyboard like a starving person about to sit down to a big, fine meal.

Field kit in hand, Nick followed Denard back to her office, where she photocopied the document and handed it toward Nick, who asked, "Would you mind if you kept the copy, and I took the original?"

"Well . . . I suppose. But why do you need the original?"

"We might have to have a handwriting expert look at it, and it'll be easier to work with the original."

Her expression was astounded. "A *handwriting* expert? You really think so?"

He shrugged, and gave her a little smile. "Just covering the bases."

She returned the smile, almost shyly, and handed over the original. He gave it a quick scan, then tucked it into an evidence envelope and slipped it inside his kit.

"Thanks," Nick said. "Now, shall we try to find Ben Jackson?"

"All right," Janice said. "Better start back at his work station."

But when they got there, Jackson still wasn't there. Catherine was just finishing up, packing her silver case.

"Anything?" Nick asked.

"Got some prints," she said, pulling off her latex gloves. "From the keyboard, desk, and even the edge of the cubicle itself; not much more. Tomas may be able to tell us something after he goes through the computer. You didn't happen to run into the elusive Mr. Jackson, on your journey, did ya?"

"Nope. But I have the original from the sign-in book. Ms. Denard kept the copy. We were kind of hoping he'd be back in his roost by now."

Catherine shook her head, red-blonde arcs of hair cutting the air. "Haven't seen him or anyone else."

Nick turned to Denard. "When we do locate Ben, is there somewhere we can talk to him alone?"

Denard made a vague gesture. "Break room is right around the corner, when you leave my office."

Nick nodded. "I know we've been imposing, but would you mind tracking Ben down for us? Asking him to meet us there?"

She nodded curtly, professionally; Denard was clearly happier when given a task. "I'll take care of it."

"And if you run into our wandering boy, Sergeant O'Riley, would you guide him to the break room, as well?"

"No problem."

When the office manager was gone, Catherine and Nick—field kits in hand—went the opposite direction through the covey of cubicles. Shortly, he was pushing open a door holding it open for Catherine as she stepped into the break room. Which was larger than Nick would have expected for this facility, with round, dark-wood-topped tables and conference-room-style padded chairs positioned around the twenty-by-twenty-five-foot room. Against one wall was a big-screen TV, and along another a long counter with microwave, an espresso machine, a stainless steel sink and an assortment of condiments. At the far end of of the counter a full-size refrigerator and a Coke machine stood guard. A smoked-glass window ran the length of the far wall and let in just enough sun and a nice view of a back-parking-lot basketball court.

"So this is what it's like to have perks," Nick said, setting his case on one of the tables.

"No kidding," Catherine said, doing the same with her kit. "If our break room was set up like this, I'd pitch a tent and move in."

Janice Denard didn't keep them waiting long. Barely five minutes after she had left them, she entered and held the door open for the young man they'd waited for.

The individual Nick took to be Ben Jackson stood well over six feet tall, carried over two hundred seventy pounds on a wide frame, yet moved with a grace a man half his size might envy. The artist's brown crewcut above an ample forehead gave him a collegiate look; his brown eyes were bright, alert.

"Detectives Willows and Stokes," Denard said, "this is Ben Jackson. . . . No sign of your sergeant."

"Thanks," Nick said to Denard, not bothering to correct the "detective" designation. But to Jackson, Nick said, "I'm Stokes, she's Willows. From the crime lab."

Jackson nodded at Catherine and seemed to want to shake hands, but thought better of it.

"Thank you again, Ms. Denard," Catherine said.

Denard took the hint and backed out of the room, pulling the door closed as she went.

"Have a seat," Catherine said to Jackson in a pleasant but not particularly friendly fashion. The man headed to a table, walking with the slightest hint of a limp.

Nick and Catherine sat on either side of the young man at one of the round tables. Still pleasant, Catherine said, "You're pretty casual." She gestured around the room. "I would've taken this for a shirt-and-tie kind of place."

Jackson shook his head. "Only if a client's coming in."

"Don't have to be a detective," Nick said, affably, "to figure you played some football."

Jackson smiled a little. "Second-string guard at Iowa State." His voice soft, his words measured. "You?"

Nick gave him half a grin. "Texas A&M, fourth-string tight end."

Jackson nodded, and seemed a little more at ease. Which had been the purpose of Nick letting the guy know they were both ex-jocks; further, their glory days had been more in high school than in college. Nick's football career, he was well aware, ground to a halt because he was too short and too slow. Jackson certainly wasn't too short and Nick—reflecting on the man's limp—wondered if that's what had kept him from moving on; hell, the guy had size enough for the pros.

Catherine—obviously seeing the rapport between the two ex-jocks—caught Nick's eyes and tightened hers, in a signal for him to take the lead. He responded with a nod so tiny Jackson surely didn't notice it.

"If you'll excuse me," Catherine said, and she went to her crime scene case on a nearby table and opened the lid.

"How long have you been with Newcombe-Gold?" Nick asked, drawing Jackson's eyes away from what Catherine was up to.

"Not quite a year."

"Like it here?"

Jackson nodded. "Very cool people, and the work is challenging."

Casually, Catherine asked, "Were you here over the weekend?"

"No." Jackson sat up. "Look, is that what the investigation's about? Something that happened this weekend?"

Ignoring the question, Nick insisted, "Tell us where you were this weekend."

Jackson looked hard at Nick, and then did the same with Catherine, before answering. "What exactly am I suspected of?"

Nick glanced at Catherine, who lifted an eyebrow. Looking back at Jackson, Nick said, "We didn't say we suspected you of anything, Mr. Jackson. Maybe Ms. Denard mentioned, we talked to everyone at Newcombe-Gold, yesterday, except for the handful of you who were away for whatever reason."

"Yes. She did mention that."

Nick smiled blandly. "Good. Now. We just want to know why you didn't work this weekend. . . . I understand you usually come in at least part of Saturday."

His expression skeptical, Jackson said, "My wife and I flew back to Iowa—Des Moines to be exact, to visit her mother."

Catherine wheeled, arcs of hair swinging. "I thought you were in Idaho."

Jackson frowned. "Who told you that?"

"Ms. Denard."

"Oh, well. That's a common mistake. They make it around here all the time."

Catherine gave Jackson that beautiful smile of hers that she reserved for suspects who were making her suspicious. "What mistake is that, Mr. Jackson?"

"I'm from Idaho. But I went to Iowa. I met my wife at Ames—at college. Her family's from Des Moines. Idaho, Iowa, they mix it up."

"Ah," Catherine said, as if he'd just told her an enormous whopper.

Nick said, "You left when?"

Thrown a little by Catherine's attitude, Jackson said, "Friday night after work . . . and we just got back, late last night."

Catherine tossed the question casually over her shoulder: "Anybody in Iowa besides your in-laws see you in Iowa?"

"About half the staff of Mercy Medical Center," Jackson said, a hard edge in his soft voice. "My mother-in-law went in for a mastectomy—that's why we went back to Iowa."

"I'm sorry," Nick said, genuinely.

If Catherine felt sorry, she didn't show it; she was pulling no punches: she tossed one of the evidence bags containing the child porn pictures onto the table.

"Ever seen anything like this before?" she asked. She did not sit, hovering ominously. "In Iowa? Idaho? Vegas?"

Jackson's face drained of blood as he looked down at the photo. "Oh, my God. Take that away. Please!"

Neither Catherine nor Nick complied.

He swallowed thickly. "Is that what this is about? This isn't me. What does it have to do with the agency, anyway?"

Nick and Catherine exchanged glances.

Then Nick said, "Can we trust you to not talk about this to anybody?"

Jackson looked from one to the other. "Of course you can. This kind of thing is a crime. I know that. Jeez!"

Nick nodded, then gestured to the photo. "Several of these were found in a printer here yesterday."

"Here? Damn! What kind of perv would—"

"According to the log," Nick said, "the print order originated from your work station."

His eyes bulged. "My—"

Catherine said, "On Saturday."

Jackson pressed a hand to his forehead and rubbed it down his face as if he were trying to wipe the features off. "Oh, man. . . . I was in Iowa, there are fifty, a hundred people who either saw me at the hospital, or in one of the airports, or for that matter on the plane!"

Nick asked, "Anybody else ever use your work station?"

"No. Not that I know of, anyway."

"Could they use it without your knowledge?"

Shrugging, Jackson said, "Sure, I suppose—if they had my password. Which they don't."

Catherine cocked her head, smiled, more to herself than to the others. Then she asked, "So—nobody knows your password?"

Jackson shrugged. "Well, maybe—I mean, the passwords *are* assigned to us."

Nick asked, "Do they ever change?"

"Sure—every month, sometimes even less. Last time was three weeks ago." Catherine said, "Your current password . . . is it SOL20DAC?"

Jackson's mouth fell open. "Well, I . . . God. I think that's it."

"And was it 2DEC47 before that?"

Jackson leaned forward. "How the hell could you know that?"

Catherine held up a small evidence bag in which a pink post-it resided, with SOL20DAC written above a crossed-out 2DEC47 and two other crossed-out numbers. "This was on the underside of your gel wrist protector. It is hard to remember a password when they change it on you all the time."

"What the hell did you do?" Jackson said, too stunned to be angry. "Go through my cubicle?"

Catherine beamed at him. "That's right, Mr. Jackson."

"But that's my personal space . . ."

"Actually," Catherine said, "it's not. Your cubicle is the property of Newcombe-Gold."

"But don't you need a search warrant?"

"We presented the agency with a warrant yesterday. . . . You said it yourself, Mr. Jackson." Catherine snatched away the offensive photo. "This is a crime. And we're investigating it."

Jackson's forehead had gathered into a frown of thought, but something in the flummoxed man's eyes said no thought was forming.

Finally Catherine sat down beside Jackson, and her manner softened, her tone, too. "That's why I'm reasonably certain you're not responsible," she said.

His expression brightened. "Really?"

She nodded. "Somebody knew where you kept your password, and they used that information to use your work station to print off these pictures."

"So, I'm in the clear?"

"I'm afraid I can't go quite that far. We'll check your story, Mr. Jackson . . . but you can rest easy, I think. You seem to be telling the truth."

A slow, relieved sigh preceded the man's next question: "If I might ask, why are you so sure I'm innocent?"

Nick said, "The airline'll have a record of you. It won't take any time at all to check that. The hospital staff in Des Moines will back up your story, too . . . if it's true."

"It's true!"

Nick smiled gently. "I believe it is. Relax, buddy."

Jackson nodded and seemed to relax for the first time since he entered the room. "You can ask my wife, but . . . go easy, would you?"

"About the pornography?" Catherine asked.

"I wasn't thinking of that. She'd know that's not me. She'd never believe that of me. I meant, take it easy in general. . . . She's a wreck, after this weekend."

Finally genuine concern colored Catherine's voice as she asked, "And how is your mother-in-law doing?"

He let out another sigh. "Well, she's still got some chemo to get through, but they say she's through the worst of it."

Silence hung in the air; having a little normal real life, even tinged with tragedy, interrupt the case seemed to provide a grounding influence, somehow.

Finally Nick said, "Mr. Jackson—Ben. You may still be able to help with our case."

His eyes grew alert. "Sure. Name it."

"Think for a second. Got any idea who would . . . or could . . . have used your work station?"

Glumly, Jackson shook his head. "Nobody and anybody. They don't put locks on cubicles."

Nick's eyes narrowed. "This may sound funny, but . . . you have any enemies here?"

"Enemies? No—hell, I don't think I've been here long enough to get anyone pissed at me, yet. Besides, all I do is grunt work. They won't let me near anything important until I've got more experience. . . . Doesn't bother me. I mean, that's the business. That's *any* business."

Catherine asked, "Anybody been hanging around your cubicle lately?"

Jackson considered that, but shook his head. "No more than usual."

"I'm thinking," she said, "somebody who wasn't all that interested in you, but suddenly starts dropping by, to shoot the breeze."

"I see where you're coming from, Ms. Willows—but no."

"What about somebody who happened to be around when you were checking your password? Either refreshing your memory with that post-it, or just keying it in . . . ?"

"It may not seem like it, but I tried to be discreet

and not check it when anybody was around. After the first couple days with a new password, I generally have it down."

"You weren't sure when I first asked you."

"I know, but . . . it's different, typing it in. My fingers remember, you know?"

Nick took another tack. "Who knew you were leaving town for the weekend?"

Another head shake. "I don't have any idea."

"Well, who did you tell?"

"Janice and Roxanne and maybe a dozen or more friends here. And Janice got it wrong, right? But on the other hand, a lot of people knew my mother-in-law was sick and they asked about her. I might have mentioned it to as many as twenty people. Newcombe-Gold has been like an extended family for Laura and me. Everybody here is like family. Sounds like a cliché, but here it happens to be true."

"One more question."

"Shoot."

"Can you tell us why something printed on your computer would print on Mr. Gold's printer, instead of the one in your cubicle?"

The young man thought about that, but for only a moment. "The last thing I did Friday was a drawing that Mr. Gold was taking to Los Angeles with him. It was a mockup for a client there, sort of a rush job . . . but really not important enough for any of the senior artists to do."

"Okay, but that doesn't answer the question."

"Actually, it does. I was late to pick up Laura to get to the airport. So, instead of printing it off in my cubicle, and hunting down Mr. Gold, I just sent the drawing to his printer so he'd have it before he left. I didn't bother to change my printer selection back to mine before I left. Slipped my mind, actually."

Nick nodded. "Makes sense."

"All right, Mr. Jackson," Catherine said, on her feet again. "May we fingerprint you?"

"I guess. But why?"

"We're going to end up fingerprinting everybody, but you're important, because your work station was used. We have to be able to separate your fingerprints from whoever did this."

"Sure, I understand. Go ahead."

Catherine fingerprinted Jackson efficiently, then handed him a paper towel. "We're going to ask you to not talk about this investigation with anyone."

"Sure, but why?" Jackson used the paper towel on his fingertips, only the ink wasn't coming off easily.

"Publicity for one," Catherine said. "How would Newcombe-Gold's clients feel about this kind of investigation centering on the agency?"

"Oh. Yeah . . ."

"But there's another concern," Nick said. "Your coworkers."

"What about them?"

"You're the first person we've interviewed privately. That was in part because you weren't here yesterday, when the other interviews were conducted out in the lobby; but it might not look that way to your co-workers."

He gave them a blank stare.

Catherine asked, "How do you think they would

feel about you, if they believed our investigation had focused on you and your work station?"

Jackson stopped working on cleaning his fingers for a moment. "Shit."

"Well put," Nick said.

Studying his blue fingers, Jackson seemed strangely lost.

"Come on," Catherine said, taking pity, withdrawing a small bottle out of her case and leading the big man over to the sink. "Put your hands in the sink."

She opened the lid and sprayed the contents of the bottle on Jackson's hands.

"What is it?" he asked.

"It's what we in the crime lab call 'soap.' Good old-fashioned soap—you can wash up and no one will know what happened in here."

His expression was grim. "You . . . you think my co-workers are going to suspect me, don't you?"

Catherine shook her head. "They have no reason to; and by the time people find out what we're investigating, we're hoping to have the guilty party in custody."

As the big man aggressively dried his hands, Nick approached him. "May we have your discretion in this matter, Mr. Jackson?"

"You've got it. . . . Can I get out of here?"

"You can," Catherine said.

Nick offered his hand and the two ex-jocks shook. "Thank you for your cooperation, Ben."

"No problem," the big man said. "Just do me a favor and catch the guy."

"Our pleasure," Catherine said.

Not long after Jackson left them, O'Riley finally found his way to the break room, but he was not alone—an African American with a shaved head followed him in. O'Riley gestured to their new guest.

"This is Jermaine Allred," the detective said. "Mr. Allred, this is Catherine Willows and Nick Stokes, CSI."

Allred, whose manner was self-confident, gave them a guardedly friendly nod. Like Jackson, Allred was dressed casually, a white business shirt untucked over faded jeans, the top few buttons ignored.

"So you're the crime lab," he said, and stuck out his hand toward Nick who shook it; then Allred shook hands with Catherine too. "I always watch those forensics shows on Learning Channel, cable, you know. Fascinating stuff."

"I'm going to see if the other guy's here yet," O'Riley said.

"All right, Sarge," Nick said, and O'Riley went out. Nick continued: "Mr. Allred, we're not the crime lab, but we are criminalists *with* the crime lab. And it is fascinating work."

"Hey, havin' a cool job is . . . cool. Very cool indeed."

Catherine, already bored with this, started right in: "Well, you missed *your* work yesterday."

Allred smiled, shrugged. "They call in the cops over that now?"

Catherine smiled back. "I was hoping for an answer, not a flip question."

"Hey, sorry, no disrespect meant."

Allred helped himself to a chair at one of the tables. The CSIs remained standing.

"I had the flu," he explained with an elaborate *so-sue-me* shrug. "Started gettin' sick on Friday, laid up in bed, whole damn weekend. Still had it yesterday, so I stayed home."

"Doctor's excuse?" Nick asked.

"No."

"Anyone see you?"

"My wife saw me. My two kids saw me."

"That's a good start. Anybody else? Anybody not family?"

Allred thought about that. "No. I mean, I don't socialize when I'm sick. When I wasn't in bed I was, you know—either sittin' on, or bendin' over, the throne."

"I've been there. But think. No one stopped by?"

Allred shook his head, but then his eyes widened. "Saturday afternoon, my wife took the kids to a movie. . . . They get noisy, and she wanted me to get some sleep. While they were gone, the doorbell rang, and it just kept ringing . . . kind of insistent, y'know? I managed to haul my sorry ass to the door. It was Patty's Avon lady dropping off a bag. She normally wouldn't do it on a weekend, she said, but she was in the neighborhood so she stopped by. *She* can tell you I was home."

"Good," Catherine said, standing by the fingerprint station she'd set up on the nearby table. "That's a nice solid alibi, Mr. Allred. You know what would *really* put you in the clear with us?"

Allred nodded, smirking humorlessly. "All right, let's do it." He held out his hands. "Get it over with."

As Catherine took Allred's prints, Nick kept talking to the man. "How long have you been with the agency?"

"Twelve years."

Catherine did his left hand.

"What do you do here, Mr. Allred?"

"Call me Jermaine. I'm an artist."

"You work with clients?"

"Sometimes. It depends."

She did his right hand.

Nick asked, "You know the name of that Avon lady?"

Allred shook his head. "I should, but I don't remember. Patty'll know."

When they were finished, they gave Allred the same speech about discretion, then sent him on his way.

Interviewing Ruben Gold and Roxanne Scott would have to wait until the two came back next week, but that didn't bother Nick. They would get to them and, in the meantime, there was only one more name to go on yesterday's M.I.A. list. And soon O'Riley was parading in the last of the three employees they had missed yesterday—Gary Randle.

Randle was sneaking up on forty, with short, curly dark hair sliding back on a roundish head with evenly spaced features, brown eyes that laughed a little and an easy, expansive white smile. Like Allred, Randle wore faded jeans but his shirt was a black Polo and tucked in. He wore loafers and no socks.

After the introductions, O'Riley and Nick sat at the table with the man while Catherine lurked near the field kit.

Nick said, "I understand you were on a sales call yesterday."

Randle's grin seemed shy and self-effacing. "Yeah—

stretched into a long one, and I had to let the client beat me at golf before he'd give in."

"Tough job," Catherine said lightly.

Shrugging, Randle said, "Actually, sometimes it is. I had to let him win, and yet make it look like I *wasn't* throwing the match."

Catherine was still shaking her head at that answer when Nick asked the next question. "So—when did you get back to the office?"

Another shrug. "I didn't. I went straight home from the golf course. It was late, and why should I?"

"How do you mean?"

"I mean, hell—I had a hundred-thousand-dollar sale in my hip pocket."

O'Riley asked, "Were you in the office over the weekend?"

"Why?"

Nick said, "I'm sure you've heard about our investigation. It has to do with that."

"Yeah, but I haven't heard what the investigation's about."

"That's because we're trying to keep that confidential."

"Well, then, why don't I keep my whereabouts this weekend confidential."

O'Riley glared at Randle. "We can do without the smart mouth."

Randle laughed. "You're kidding, right? You come in here, start asking me questions about . . . *something* . . . but you won't tell me *what* that something is . . . and you expect me to answer?"

"If you're innocent—"

"Go to hell." He stood; the affability had been replaced with cold anger. "This has nothing to do with innocence—this has to do with your goddamned gestapo tactics."

O'Riley stood. "You want to take it down a notch, sir?"

"No," Randle said, and got right in O'Riley's face. "I don't. Am I supposed to be scared of you, or that haircut?" He took a step away from the big cop and directed his next demand to Nick: "Either tell me what the hell this is about, or I walk."

Nick didn't know what to say, and glanced at Catherine, who said to Randle, "We need to get your fingerprints."

"Let's see. . . . How about: no."

"We can get a court order."

"Go for it. In the meantime, I'm outa here." Without another word, he bolted out.

O'Riley, seething, turned to Nick and Catherine.

But both of the CSIs were smiling.

"What are *you* guys grinnin' about?"

Catherine already had her cell phone out and was punching buttons. "I'll get the court order and be at his front door before the end of the day," she said.

Nick put a hand on O'Riley's shoulder. "Lighten up, Sarge. We've finally got a real suspect."

6

SARA SIDLE TOOK ANOTHER BITE OF HER SANDWICH—
turkey on whole wheat with lettuce and sprouts—
and chased it with a swig from her bottle of kiwi-
strawberry Snapple. She was sitting in the break
room eating her lunch, or anyway what she thought
of as her lunch: funny way to describe her three a.m.
meal; but in the middle of shift, what else was there
to call it?

Doc Robbins appeared in the doorway, leaning on
his metal crutch; an arched eyebrow sent Sara a signal
that something, besides just that eyebrow, was up.

"Care to hear the report on Candace Lewis?"

She looked down at the remnants of her sandwich.
"Should I finish my sandwich first?"

"Depends on whether you want these results on a
full stomach or not. Would you round up Grissom and
Warrick, and meet me in the morgue?"

Sara said, "We'll be right there," and stuffed the
stub of the sandwich in her mouth. She was not by
nature squeamish.

On the other hand, Robbins was well aware of that fact. . . .

The coroner disappeared and Sara chugged the last of her drink. She sat, for a few moments, just taking that midshift moment to recharge, before bounding off to find the other two CSIs on the Lewis case.

And in less than ten minutes, the three criminalists and the Chief Coroner stood in a loose circle around Candace Lewis's sheet-draped body displayed on the cold metal surface of the table.

"Let's start with the cause of death," Robbins said.

"Ligature strangulation," Warrick said.

"Right." Robbins looked at the CSI. "Care to take a guess at the ligature?"

With a quick sideways look at Grissom, Warrick said, "Uh, we don't do 'guesses,' Doc."

Grissom twitched the tiniest smile as he exchanged a glance with the coroner, who said, "Make an educated guess, Warrick, just for me—you're my guest, after all."

Sara watched as Warrick pulled back the sheet revealing Candace's face and neck.

Warrick leaned closer to the body. The flesh of Candace's throat showed bloody gouges as well as massive bruising and something else . . .

. . . a pattern that wasn't quite discernible.

Sara wondered what Warrick—and for that matter, Grissom—would make of that.

"Some kind of chain, maybe?" Warrick offered.

Robbins turned to her. "Sara?"

She glanced at Grissom, who nodded his permission; then she shrugged. "Seems about right—don't know what else it might be."

"Gil?"

Grissom bent over the body, his Mini-MagLite materializing to light the dead woman's throat. He studied the brutalized flesh for several long moments, touched a portion of the wound, looked at his finger, then rubbed it against his thumb.

"A chain," the CSI supervisor said. "An oiled bicycle chain."

"And we have a winner," Robbins said dryly.

Sara leaned in to study the woman's throat more closely. Her colleagues were right: the design bruised into Candace's neck did resemble the markings of a chain, and a bicycle chain at that.

"Weird choice for a weapon," she said, with a quick facial shrug.

"Not a studied choice," Grissom said. "Probably a weapon of opportunity—her assailant kidnapped her, and probably meant to keep her alive . . . that's why there was never any ransom demand."

Eyes narrow, nodding just a little, Warrick said, "But something went wrong."

Grissom nodded back, curtly. "Something went wrong. She angered him . . . or tried to escape, or call for help . . . and the only thing he could do was kill her with the first thing he could lay his hands on."

Gesturing, Robbins added, "If you look at her hands, you can see evidence she fought back—tore her nails, lacerated two fingers."

Glancing down, Sara could see the tattered nails and the dried blood around the gashes in her fingers.

Then she felt Grissom's eyes on her.

Gently, Grissom asked, "Can you see it, Sara?"

"Yes. . . . Yes, I think I can. . . ."

Candace is scared.

She's in a darkened room and all she can see is shadows. She starts to run, hoping to escape and crashes into something . . .

. . . and finds herself in the arms of her kidnapper!

Screaming, kicking out, she strikes him in the groin and he releases his grip on her. As she turns to run in the opposite direction, he fumbles around and picks up a bicycle chain, looping it over her head and pulling it tight around her throat.

Candace tries to get her fingers under the chain but her nails break off and the metal bites into the flesh of her fingers. She feels herself getting weaker, the pressure intense on her neck, the pain nearly blinding as her lungs scream for oxygen. Bursting stars appear at the corners of her vision and, as she closes her eyes, little colorful fireworks explode behind her lids.

Slowly, blessedly, the pain eases, the burning in her chest lessens, and her vision blurs, the colorful little explosions blinking, winking, on and off now. It's like trying to watch fireflies on a foggy night, but the tiny lights get lost in a mist that grows, turning ever darker until all she can see is peaceful blackness.

"That's how she might have experienced it," Sara said.

"What about *him?*" Grissom asked. "What about our kidnapper, our killer?"

"Well . . ." Sara began.

He has slipped up, his prize nearly escaping. . . .

When she kicks him, the world seems to implode for a moment; but he can't let the pain consume him, he must prevail. She is his—he's worked so hard to obtain her, to possess her, he simply has to hold onto her now.

He gropes around on the nearby toolbench in the pitch-dark room; his fingers touch the cold steel of the bicycle chain. He knows what it is instantly—he'd been working on the bike when he finally nabbed his "guest." He snatches up the chain, manages to get it over her head and around her neck.

She struggles at first, struggles hard—gotta hand it to her, she's a fighter . . . that's part of what drew him to her in the first place. No ordinary girl for him. . . .

Slowly his strength wins out, and her weight falls against him as she sags backward, taking him to the floor with her, the chain still taut around her neck. He realizes at once that something's wrong.

He didn't mean to kill her—merely to subdue her; but now she wasn't fighting, in fact . . . she didn't seem to be breathing.

He loosens the chain, puts a hand to her throat—no pulse.

He had hoped to keep her alive. Alive, she could come to finally feel the love for him that he felt for her. But even though she was dead, she would be his now, all his, compliant at last. Cooperative. Behaving herself.

Now, she's his forever.

"Good," Grissom said to Sara. "Good. . . . What else have you got, Doc?"

Robbins sighed, gathering his thoughts. "Preliminary tox screen is negative, but we're still waiting for the final report. As we posited, there's evidence of necrophilia. The jaws were broken post-mortem, to allow for easier entry."

"The tearing around her vagina?" Sara asked. "Is that the same . . . ?"

"Also post-mortem—though I'm sure he assaulted her before her death. There's bruising that could only have occurred when she was alive. SART exam had nothing."

Warrick asked, "Why'd he get rid of her now?"

"Take a whiff, Warrick," Grissom said. "That's not springtime."

"Gil's right," Robbins said. "To put this as delicately as possible, Ms. Lewis was becoming a touch too . . . ripe."

Sara frowned. "Would a man obsessed in this fashion even be aware or concerned about that?"

"Within his obsession," Robbins said, "possibly not. But psychotics are exceptionally good at compartmentalizing, and often able to function and blend into normal society, with relative ease."

Still frowning, Sara said, "I don't get your point, Doc."

But it was Grissom who provided the answer: "The stench may not have bothered our man, but the neighbors, the postman, the meterman, most certainly might be expected to notice. He's cognizant enough of the realities of day-to-day life in the real world to be aware of such things."

Robbins picked up the thread. "She'd ripened past keeping her in the house or apartment or garage he was holding her in. He had to get rid of her, so he did what he could think of."

Sara nodded. "Left her by the side of the road."

Grissom asked Robbins, "Any idea how long she's been dead?"

"He tried to preserve her, but he wasn't very successful," Robbins said. "Rigor has come and gone and there's some post-mortem lividity."

Rigor mortis started as little as two hours after death, Sara knew, and was generally gone within forty-eight to sixty hours; post-mortem lividity meant that the blood had begun to pool after the heart stopped pumping.

She asked, "You figure he kept her lying on her back?"

The coroner shook his head. "The lividity is concentrated more in the buttocks and lower back. She was reclined at least slightly, and since the killer tried to preserve her, I'm going to say he probably kept her in a bathtub or perhaps a trough of some kind. There's also some marbling."

Marbling was a part of the putrefaction process; the veins took on a purple or bluish pigment under the skin, due to the decomposing blood.

Robbins asked a question: "How long has she been missing?"

Grissom said, "Three weeks—give or take a day or two."

"She's probably been dead half that time, anyway."

That was all Robbins had for them, for the moment.

"As the tests start coming back," the coroner said, "I'll have more for you."

"Don't by shy about staying in touch, Doc," Grissom said. "The politics of this smell worse than your patient."

"Not like you, Gil," Robbins said, "getting involved in politics."

"I'm not involved in politics." The CSI supervisor lowered his gaze upon the dead woman; with the science out of the way, his guard was down, and Sara could see the pity in his eyes. "Unfortunately, Ms. Lewis here *was.*"

Then Grissom began issuing orders to his team members: "All right, let's split up. Warrick, find out what you can about the piece of taillight."

"All over it, Gris."

"Sara, get that missing persons file and go over it like a crime scene."

"Ecklie's shift drew that case, you know."

"I know. I just don't care. Go over that file, make sure we know all we can, and meanwhile, I'll check with the labs. End of shift, my office."

When Sara arrived at Grissom's office some three hours later, the door was open, but neither her boss nor Warrick were there; for a fleeting instant, she had the feeling that the meeting had been moved and no one had bothered to tell her. A little kneejerk paranoia was starting to kick in when Warrick ambled up from his tiny office.

"Where's Gris?" he asked.

Hanging just outside Grissom's door, she shrugged. "Just got here myself. Find anything?"

"Maybe. How about you?"

"I think so."

Warrick chuckled. "You notice how gun-shy Gris has made us, about forming our own opinions?"

She grinned. "Tell me about it."

That was when Grissom arrived.

"Inside," he said.

They entered his office and spread out, Grissom sitting behind his desk, Warrick leaning against a set of shelves to the left of the entrance, Sara remaining near the door where she could see them both.

Grissom began speaking without preamble: "The trace lab is working on the carpeting and the duct tape."

"Anything yet?" Sara asked.

"Results from the mass spectrometer say that the carpet is made of polypropylene-olefin."

"Gezzundheit," Warrick said.

Grissom gave Warrick the look he seemed to reserve for those times when his young CSIs exhibited humor too sophomoric for his tastes. "It's actually a good thing."

"Why?" Sara asked.

"Only about twenty-two percent of manufactured carpeting," Grissom said, not referring to any notes, "is made from that particular compound."

"Which narrows our search," Warrick said.

"Which narrows our search. What did you two find out?"

Warrick and Sara traded looks, then she nodded at him to go first, which he did.

"The plastic is from a taillight; we were already pretty sure of that. But I found a partial part number stamped on the inside, and ran that."

"And?"

"And the piece of plastic came from one of three types of cars: a 95–01 Chevrolet Monte Carlo, a Chevy Lumina from the same years or a Chevy Impala from 2000 or 2001."

Grissom frowned in thought. "What did Mr. Benson say he saw?"

Also not referring to notes, Warrick said, "A white Chevy, possibly a Monte Carlo."

Sara said, "Could we possibly have actually found a reliable eyewitness?"

"Let's not jump to that conclusion," her boss said. Then he asked Warrick, "How many 95–01 white Monte Carlos registered in Clark County?"

"Car's only five years old, so there's quite a few. White ones? Just under a hundred. All Monte Carlos, Luminas and Impalas that fit the profile, and all the others—just in case our eyeball witness got the color wrong, or the car had been repainted—there's just about a thousand."

"Tell me you started with the short list."

"I did. Already put it on the radio—patrol cars'll be watching for a car that matches."

"Good."

Warrick twitched a smile. High praise from Grissom.

Who moved onto to his other CSI, saying, "Sara?"

"Biggest news is Ecklie's people found definite evidence that Mayor Harrison was having an affair with Candace Lewis."

Grissom sat up. "How definite?"

"Well . . . real definite. Like, his DNA was in her bed."

Grissom's mouth dropped open like a trapdoor; the CSI supervisor rarely expressed surprise so blatantly. And the normally laid-back Warrick straightened up, the usually half-lidded eyes wide open.

"Ecklie's people," Grissom said, in a measured manner, "found His Honor's DNA in Candace's bed . . . and said nothing?"

Sara shrugged. "I don't know about that. File doesn't indicate whether or not they informed the sheriff or the FBI or either or neither . . . no notes in the file mention anything to that effect."

Warrick let out a bitter chuckle. "Well, at least Ecklie didn't leak it to the press."

Sara had not followed the story intently, but anyone in Las Vegas—really, anyone in America with cable or access to a newsstand tabloid—knew the parameters of the case.

And for conclusive evidence of an affair between the Mayor and Candace to be the one bit of information about the case to have fallen through the cracks . . . well, that was unthinkable. The hell His Honor was currently living through would have been multiplied by a factor of ten.

Grissom's eyes were grim. "Warrick, stay on the carpeting and the car." Turning to Sara, he added, "Get that file—we're calling on Sheriff Mobley."

Ten minutes later, Sara was standing in the sheriff's outer office; her "day" was supposed to be over, and the city government's was just beginning. A recent City Hall renovation had garnered the sheriff the extra room and his civilian secretary, a very efficient-seeming woman in her forties, was doing her best to convince Grissom he couldn't enter Mobley's private office.

"You simply can't go in there," she said again, her voice growing more shrill.

But the preoccupied Grissom was already almost past her now, his hand on the knob of a door marked PRIVATE, and only when the woman gripped him by the arm did he turn to acknowledge her presence, despite the fact that probably most of the building had heard her all-but-scream at him.

"What is it you want?" he asked, frowning mildly.

"I said you *can't go in there*—Sheriff Mobley is in a very important meeting and doesn't wish to be disturbed."

"I'm afraid he's going to be," Grissom said, "when he sees this." He held up the file folder. "You tell Sheriff Mobley that Gil Grissom from CSI has discovered suppressed evidence from the Candace Lewis case . . . and see if he doesn't make time for me."

At that instant Mobley's door opened and the sheriff stood framed there, red-faced with anger, inches away from Grissom. "What the hell is going on out here?"

Grissom brandished the manila folder. "Did you know about this?"

The two men moved deeper into the office; the secretary was fading back, confused and alarmed. Sara kept her position on the periphery, fascinated to see Grissom in such an emotional state. Others might have assumed Grissom was as cool as usual, but Sara could sense the rage.

"Did I know about what?" Mobley snapped, defensively. Then, taking it down a notch, the sheriff added, "I honestly have no idea what you're talking about, Gil."

A short, pudgy man in a crisp suit and tie, his fla

face decorated with a beaky nose and black-button eyes, stood eavesdropping in the doorway. Sara did not know this man, but his grimace and generally dismayed expression indicated he recognized the file folder, even if the sheriff did not.

"This," Grissom said, indicating the folder, "is the report Conrad Ecklie's people did on their search of Candace Lewis's apartment."

The pudgy little man stepped into the room and said, "You two gentleman have things to talk about— I'll stop back later, Sheriff."

"Don't rush off on my account, Mr. Anthony," Grissom said with an acid smile.

"See you later, Ed," the sheriff said, absently, and Anthony hurried across the office, flashing a nervous smile at Sara before he rushed out and was gone.

Interesting, Sara thought.

"Mrs. Mathis," the sheriff said to the secretary, "please step out into the hall, and make sure no one enters."

"Yes sir," she said, her confusion apparent, but she complied.

They did not move into the sheriff's office, remaining in the outer reception area, as if this were somehow neutral turf. The sheriff seemed calmer, now. "I didn't know there *was* a report from the Lewis woman's apartment. I thought they were still waiting for lab results."

Grissom winced. "For three weeks?"

"Well, don't some of your lab results take a long time?"

That slowed Grissom down. He flapped the air with the folder. "You didn't know about the report?"

"Gil, you have my word."

Grissom said nothing for a moment; he was studying the sheriff as carefully as he might a specimen on a slide. Then he said, "How is it that you never saw the crime scene report from the highest-profile missing persons case we've had in years?"

Mobley thought about that, and the irritation in him was building—and Sara didn't sense the irritation was aimed at Grissom.

Finally the sheriff said, "Frankly, I don't know— let's find out."

Mobley went to the door and opened it, scaring his secretary a little, as she stood out there awkwardly waiting. "Mrs. Mathis," he said, "come back in and find out where Conrad Ecklie is—and tell him I want to see him immediately."

"Certainly, sir," Samantha said, slipping in, moving past the sheriff and returning to her desk.

Mobley was heading toward his inner office, motioning in a manner that wasn't unfriendly. "You two come in," he said, "and let me have a look at that report."

Now it was Grissom who hung back. Sara was surprised to note an expression of confusion on the boss's face—it wasn't common.

"What is it?" Mobley demanded.

Grissom shrugged. "You've recused yourself from this case."

"Gil!" Mobley blurted. His eyes were huge and rolling. "For God's sake, man, you can't have it both ways. Either you *want* me to see that report, or you don't!"

"You're a suspect, Brian."

"Well, I think you've already made that clear," Mobley said sarcastically.

Grissom's tone seemed tentatively conciliatory. "What I need is for you to tell me the truth about this report. I need to know if you've *already* seen it."

The secretary was on the phone, trying to make her call to Ecklie.

"You have my word, Gil, I haven't. I have never seen any crime scene report about Candace Lewis. Now, damnit . . . come in."

As Sara and Grissom entered Mobley's inner office, the CSI supervisor handed the sheriff—who had shut the door—the manila folder.

Seated behind his desk now, Mobley opened the folder, slow-scanning contents; then he looked up disbelievingly at Grissom and Sara, who stood in front of his desk.

"Sit," the sheriff said, his voice weary, and they did, as Mobley went back to the report to read it more carefully.

When he'd finished, the sheriff looked across at the two CSIs. "They found Harrison's DNA in her bed?"

Grissom nodded.

Sara couldn't tell how her boss was reading the situation, but to her, Mobley seemed completely, honestly surprised. She believed the man had never seen the report before; and, if he had, Sheriff Brian Mobley was a better actor than the vast majority of liars the CSIs encountered. And they had encountered quite a few.

Before the discussion could even begin, a soft knock came at the door.

Mobley said, "Come in," and Mrs. Mathis ushered in dayshift CSI supervisor Conrad Ecklie. The secretary disappeared, but Ecklie froze just inside, apparently surprised to see Grissom and Sara.

"Come in, Conrad," Mobley said.

Ecklie nodded to the other two and stood next to where Grissom was seated.

"Good morning, Sheriff," Ecklie said. "I understand, there's a matter of some urgency . . . ?"

Mobley tossed the report across the desk. Ecklie looked down at it; his eyes and nostrils flared. "What's this?"

"Nothing much," Mobley said. "Just the Candace Lewis crime scene report."

Ecklie seemed confused. "What do you mean?"

"Do I stutter? How much more clearly do I need to put it? This is the Candace Lewis crime scene report!"

"But . . . Sheriff . . . Brian . . . I gave that to you weeks ago."

Sara and Grissom exchanged glances, then turned back to the sheriff, Grissom saying sharply, "So then, you *have* seen it?"

Mobley shook his head vigorously. "No." Then to Ecklie, he demanded, "Conrad, why the hell are you lying about this?"

Both Mobley and Grissom were glaring at the dayshift supervisor.

Who seemed beside himself. "But I'm not! I'm not lying—what possible reason would I have to lie about that?" Ecklie looked pleadingly at Grissom. "I know we've had our little problems, Gil—but the sheriff . . .

this must be some political maneuvering. If one of us is lying, it has to be him!"

"Goddamnit," Mobley began, thrusting to his feet.

Eyes moving quickly from Grissom to Mobley and back again, a desperate-sounding Ecklie said, "I'm telling you, Grissom, I brought that up *personally* to this office, two weeks ago!"

Mobley, almost shouting, said, "And you claim you gave this to me, personally?"

"Yes! I . . ." Ecklie's mouth went slack. "Actually . . . no. No, come to think of it . . . no. I didn't."

"Did you or didn't you give the report to the sheriff?" Grissom demanded.

Pitiful now, Ecklie said, "I gave it to him . . . but I didn't give it to him."

No wonder, Sara thought, *Grissom always seemed on the verge of tearing his hair out, when Ecklie's name came up. . . .*

"Care to explain that?" Grissom asked, outwardly calm; but one of the hands in his lap had, Sara noted, involuntarily balled into a vein-throbbing fist.

Taking a deep breath, Ecklie alternated his gaze from Grissom to Mobley and back again. "I was bringing it to the sheriff, when I ran into Ed Anthony in the hallway."

Grissom sat up; Mobley's face fell.

Ecklie was saying, "We got to talking, some political chit chat or other, and Ed volunteered to deliver the report to the sheriff for me. . . . You were in some kind of meeting, Brian."

Mobley sighed and fell into his chair, hanging his head.

"And you handed that little toady a confidential report," Grissom said. It wasn't really a question. . . .

"He . . . he was already coming this way," Ecklie said, with an elaborate open-handed defensive gesture. "Told me the sheriff was busy in a meeting, and . . . anyway, it's not like that was the only case we had on our plates . . ."

"Just the biggest case in Vegas so far this century," Mobley said softly.

Ecklie swallowed and continued: ". . . and besides, the report was going straight from here to the FBI. After all, at that point it was just a kidnapping."

Sara couldn't believe anyone could, with a straight face, say "just a kidnapping"; but she knew better than to get into this.

Mobley's fist banged off his desk.

Sara jumped a little and Ecklie flinched; Grissom had no reaction.

The sheriff's face had turned a delicate shade of pink, definitely on its way to the full-blown red-faced rage for which the sheriff was famous.

Mobley used the intercom to tell his secretary: "Mrs. Mathis, get Ed Anthony back up here, now!"

Within minutes—long, strained minutes, during which Sara, Grissom, Ecklie (seated now) and Mobley waited silently, the sheriff's rage palpable—a timid knock came to the door.

"Come in!" the sheriff bellowed.

It was not the most inviting invitation Sara had ever heard. . . .

The door squeaked open and Ed Anthony's hair-challenged head poked through the narrow opening; the political adviser's eyes were bright, or was that just . . . fear?

"Wanted to see me, Brian?"

"Get your ass in here, Ed."

Swallowing, the aide shut the door gently and padded over, standing beside Sara, his hands fig-leafed before him. "Problem, Sheriff?"

Mobley picked up the manila folder, shaking it nastily. "Did Conrad Ecklie give you this report, to pass on to me?"

Anthony nodded meekly. "Why? Is that a problem?"

"Well, you didn't pass it on to me, did you?"

"No . . . I didn't."

"Do you *know* what's in this report?"

The political hack looked everywhere but at the sheriff. "Yes. I, uh . . . gave it a read."

He might have been talking about the latest Stephen King novel.

Grissom turned Anthony's way and said, pleasantly, "And then you decided to hold it back until the election—so you could use it to smear Mayor Harrison?"

Anthony said nothing.

"That," Mobley said tightly, "is tantamount to withholding evidence."

"No! No, I was protecting you, Brian."

"Protecting! You're about to screw my career over!"

"Not at all." Anthony patted the air, placatingly. "I was *attempting* to help you. Information of that sensitive a nature needs to be released carefully, at an opportune time. Correctly used, that's the ammunition we need to—"

"*We?*" Mobley interrupted, on his feet again, hands flat on the desk. "There is no 'we,' Ed. You're fired."

"Brian, I understand that you're concerned. And we both know you have a temper. I'm going to advise you count to ten and—"

"You're not going to advise me about shit, from here on out!"

"Brian . . ."

"Get out! *Get out!*"

And now Anthony was almost running to the door.

But Mobley froze him: "And don't even *think* about leaving town, because if I can find a way to bring charges against you for this, I will."

At the door, with a little space between them now, Anthony suddenly summoned some anger of his own. "For what, Brian? For trying to get your hot-headed ass elected mayor?"

Sara was not quite able to process that mixed image.

"No," someone said, calmly.

Grissom.

His voice was quiet, the serenity of it causing the other two men to stop shouting and gape at him: "For aiding and abetting. For possibly turning Candace Lewis's kidnapping into a murder."

Anthony gestured to himself, his eyes enormous, almost as enormous as the fear in his voice. "I . . . I . . . *I* didn't kill her!"

Grissom's tone remained placid. "You withheld key information from our top law enforcement officer . . .

the sheriff, here . . . information that might have saved her."

"You can't know that."

"You're right, I can't, I don't—and now? None of us ever will."

Finally Grissom stood, turning toward the former aide. His voice was so unthreatening that it went beyond any threat: "But I will tell you this, Mr. Anthony. Without your interference, that young woman might still be alive. . . . A fact that will not reflect well on your candidate—Sheriff Mobley."

"Out, Ed," Mobley said, sounding fatigued. "Just go."

Face white with alarm, features slack with defeat, Anthony slipped out.

Turning his attention to Ecklie, Mobley said, "You know better than this, Conrad."

Ecklie nodded; the normally egotistical supervisor now seemed humble. "What can I say? I was careless. I screwed up."

"Yeah, you did."

"Brian, I appreciate this . . . you being so understanding."

"You're welcome, Conrad—three days' suspension. No pay."

Swallowing hard, Ecklie accepted his punishment in silence.

"Go home, Conrad. And if you breathe a word to the media, I'll fire your ass, too."

Nodding, Ecklie left the office, his eyes never landing anywhere near Grissom and Sara.

With just the three of them in the room, the silence seemed deafening. Finally, Mobley was the one to shatter it. "I know," Mobley said, "I don't have to tell the two of you what to do."

Still on his feet, Grissom nodded, picked up the report and headed toward the door, Sara following him. They were almost there when Mobley's voice stopped them.

"Am I in the clear as a suspect yet?"

Turning back, Grissom said, "Not yet."

"DNA?"

"Don't have those results yet."

"I suppose it would be mean-spirited to hope it turns out Ed Anthony did it."

Grissom managed a miniscule smile. "Not really, considering it would probably kill you politically."

Mobley grunted a laugh. "Sometimes, Grissom, having an apolitical asshole like you on the team is a real benefit."

"I appreciate the compliment, Brian. And if it helps—I believe you're innocent."

"Don't tell me that's a hunch?"

"An educated one. Just don't tell anybody."

The sheriff tried to smile but couldn't quite muster it.

In the hall, all business, Grissom said to Sara, "We need a search warrant for Mayor Harrison's house and home."

Sara frowned. "Will a judge give us a warrant based on that DNA evidence?"

Shrugging, Grissom said, "Not only were they having an affair, we also have His Honor's fingerprints in her car, day she disappeared. Go to Judge Giles—he'll listen to reason."

"All right."

They were still walking down the hall when Grissom's cell phone chirped. He took it from his belt, punched a button, and raised the phone to his ear. "Grissom."

He listened for a while.

Then he said, as they walked along, "All right. Sara and I have something to do here. . . . Well, that'll make Mobley feel a little better, anyway."

He listened again, Sara unable to read him.

"All right—stay in touch." He punched the end button then and replaced the phone on his belt.

They walked a little and then Sara asked, "Do I have to beg?"

"That was Warrick—he got carpeting samples from the sheriff's house. None of it matches our remnant."

"That's good news, I guess. For Mobley, anyway."

"One step at a time," Grissom said. "We still have other suspects."

"Like the mayor."

"For one. Now, let's get that search warrant and ruin Mayor Harrison's day."

7

GARY RANDLE'S BELLIGERENCE WAS NOT ENOUGH TO EARN Catherine Willows a search warrant for the suspect's house. But it did provide extra weight in landing her a court order for fingerprinting the Newcombe-Gold employee, which meant—the courthouse being the courthouse—the process took till Wednesday morning. In the meantime, however, Catherine and Nick had learned a good deal about the advertising man.

A few quick calls Tuesday evening had confirmed that Randle had indeed been in the agency offices over the weekend. Janice Denard and several other employees all remembered seeing him, though none could verify whether he'd been working at his own desk or had perhaps been in Ben Jackson's cubicle. And no one seemed to know what project Randle might have been working on.

For all Janice Denard's efficiency, Catherine had the feeling that Newcombe-Gold was a pretty loosely run ship.

When the court order came through this morning,

Nick had talked Catherine out of accompanying him to take the man's fingerprints.

"Really, Cath," Nick said. "It's not just necessary—how many CSIs does it take to screw in a light bulb, anyway?"

"AC or DC? Fluorescent or incandescent?"

But in the end, she sent Nick off to Newcombe-Gold, by himself.

Probably a good call. She was still pissed at Randle for balking and making such a scene, yesterday. Sure, the man was well within his rights; but there was just something about the guy that got her hackles up. Her presence might only serve to accelerate a simple fingerprinting into another scene. . . .

Thanks to some speedy imaging work by Tomas Nunez and his trusty compu-posse, the ad agency would be back at work some time this morning. They were using copies of their old drives, but all their information was there, and they could return to business as usual. At least that problem was out of the way, and it would encourage Newcombe-Gold to be even more cooperative in what could prove to be difficult days ahead.

While she waited for Nick's return, Catherine for the third (or was it the fourth?) time went through what they had learned about Randle, thanks to investigative work by O'Riley, who had talked to neighbors and other agency employees, and seen to the routine computer checks.

Divorced from an alcoholic ex-wife named Elaine, Randle had sole custody of their fourteen-year-old daughter, Heather; he volunteered as a youth counselor at Scenic Peak Presbyterian on Del Webb Boulevard in Summerlin. He and his daughter lived in a two-story stucco home on Crown Vista Lane, not far off Fort Apache Road and Prize Lake Drive.

Randle had originally lost custody of the girl in the divorce, but when Elaine was charged with DUI and reckless endangerment of her daughter, the father had gotten the child back with little trouble. For her part, the ex-wife seemed to have kept her nose clean since her last arrest five years ago. Court records showed that she still had contact with her daughter, through supervised visits.

Looking vaguely nautical in today's ensemble of white Polo with horizontal navy stripes and navy Dockers, Nick Stokes came jauntily back in, waving a white card. "Stop the presses—got the dude's prints, right here."

"When you say 'dude,' are you trying to make me feel young?" Catherine asked, swinging around in her chair. "Because it's not working. . . . Let's get these loaded in the computer."

"You got it."

They were in the corridor in seconds.

Nick said, "And I'm just saying 'dude,' 'cause I'm just . . . saying dude."

Catherine stopped abruptly and so did Nick, who looked at her wide-eyed as she touched his chest with a forefinger. "Nicky, never forget—it's all about me."

He grinned at her. "Sometimes that does slip my mind."

They were on the move again, Catherine saying, "I want to know ASAP if there's a match."

"Wouldn't it be nice if we could nail this guy."

Catherine looked sideways at him. "You think he's guilty?"

"I don't think anything! . . . I just meant . . . Well . . . he *is* a good suspect."

"He's a great suspect."

"That's doesn't make him guilty, Cath."

"No. Of course not."

"Only the evidence can do that."

"Right, Nicky. Hey, we're cool."

"You don't think . . . 'cause of . . . your daughter . . . My background, and . . ."

"Nick! We're professionals."

They had already fed the prints of all the other employees into the computer; and of the two sets of prints on Ben Jackson's keyboard, one belonged to Ben himself, and the other set remained unknown.

"Either Randle is our match," Nick said, "or . . ."

"Or we're back to square one. I hate going back to square one."

Nick shrugged as they turned the corner on the corridor. "Maybe not square one. Ruben Gold left town Friday, yeah, but we should still look at him, talk to him . . . and Roxanne Scott was in the office on Saturday."

Catherine threw a smirk at Nicky. "And if neither of them pans out?"

Another shrug, but less upbeat. "We really are back at square one."

Catherine dreaded that—starting over, and maybe looking outside the company somehow. Newcombe-Gold employed a rent-a-cop security outfit, which

O'Riley was looking into; maybe some security guard had . . .

But Catherine knew she was getting ahead of herself. First things first.

While Nick took care of the fingerprints, Catherine checked in with Nunez. The computer expert had returned the ad agency's equipment, but he was still sifting through the copies he'd made for himself.

She found the tall, unlikely computer geek still in the garage where he and his crew had first set up. The others were gone, and Nunez was left to wade through the mountain of information on his own.

"What's new?" she asked, giving him a smile.

Glancing up from the screen of his monitor, he said, "You clearly haven't heard."

Catherine frowned. "What haven't I heard?"

"Hey—I'll tell you, but don't shoot the messenger."

"Well, not to kill, anyway. *What*, Tomas?"

"Mobley took me off your case. . . . Temporarily! Just temporarily. . . ."

Catherine felt red-hot anger rising inside her, but she managed not to detonate all over Nunez. "And why would the esteemed Sheriff Mobley do *that?*"

He sighed, shrugged. "Sorry—but some thoughtless asshole hacked into a bank last night, and the sheriff's got me on that. I'll start working your stuff again, ASAP—but Mobley's on my tail to find this hacker, stat."

"Gee, I wonder if this bank has a president or chairman of the board who's a potential contributor to Mobley's mayoral campaign or anything . . ."

"Hey, I don't do politics!"

Her hands came up in front of her and she pressed them together, her knuckles turning white.

"Easy, Cath—it's not all bad news."

"Improve my mood. Quick."

Nunez did his best: "We imaged and processed all thirty hard drives using Encase, version four."

Catherine nodded—she'd heard of, though never used, the Guidance Software product. She knew it allowed for bit-by-bit copying of hard drives, zip disks, USB devices, even Palm Pilots.

"Then," Nunez was saying, "I verified the copies using an MD5 Hash algorithm."

"Of course you did," she said, invoking a light humor she didn't feel, both of them knowing she had no idea what an MD5 Hash whatever-the-hell was.

"It's like a digital fingerprint," Nunez said. "The odds of two files having the same hash value and *not* being identical is two raised to the 128th power, or 340 billion billion billion billion to one."

She shook her head. "You can't get better odds anywhere in Vegas."

"Not unless you're the house. Cath, that's about the same as winning the LOTTO four in a row."

"So, we're sure you got everything then."

"Damn sure," he said. "And that's not just the files—it's deleted files, file slack and unallocated space. If there was ever kiddie porn on any of these machines, I'll find it."

"That's good news. But when?"

"Either when I catch the bank hacker, or when Mobley decides to let me get back to it."

"Before the interruption, did you find out anything?"

Nunez nodded. "The hard drive in Ruben Gold's computer was negative for any child-porn pics."

"Okay—that's a start."

"I couldn't find any pictures on any of the client computers, either."

"Client computers?" she asked.

"The other machines in the network."

"So how did our pictures get there?"

A shrug. "Lots of possible ways—I just don't know which one yet."

Not liking the sound of this, Catherine made sure she was following Nunez, asking, "So there's no porn on any of the computers?"

"Not even a casual hit on an adult site. And just to make sure, I ran an E-Script to carve all the jpegs out of each hard drive—and none of those resembled the ones from the printer."

She knew jpegs—that is, .jpg files—were the common photo format for pornographers to use. "But did the print order come from work station eighteen or not?"

His answer didn't really sound like an answer to the CSI: "I searched the network server hard drives."

Striving for patience, Catherine nodded as if she followed this. The truth was, her daughter Lindsey probably knew more about the actual workings of the machines. Embarrassing as it might be to a scientist like Catherine, the guts of the things were completely foreign to her. Nunez, however, was babbling on: "I found print files showing pictures angel1.jpg through angel12.jpg were sent to Ruben Gold's computer."

"Which led to?"

"Me looking in the network logs and finding that the pictures came from a client computer using an IP address of 1.160.10.240."

"Okay—I can't even *pretend* you haven't lost me. . . ."

"An IP address is an identifier for a computer or a device on a TCP/IP network. These networks route messages based on the IP address of the destination."

"The destination," she said, "not the sender?"

He nodded. "Don't panic just yet—there's more. Date and time stamps on the print file showed that it was created early Saturday morning. Then the IP address found in the server log showed that it came from client computer number eighteen."

Relief flooded through her. "So—we were right; and everything you've done has cemented that."

"That would be a great big *si.*"

"But on the other hand, we really haven't gotten any further."

Nunez's face fell, a little. "No, we really haven't . . . and as long as Mobley's got me on this bank hacker, we're stalled."

"If you can steal a little time for me . . ."

"I will. You know I will.

"Thanks, Tomas."

Exasperated, Catherine strode off.

She found Nick hunkered in front of the AFIS computer.

Without waiting for him to look up, much less report, she launched into her tirade: "Mobley took Tomas away from us to track down some bank hacker!"

Nick shrugged. "Grand larceny trumps kiddie porn, I guess."

"Trumps kiddie porn?" she fumed. "Are you serious?"

He gave her a sideways look, then turned to face her. "No. I wasn't."

But she was already off the runway, and there was no coming back: "Just because this isn't a murder or a crime involving money, Mobley's willing to stick these abused kids on the back burner! Well I sure as hell am not!"

Nick patted the air in front of him until she lapsed into silence. "Why—do you think *I* am?"

"No, but . . ."

Reasonable as Nicky was being, Catherine could not stop the white-hot anger coursing through her. An urge to tear the lab apart caused her to tremble and she fought to stay in control. She fell into the chair beside Nick and she sensed his hand on her shoulder.

Her frustration was palpable now, a heaviness in her body, a rage in her brain, and a thickening of her tongue. She felt tears flowing. "Shit! Shitshitshit! . . . If you tell Grissom I broke down, I'll . . ."

"Hey, dude," Nick said gently. "Your secret's safe with me."

She laughed a little, though still crying, and Nick got her some Kleenex. She said, "It . . . it's jus . . . just . . . I'd like to track down that bastard Mobley and curse him into next week. . . ."

"I hear you."

"Nicky, those girls in those photos—they're barely older than Lindsey!"

"I know."

"And the department just doesn't seem to care."

"I know that, too."

And she fell into his arms, she in her chair, he in his, and patted his back, as if he were the one crying.

He pushed her away, and smiled at her, providing more Kleenex. He reserved one for himself, but his voice was strong as he said, "We'll solve this. We will solve it. Now—how about some good news?"

Her trembling had subsided a little. "Yeah. Yeah, some good news . . . I could use it, I could *really* use it. . . ."

Nick's grin was almost pixie-ish. "Gary Randle's prints . . . are a match."

"Oh, Nicky. That's great. I told you he was a good suspect."

"No, you said he was a great suspect."

She drew in a deep breath—she felt as though she'd been held under water for too long, and only now was just bursting through the surface.

Nick said, "Those were his prints on the keyboard in Ben Jackson's cubicle."

"How about AFIS?" she asked, meaning the national fingerprint database.

"I put him through," Nick said, "but he's got no priors."

"It's enough for a search warrant. We can get inside that house now!"

"Yes we can," he said, nodding. "Make the call, Cath. And I'll get O'Riley up to speed."

An hour later, the CSIs were back at Newcombe-Gold, moving single-file down the corridor toward Randle's office with Nick in the lead, holding a wad of papers in one hand and his CS case in the other. Catherine, carrying her own case and more papers, tagged right behind him with O'Riley trailing her. As the procession approached the conference room, Janice Denard stepped out in their path.

"Did you find out anything?" she asked.

"Still digging," Nick said, with a nod of hello, and then walked on.

The blonde office manager fell in beside Catherine, who said, "Getting closer," then handed the woman a copy of the new search warrant.

Denard dropped out to read the document, while the others kept going. The half-glass front wall of his office warned Randle of their approach and he was out of his chair even before they were completely through the door.

"Now, goddamnit, this is harassment!" He was coming around the desk as he spoke. "Didn't you already get your damned fingerprints?"

Nick stood and faced the ad man. "And I do appreciate your cooperation, earlier; and you don't even have to answer our questions, about whether or not you were here this weekend—we already know you were."

O'Riley stepped up, taking a referee's position, as the two men continued the tense exchange.

"So I was here! Damn it, I work here!" Today, the

adman wore an expensive charcoal suit, white shirt and a red and blue diagonally striped power tie.

"You know," Catherine said from the sidelines, in a tone that pretended to be light, "you might want to ease up on the attitude. . . . It's not going to reflect very well."

Randle glared over at her. "What are you talking about?"

But it was Nick who spoke next: "It's not just that you were here this weekend, Mr. Randle—but that you also used Ben Jackson's work station." The CSI held up the sheaf of papers. "We matched your fingerprints."

Randle's anger evaporated and he laughed out loud, as he took a step back, as if reappraising not just the situation but these law enforcement officers.

"You're kidding, right? Is *that* what this is about? Me using some poor schlub's computer, while he was out of town for the weekend? Is this some weird crackdown Gold or Newcombe instigated?"

Catherine stepped forward. "Actually, it *is* about you using some poor schlub's computer over the weekend. And it is police business."

She held one of the pornographic printouts out, just inches from his face.

Tightly she said, "Specifically, it's about you using Ben Jackson's computer to print this out, and a dozen more like it. . . . Why, Mr. Randle! . . . You're not laughing anymore."

And he wasn't. His laugh had died in his throat as his eyes focused on the photo. He swallowed thickly and stumbled backward, till his desk stopped him.

"You . . . you think I did *what?*"

And his anger returned, the man recovering quickly, stepping forward, eyes flaring.

"You think I printed this filth—off company property? And that I did it with, with . . . sick shit like this? I have a daughter, a young daughter! You people are sick. You can't honestly believe . . ."

The man's eyes traveled from the photo to Catherine's and locked—she did her best to tell him, with her eyes, that that's exactly what she did believe. And he appeared to get the message.

He half-sat on the edge of the desk, clearly staggered.

Nick stepped forward. "You want to tell us what you printed out on Saturday? If it wasn't these photos?"

Randle's eyes, not so confident now, went to Nick's stony face. "You can't believe that I . . ." Then he shook his head. "I can tell trying to get through to you people is useless. You've already made up your minds."

Nick frowned. "Mr. Randle . . ."

"I'm not saying another word till I've spoken to my attorney."

O'Riley, still standing nearby like a ref, said, "That's your right, sir," but the respect of the words took on a chill, thanks to the detective's cold eyes.

Catherine said, "Give Mr. Randle the warrant, Nicky."

Nick did, saying, "As the true owners of this office, Newcombe-Gold's representative, Janice Denard, has already been served with this warrant; but out of consideration to your rights, this is a copy for you."

"Thank you very much," Randle said, oozing sarcasm as he took the piece of paper; but the voice was edged with anxiety now.

Then Nick handed the man a second warrant. "And this one is for your home."

Randle didn't accept this warrant, at first, looking at the paper as if Nick were offering a glass of poison. Still half-sitting on the desk's front edge, the adman fell into an uneasy silence. Nick held out the paper; Randle stared at it. Nick said nothing; Randle said nothing.

After seconds that seemed like minutes, Randle took the paper, reluctantly, and said, "I'll have to call my lawyer. Any objection?"

"Of course not," Nick said.

The man removed his cell phone from his suitcoat pocket.

Moving quickly, Catherine snatched the device from his hand. "But not with this!"

"What the hell?" Randle exploded. He was on his feet now, glaring at Catherine, his eyes wild. "Are you crazy? You can't stop me from calling my attorney!"

"Wouldn't dream of it," she said sweetly. "But we're going to place that call for you."

He looked baffled. "*Why* in hell?"

Catherine's eyebrows lifted. "Perhaps because we didn't just fall off a turnip truck. We're aware that you may set things up to wipe your hard drive, at home, clean—with just a phone call."

His eyes rolled. "You're insane—why in hell would I destroy my own computer? Why would I have it set up to do so with . . . a *phone call?*"

"Mr. Randle, if you're a trafficker in child pornography," Catherine said blandly, "you'll know the answer to that. If not, I suggest you allow us to do our job, which if you're innocent will include clearing you."

"Oh, I can see you're on my side!"

Nick stepped up. "Your lawyer's name, Mr. Randle?"

"Jonathan Austin."

"You have a phone book?"

"Bottom right hand drawer of the desk."

"Would you get it out for us, please?"

Shaking his head, sighing, Randle said, "Christ, I *know* the number!"

Nick's voice turned hard. "The phone book, Mr. Randle."

Randle walked behind the desk, with O'Riley following, watching him carefully. The ad man fished the thick Yellow Pages directory out of the drawer and handed it over. Nick thumbed to ATTORNEYS and found the listing for Jonathan Austin. Using the phone on Randle's desk, he dialed the number, waited for the ring, then handed the receiver to Randle.

The adman waited a moment, then into the phone, he said, "Mr. Austin, please."

He listened.

"Yes—Gary Randle."

Another beat passed.

"Jonathan? Gary Randle." He went on to explain the situation, then listened for a while. "I can't stop them? . . . Fine, fine, please, just get here as fast as you can. These officers are less than sympathetic. . . . I'm at the office." He hung up the phone and announced, "My attorney will be here in fifteen minutes."

Catherine was in the process of sealing an evidence bag in which Randle's cell phone now resided.

Randle had a whipped look. "You're keeping my *phone?*"

She said, "Until we know it's not part of the case, yes."

The adman heaved a weight-of-the-world sigh, but said nothing.

"Mr. Randle, why don't we step into the hall?" O'Riley suggested.

Shaking his head, Randle said, "No, I prefer to wait here."

"That may be," O'Riley said, and held out a hand in a "this way" gesture. "But we need to let the crime scene investigators do their job."

"It's my office! It's not a *crime* scene. . . ."

Catherine flashed a smile that had little to do with the usual reasons for smiling. "We'll let you know."

Shaking his head bitterly, Randle followed the detective into the hall, where the two men stood and watched through the glass as the CSIs worked. She could feel other eyes, from cubicles and offices, more discreet—she never caught anyone looking directly—but very much there.

Catherine took a good look around Randle's office as she and Nick pulled on their latex gloves. Only slightly smaller than those of Newcombe and Gold themselves, Randle's office had a distinctive starkness. The glassed front wall had a curtain, open now; but the other three walls had no windows and no hanging pictures. Bookshelves lined the right wall and the back wall was bare but for a small section of awards-arrayed shelves. Near the left wall stood a large, tilted drawing table with comfy wheeled chair, and beyond that, near the front, was a stand with a television and DVD/VCR combo machine.

Odd so visual a person would leave his office so spartan, Catherine reflected; perhaps the man preferred to keep his mind clear of other people's images to make way for his own. On the other hand, Catherine wasn't sure she even wanted to know what kind of images might be found in this man's mind. . . .

She eyed the thick wall-to-wall carpeting, thinking she might have Nick hand-vac the major traffic areas, though footprints in here were probably useless, especially after they'd all tromped in on top of any others.

Two wing chairs faced the huge mahogany desk and behind them, pushed up against the front wall, stretched a green leather sofa. The desk top had some files open on it, a phone, banker's lamp and a framed picture.

Catherine got behind the desk to see a photo of a curly-haired blonde girl about twelve, standing beamingly with Randle, an arm around her—his daughter, she supposed. Considering the nature of this case, she decided to confirm that. She picked up the photo, turned it toward Randle and O'Riley, visible through the window out in the corridor; the open doorway carried her voice to them: "Your daughter?"

Randle nodded. "Heather."

Putting the photo back, she asked her partner, "You want the desk or the bookshelves?"

Nick took one look at the shelves crammed with books and magazines—the lone sign of mess or disorganization in the whole room—and said, "Mind if I take the desk?"

"Nicky, you're such a wimp," Catherine said good-naturedly.

"When you say 'wimp,' " Nick said innocently, "are you trying to make me feel old?"

They exchanged small smiles and got to work. The shelves looked to be mahogany, as well—five high, spread to different heights, the top two housing books with titles including *Error-Free Writing* and *Strunk and White's Elements of Style*, plus a dictionary, thesaurus, desk atlas and numerous art books, some of which were oversize and even massive. She pulled one down and absently thumbed through the pages. One picture—a nude—caught her eye. At first she thought it might be evidence, then she realized it was an image that could be found in her own home: one of the Helga pictures, by artist Andrew Wyeth.

After returning the book to its place, Catherine went through the rest of the volumes methodically; she moved down to the third shelf and sorted through seven three-ring binders, filled with drawings and other artwork from different ad campaigns, a number of which she recognized. The man had talent. As she prepared to go through the magazines in three piles on each of two bottom shelves, she sensed something, turned and saw Randle glowering out in the corridor.

Nick called, "Any luck, Cath?"

She looked Nick's way and saw him bent over the center drawer of Randle's desk. "Nothing so far. You?"

He shook his head. "Nada."

Glancing back at Randle, Catherine said, "Keep at it—I got a feeling he's watching us just to see what we'll find."

"That's natural, Cath."

"Maybe."

Her eyes were still on Randle as a tall, silver-haired gent strode into view and shook hands with the ad man, placing a hand of concern on his client's shoulder—this was his attorney, no doubt. Concentrating on the job before her, Catherine returned to the shelves.

She was riffling through the second pile on the fourth shelf when she froze. . . .

In the midst of all the copies of *Advertising Age, Mediaweek* and *Brandweek,* the CSI caught a glimpse of gray crammed between two pages of a copy of an *Adweek.*

"Nick."

"What?"

"Get the camera—take a picture of this."

In a few seconds he was next to her, the thirty-five millimeter poised. "Whatcha got?"

She allowed the magazine to fall open and—tucked there, between a full-page picture of a woman holding a beer bottle and a story of the ad company that created the campaign—was a cobalt-gray zip disk with no label. As Catherine held her position, Nick took several shots of the disk and magazine.

Then Randle was standing beside them, his eyes wild.

"That's not mine!" His voice was as loud as it was

angry, as angry as it was defensive. "I don't know what it is, or how it got there!"

His attorney came quickly up behind him. An impeccable, distinguished man in his early sixties, the attorney said, "Gary, be quiet. Not another word."

Randle turned to the lawyer, immediately ignoring his advice. "Jonathan, I don't know how that got there—I've never seen it before."

Austin—his eyes a washed-out blue though bright with intelligence, his handsome features marked by a narrow nose and thin lips—gritted his teeth, his words cold and measured. "In other words, that disk may be nothing at all."

Not quite getting what his lawyer was reaching for, Randle said, "I suppose, but—"

Cutting him off with both words and a chopping gesture, Austin said, "If it's nothing, we don't want to get all worked up about it—do we, Gary?"

Finally getting it, Randle clammed and allowed Austin to usher him back out into the hallway, where a whispered conference consisted mostly of the attorney talking. As they'd gone out, O'Riley had come in.

The detective said, "But *is* that something?"

"Our boy sure behaved like it is," Catherine said. "But until we get it to Tomas in the lab, we won't know . . . that is, if Tomas can work us into the sheriff's busy schedule."

O'Riley made a face. "Guy gives me a pain," he said, meaning Mobley.

Catherine and Nick searched for another twenty minutes, thoroughly going over every square inch of the office, even bringing in step ladders and looking above ceiling tiles; but, beyond the mysterious zip disk, they found nothing special.

"We done?" Nick asked.

Catherine took one last look, then said, "Yeah—let's head for la Casa Randle."

"You're spending way too much time with Tomas. . . ."

In the corridor, they informed Austin and Randle of their intention, loaded up their gear and a small caravan took off for Crown Vista Drive: CSI Tahoe in front, then Randle and Austin in the lawyer's Jaguar, finally O'Riley's Taurus. Nick caught the Beltway and followed it around to Flamingo, taking that to Fort Apache Drive. From there the twisty streets of the Lakes development swooped around, until the Tahoe drew up in front of 9407 Crown Vista Drive.

Nick parked, Austin's Jag pulling up into the driveway of a three-car garage, itself bigger than the average house in Vegas. O'Riley parked on the street directly behind the Jag in the driveway: if Austin wanted to leave before the LVMPD was finished, he'd be backing over his client's lawn to do so.

The two-story house was impressive in size but otherwise typical of the desert town—cream stucco with a red tile roof—and not what Catherine expected, simply because it *was* so typical, particularly of the Lakes area. Someone artistic, like Randle, might well live in a residence with a little more flair or style.

The front yard, richly green and well manicured, did have the touch of a Chinese elm, a small mulch-filled circle of stones surrounding it. Two pillars held up a second floor that stood out over the entrance and left the front door and the two skinny windows on its either side in perpetual shade. An afterthought of a sunroom seemed to lean against the side of the house, just to the right of the entrance.

O'Riley followed the lawyer and his client to the door, while Catherine and Nick were getting their equipment out of the back of the Tahoe. By the time the CSIs caught up, they found Austin, O'Riley and Randle off to one side of the large stoop, the ad man pulling nervously on a cigarette.

O'Riley gestured in a presentational manner. "Unlocked, and all yours."

Catherine asked, "You're not coming in, Sarge?"

"Think I'll keep the counselor and his client company."

Austin said, "I've advised Mr. Randle to stay out of your way. If you need to know where something is, need any help with anything . . . just let us know."

"Thank you, Catherine said, tugging on her latex gloves. Nick already had his on. The white steel door opened onto an entryway that bled at right into a suitably airy sunroom with lots of rattan furnishing; at left, stairs hugged the wall on their way to the second floor. Just past the sunroom a door was open onto a half-bath, opposite which was a door that Nick discovered led to the vast garage.

Much of the downstairs was essentially behind the garage. Catherine entered a galley-style kitchen with a breakfast bar on the far side opening into a great room with an overstuffed sofa, two overstuffed chairs, a thirty-six-inch TV and a set of black shelves that held a monster stereo system. Large windows on the back wall showed the blue water of a swimming pool out-side.

"Pays to advertise," Nick said.

"No," Catherine said. "People pay *to* advertise."

A hallway led to a large bedroom that—judging from the male feel of the room and a work area in the far right corner, with drawing board—had to be Randle's.

"Upstairs or down?" Catherine asked.

Shrugging, Nick said, "Up."

Catherine started by examining the bedroom work area. A large if prefab-looking desk accommodated a desktop computer, printer, scanner and zip drive. The latter zip was of particular interest—Randle could have downloaded the kid-porn images at home and conveniently taken them to work on that disk they'd found in his office.

Taking her cue from Tomas's process at the agency, she photographed all the equipment and wiring, then one by one disconnected the various pieces.

Two hours later, the sunroom encompassed a pile of evidence they'd take with them: the bedroom computer and all associated media; a laptop Catherine had found in a corner next to the sofa in the great room; another PC tower from a computer Nick had located upstairs; and, not insignificantly, two boxes that Catherine had discovered in Randle's closet.

One box was filled with hard-core porn magazines as well as photo albums that showed Randle and at least a dozen other people in various sexual situations. The other box was stuffed with triple-X DVDs and videotapes. On first pass, the magazines—evenly divided between newsstand magazines like *Hustler* and *Penthouse* and harder material available only in "adult" bookstores or on the net—seemed to contain nothing but photos and stories of and pertaining to adults.

Likewise, the photo albums showed nothing but adults having sex—swinger-party Polaroids. Catherine knew that the lack of children or young teens in this material didn't mean a great deal, though the magazines and albums did reflect a strong interest on Randle's part in sexually oriented material. That, of course, didn't make him a child pornographer or even a consumer of child pornography.

About half an hour into the search, Nick had invited Randle and his attorney—and O'Riley, of course—to come in and sit in the kitchen, where they had coffee and watched CNN.

As Catherine and Nick were preparing to load the property up, Randle must have got a sense of it, because the lord of the castle came in with his lawyer trailing quickly behind (and O'Riley ambling thereafter).

Randle's eyes widened at the sight of the pile on the sunroom floor. "Isn't this a little excessive. . . . Oh, jeez—you're taking my *daughter's* computer, too?"

"Every computer in the house," Catherine said. "No exceptions."

"Well, hell—she *needs* that! How's she supposed to do her homework?"

Nick said, "We'll try to get it right back to you, Mr. Randle . . . but in a case like this, we're going to check every computer you could have come in contact with."

Catherine said, "That's quite a collection you've got there," and gestured to the boxes of adult material.

"What about it? It's not illegal."

"Not illegal—maybe a little damaging, when you're being investigated for a sex crime."

The attorney stepped up, asking Catherine, "Ms. Willows, isn't it? Was there any child pornography in the collection?"

"Not that we've seen thus far," Catherine said.

Nick said, "We haven't been through it all. Your client's a real collector."

Obviously as frustrated as he was irritated, Randle said, "Let me save you a step—you're not going find any child porn, because there isn't any in there!"

Catherine asked, "Would you care to comment on the photo albums? Pornography is one thing; but you obviously take a . . . proactive interest."

The attorney touched Randle's arm and said, "You don't have to explain yourself, Gary. We'll discuss this—"

But Randle said, "I have nothing to hide, Jonathan!"

"I know you don't, but—"

Randle looked directly at Catherine. "You see, my ex-wife—"

"Elaine."

His eyes tightened, when he realized Catherine knew his ex-wife's name; but he pressed on: "Yes, Elaine. . . . Elaine and I were, for a time, in . . . how should I say this . . . a certain lifestyle."

"Swinging," Catherine said. "Wife swapping? Group sex?"

His eyes fell to the floor; he nodded. "I'm not proud of it. It was kind of an experimental phase we were both going through. We'd both had affairs, and got back together, and we thought maybe . . . I don't know. We'd save the marriage somehow, by this . . . openness. Anyway, it was a mistake. In fact, in the end, I think that . . . activity . . . was what led to Elaine's drinking getting out of hand."

"And that phase is over?"

Randle waved dismissively. "Long since. We ditched the swinger's scene, but . . . I guess it was too late to save the marriage."

Nick said, "If it was just a phase, why hold onto the photo albums?"

"I don't know. I just did. I don't really think that's any of your business, anyway. I've been frank. Doesn't that count for anything?"

"You're not involved in that scene, anymore."

"No! I have nothing to hide!"

"Not in those photos," Nick said.

The attorney said, "Mr. Stokes!"

Catherine asked, "Your ex-wife has visitation rights, correct?"

"Supervised," Randle said, "by an officer of the court. Social worker in our case."

"So Elaine doesn't have custody on the weekends?"

"Much as she hates that, no. Her drinking burned a lot of bridges for her. She was drunk behind the wheel when she got into that accident—with Heather in the car!"

Catherine didn't think either one of them sounded like candidates for parent of the year. She handed

Randle a piece of paper. "This is an itemized list of the property we're seizing. Anything that isn't evidence will be returned, in due course."

Randle slowly scanned the list; he looked up, surprised. "What's this about a laptop?"

"The one that was next to the couch," Catherine said, "in the family room."

"No."

"No?"

"Lady, I don't even own a laptop."

"Well, that's a new one, Mr. Randle. I've heard 'I don't even *own* a gun,' I've certainly heard 'That's not *my* grass' . . . but—"

"Show me this laptop. Come on—show me!"

They did.

"Not mine," Randle said, shaking his head emphatically. "Not Heather's, either."

Nick asked, "Then how did it come to be in your family room?"

Randle's eyes were huge, though the flesh around them had tightened; a vein was throbbing in his forehead.

Catherine said pleasantly, "Well, Mr. Randle?"

For first time, Randle seemed not just put out or frustrated or irritated: he was afraid. Clearly, utterly terrified. But he managed to say, "How can I explain it? You should tell *me*—you're the detectives!"

The attorney took his client firmly by the arm. "Mr. Randle has nothing further to say about this matter. Are you going to charge him? Take him in for questioning as a material witness?"

Catherine said nothing; Nick was silent, and O'Riley, too.

"Then please take with you what your search warrant allows," Austin said, "and leave my client's home."

Catherine looked right at Randle, though her words were directed to the attorney: "Your client should not leave town. He may feel he has nothing more to say to us, but we may have much more to say to him—once we've gone through this material at the lab."

Nick's smile looked almost sincere. "You'll be hearing from us real soon, Mr. Randle. Thanks for your cooperation."

Randle and his attorney headed back for the kitchen, and O'Riley helped the CSIs load up the Tahoe with the potential evidence.

At HQ, Nunez was given custody of the computers while Catherine and Nick split up everything else. Before they really dug in, Catherine said, "Hey—before we look at naked pictures, Nicky . . . isn't there someone we should talk to, first?"

"A man of the cloth?" Nick asked, wryly.

"Not even a man *with* a cloth. . . . A woman. With an ex-husband I'm confident she'll want to tell us *all* about. . . ."

Within half an hour, Catherine and Nick—with O'Riley chaperoning—were on the front porch of a one-story house in a quiet neighborhood on Gunderson Boulevard.

The older home, with its white and gray siding, tall trees sprouting from a lush, trim lawn, could hardly compare with Randle's Lakes area residence, but it had a quiet, homey appeal. In the driveway outside a one-car garage, a black Lincoln Continental seemed slightly incongruous next to the modest but well-kept home.

O'Riley rang the bell and, as if she'd been expecting them, a woman answered.

"May I help you?" she asked, her voice midrange and sweet, almost saccharine.

O'Riley said, "Elaine Randle?"

She nodded. "Why yes—what is it? You folks have an . . . official look."

Were the remnants of a Southern accent, Catherine wondered, lurking in there somewhere?

The detective was showing his wallet I.D. to the woman, introducing himself and the CSIs.

The woman's smile vanished. "Is it Heather? Is she all right? Please tell me she's fine!"

"Yes, she is fine," Catherine said, putting some warmth in it.

"Thank God," Elaine said, and her smile returned, however tentative.

"Sorry to alarm you," Catherine said. "Hey, I'm a mom myself. Mrs. Randle, we'd like to talk to you about your ex-husband."

The smile was gone again, but she opened the door. "Please come in. Is something wrong? Is Gary all right?"

They were all inside before Catherine answered. "Your husband's all right. As for, if something's wrong . . . frankly, we don't know yet. We'd just like to ask you a few questions."

Nick said, "You may be able to help us determine if there is a problem."

"I'm not sure I understand, but I'm glad to talk to you. Can I get anyone a drink?" They declined and their hostess led them into a small, neat living room with anonymous contemporary decor. A sofa lined one wall and a couple of chairs sat at angles, one at the sofa's far end, the other across the narrow room. A twenty-one-inch TV perched on a cart in a corner and an end table separated the sofa and the nearest chair.

"There's no polite way to say this," Catherine said, having been asked in advance by an embarrassed O'Riley to take the lead with the woman. "But we need to talk to you about Mr. Randle's sexual proclivities."

A hand went to the woman's mouth and trembled there; her eyes jumped. "Oh, God . . . I thought that was behind me. What has he done? What has Gary *done?*"

How quickly they'd gotten to this point caught Catherine by surprise, and she was astonished to hear herself pleading the suspect's case, however vaguely: "We're not sure Gary's done anything, Mrs. Randle."

"Oh. Well, I hope you're right. . . ."

"Why would you think he had?"

Elaine Randle shrugged, sighed. "Gary's . . . appetites always seem to be escalating. When we were married, he just kept wanting more . . . more of . . . well, everything."

"When you were involved with him, in that lifestyle, you didn't like it?"

"No. I *tried* to like it—for Gary. For our marriage."

"Did that pressure, that stress, have anything to do with your drinking problem?"

The woman leaned forward and almost whispered to Catherine: "Could you and I talk, alone? I'm sorry, but this is . . ." She glanced at Nick and O'Riley. ". . . this is embarrassing."

"It needn't be," Catherine said. "Detective O'Riley and CSI Stokes are professionals, and they need to hear what you have to say."

"Well . . . but it's . . ."

"We gather evidence," Catherine said in a firm but friendly manner. "We don't judge."

Elaine Randle drew in a deep breath, sighed, and pressed on: "Our lifestyle involved . . . well . . . there's no other way to say it: Gary's perverted tastes. He always wanted to see me with other men, other women and finally, in groups. It was getting out of hand. It was humiliating, demeaning, and as you guessed, yes, I started drinking to cope, and eventually that got out of hand, too."

Catherine cocked her head, studying the woman. "Was Gary ever interested in younger partners?"

With a derisive laugh, the woman said, "Yes—once I hit thirty, he had an affair with a woman barely out of her teens. And, later, I could see . . . in the swinging situations? Where Gary was concerned, the younger the partner, the better."

"Really?"

She grunted a laugh. "It's almost like he's obsessed with youth—youth and sex. He was constantly looking for attention from younger women. Maybe that's not unusual."

"What do you mean, Mrs. Randle?"

"Well, he was past thirty, too, remember—younger women, girls, that was a way to prove to himself that he hadn't lost it—that he really wasn't getting older."

"How young *were* these 'girls'?" Nick asked.

Elaine Randle flushed a little. She answered Nick's question, but looked at Catherine, her voice soft. "One night, shortly before I ended our relationship, I let him talk me into a threesome . . . I'm not proud of this . . . with the eighteen-year-old girl babysitting our daughter."

Catherine sat forward. "Did Gary ever display a desire for an even younger girl?"

She frowned. "Younger than that? Teenage girls, you mean? Our daughter's age . . . ?"

The words were barely out of the woman's mouth when she froze in horror.

"Your daughter's age," Catherine said gently. "Or younger."

Elaine Randle leaned forward and gripped Catherine by the wrist; the woman's face was tight with concern. "Dear God, is my daughter safe? Are you sure Heather's *safe* with him? Where is she? Is she—"

"Heather's fine," Catherine said firmly. "We're investigating a crime where Mr. Randle works."

Fury enveloped the woman's face. She flew to her feet. "Why that no-good son of a bitch! That lousy no-good perverted son of a—"

Catherine stood and faced the woman; held onto her forearms. "Whoa . . . go slow, Mrs. Randle. We don't know anything yet—your husband may just be an innocent bystander. There are several dozen people at his agency, and he's just one of many we're looking at."

"Well, that may be . . . but he's the only one with access to my daughter!"

"Elaine?" Catherine said, locking her eyes with Mrs. Randle. "I said I was a mother, too. Do you understand?"

Elaine Randle swallowed, nodded.

"I would feel the same about my daughter," Catherine said. "I know all about the maternal urge to protect . . . and as one mother to another, I'm telling you—don't worry."

"How can I not—"

Catherine put a hand on Elaine Randle's shoulder. "We won't let anything happen to Heather. She will be safe."

8

FOR THE FIRST TWENTY-FOUR HOURS AND THEN SOME, THE "Want" on the radio for the white Chevy had been a bigger bust than the car's broken taillight.

And then a prowl car reported a white Monte Carlo with a broken tail near the New York New York casino resort. The patrolman said the Monte was headed into the hotel parking ramp and that he would follow, but by the time Warrick Brown and Captain Jim Brass arrived, both the patrolman and the Monte were gone.

Livid, Brass radioed dispatch and was told that 2Paul34—the patrol car in question—had responded to a 444 . . . "officer needs help—emergency" . . . on Russell Road, where a drunken motorist had taken a potshot at another officer during a routine traffic stop.

"Talk about good excuse," Warrick said. This was midmorning—Warrick already several hours into a double shift—so the drunk was either getting an early start or heading home way late.

Brass nonetheless looked pissed-off, though Warrick knew damn well the detective would have done the same as the patrolman—the urge to help a brother officer ran deep. Brass pushed the button on the radio and said, "Dispatch—did 2Paul34 report a license number?"

The female dispatcher's voice crackled: "1Zebra10, that's affirmative. It was a match for your partial."

"Dispatch, you have the whole number?"

"Affirmative."

"Run that for me, will you?"

While they waited, Warrick talked Brass into driving up and down every row in the parking building to search for the vehicle; there were lots of white cars, several Chevys, even a few Monte Carlos, but none the right year, nor with a broken taillight.

Soon Brass was pulling out onto Las Vegas Boulevard, where he glided aimlessly, both the detective and CSI searching for the white-car needle in the traffic haystack of the Strip, really just killing time until a computer coughed up the name and address of their suspect.

After an endless wait—about four minutes—the dispatcher came back on. "1Zebra10, that car, a white 1998 Chevrolet Monte Carlo is registered to Kyle A. Hamilton."

"Address?"

The dispatcher told him.

"Ten-four," Brass told the mike. "1Zebra10 will be 423 at that address."

"Ten-four," the dispatcher replied.

A 423 radio call meant they'd be seeing a person for information—not usually the business of a CSI, but both Warrick and Brass knew they might well be going to the home of a killer. That meant possible evidence, even—considering the nature of Candace Lewis's apparent extended stay with the killer—a crime scene.

Anyway, two heads were better than one in such a situation; also, two guns. . . .

The address was way up north, Cotton Gum Court, above Craig and off Lone Mountain Road and Spruce Oak Drive. From the Strip, even in relatively light midmorning traffic, the trip took the better part of an hour and, when they finally pulled up to the house, the distinct signs of nobody-home awaited them.

The two-story stucco with two-car garage had one of those new xeriscape yards. With the drought oppressing the area for the last two years, ripping up and replacing lawns with low-moisture plants—xeriscaping—had become more than a fad, including a way to gain rebates from the water company as the dry spell continued its stranglehold on the city's unchecked growth.

The double-wide garage door was down, the blinds were pulled tight, and the upstairs curtains were drawn; all that was lacking was some tumbleweed to plow across the landscape. Warrick followed Brass to the front door and the detective rang the bell; no answer. They tried again, and again, with the same result. They took a quick trip around the residence, but saw nothing, including peeking through the few windows that provided a view.

Brass tried the neighbors on either side. At the house to the east, the detective talked briefly to a soccer mom just getting ready to leave. She reported that Hamilton was a nice, quiet neighbor who worked days and sometimes into the evening. What job? She couldn't quite recall; sales of some kind.

When the woman excused herself and closed the door, Warrick said, "Pretty much the kind of innocuous report the neighbors give when a TV crew comes around asking about the serial killer next door."

Brass didn't disagree.

The neighbor to the west, like Hamilton, wasn't home.

"Well," Brass sighed, leaning against the driver's side door of the Taurus, looking across at Warrick. "Shall we wait him out?

"I'm into double shift," Warrick reminded the detective. "Could we get a patrol car out here, to watch for him?"

"I could arrange that. If you'd care to volunteer to answer the call from Sheriff Mobley, when he wants an explanation why we parked an officer in front of the empty house of a guy who might be a suspect, or might just be a good citizen."

Warrick thought about that, then shook his head. "Jim, this isn't just any case—it's a national story, and the sheriff's ass is on the line. I think this is one time he'd justify the outlay."

Brass stopped to reconsider. Then he said, "You know . . . you're right. And I know just how to do it."

Brass got on his cell and called a detective at the North Las Vegas PD. He filled the man in, clicked off and said to Warrick, "Guy owes me a favor. He'll send a patrol car out here and keep us posted."

"And it won't even come out of our budget. Captain Brass, nicely played."

Brass smiled a little; it was almost like he was blowing a kiss at Warrick—almost. "So what now? This is one of those cases where I gotta follow the CSI lead."

"Nice to hear you admit that. So why I don't check in with Grissom? I think he's headed to the mayor's office, and he might want us to try to catch up."

Brass's brow rose and yet his eyes remained half-lidded. "All the way back downtown, then."

"All the way back downtown."

On the way south, Warrick made the call. "Gris? Warrick—we've tracked the taillight to a possible suspect, but the guy isn't home."

"Is someone watching the house?"

Warrick filled Grissom in, and the CSI supervisor requested that his kudos also be passed along to Brass.

Grissom added, "Why don't you join us, then. Brass, too, if he's free."

"It's not like there's a bigger case in Vegas, right now. Mayor's office?"

"Office, and then house. We have warrants for both, but it took a while."

Warrick could hear the weary frustration in his boss's voice, and asked, "You mean you haven't even talked to His Honor yet?"

Grissom's voice displayed the lilting sarcasm he often lent to his understatements. "Judge Clark was reluctant to give us the warrant."

Warrick groaned. "Probably thought it was political. That Mobley was behind it."

"As if *we'd* do that kind of bidding for the sheriff."

Grissom's contempt for politics was well known not only within CSI itself but local government, generally.

"That's why it took overnight," Gris was saying. "Judge called the sheriff this morning and, devil his due, Mobley must have convinced Clark, because we finally got the ruling."

"Yeah, well, at least you got it—we'd be S.O.L., otherwise."

"We have an appointment with the mayor, at his office, in half an hour. Can you make it?"

Warrick checked his watch; and traffic looked light. "We'll meet you outside the Mayor's door in twenty minutes." He ended the call and turned to Brass. "City Hall."

Half an hour later, Warrick, Brass, Sara and Grissom were seated in the mayor's maple-paneled outer office. Comfortable seating lined the walls and it was easy to imagine the spacious office bustling; but today it was strangely quiet. Only the detective and the CSIs were present, as well, of course, as the mayor's new secretary, a man in his vague thirties, in a crisp gray suit with dark blue tie. The secretary's brass nameplate on a formidable maple desk identified him as Woo, which struck Warrick as ironic, considering the homely man was replacing the late lovely Candace Lewis, who'd been so much more than a secretary to His Honor.

"The mayor will receive you shortly," Woo said to them.

No one bothered to select a magazine to flip through. While Brass seemed (as was often the case) faintly bored, Grissom looked relaxed and focused,

while Sara appeared tense and Warrick felt somewhere between.

Celebrities, important people, were a routine part
of the Vegas landscape, and Warrick was a local boy,
after all, and not easily impressed. He'd met the mayor
before, at an LVMPD recognition dinner, but shaking
the man's hand and exchanging smiles was a different
deal than coming to the dignitary's office to serve him
a search warrant on a possible murder charge.

Woo was right: they didn't have to wait long.

After the secretary spoke softly on the phone to his
boss, he rose and opened the door and—in a show-
bizzy manner, perhaps fitting for the mayor of Las
Vegas—Mayor Darryl Harrison, in a crisply tailored
tan suit with red tie, strode into the outer office, like a
headliner bounding on stage.

Grissom and company got to their feet and the
smiling politician came to them, and shook hands
with each of them, making eye contact, but bestowing
a general greeting, "Well, this is real pleasure. An
honor. I'm so proud of what you're doing for our city."

Before the Candace Lewis case had put him under a
dark cloud, Mayor Darryl Harrison had been one of
the most popular, best-liked, most widely known
mayors in the nation. Some day his party's nomina-
tion for governor would be (or anyway, would have
been) his; and he had the sort of Clinton-esque
charisma to make the White House a real possibility,
in a foreseeable future.

You would never guess the strain he was under; his
brown eyes had a sparkle, his capped white teeth
gleamed in a smile as seemingly genuine as the chop-

pers were not. The fortyish Harrison reminded Warrick of Dean Martin just after leaving Jerry Lewis and prior to his drinking reputation: darkly tan with curly black hair, dimpled chin, and just generally the kind of matinee idol good looks that lured female voters across party lines.

Now it was time for individual greetings.

Knowing to honor rank, he went first to Brass, saying, "Hello, Jim. Been too long."

"Yes, sir."

Harrison's knack of remembering the first name of almost everyone he met—a typical but nonetheless impressive politician's trick—played up a widely felt perception that this man cared about every single person in the city. Then, turning to Grissom, Harrison said, "Gil—it's been a long time."

"Yes, sir," Grissom said.

"I think the last time we spoke was after you put that evil 'Deuce' character, away."

"I believe so, Your Honor."

"And I meant to call about that torso case—what was that woman's name?"

"Lynn Pierce."

His features assumed a grave cast. "Terrible thing. Tragic family situation." Then he beamed at all of them, flicking from face to face, saying, "I don't know why I should be so damn friendly to you people—it's the great job you're doing putting the bad guys away that gives Brian Mobley a shot at unseating me!"

Smiles and nervous laughter ensued.

He turned to Warrick. "We've met before," he said.

"Yes, sir."

"Warrick Brown, isn't it?"

Surprised, Warrick smiled. "Why, yes, sir."

"You were commended for bravery, what—two years ago? And Ms. Sidle, we haven't met. But I've kept up with your impressive accomplishments."

Sara grinned. "Thank you, Mr. Mayor. I don't know what accomplishments *those* would be. . . ."

Warrick noted the mayor didn't elaborate, and the CSI was getting the distinct impression the mayor had done some quick homework before their visit. . . .

Grissom moved his head, in that little gesture that indicated he was about to cut through the b.s., and said politely, "Your Honor? We need to talk. Privately?"

Harrison put his arm around Grissom's shoulder and began to walk him toward the open door of the inner office. Warrick, catching Grissom's wide-eyed, almost horrified response to this physicality, smiled just a little; touchy-feely, Gris was not.

Harrison was saying, "I realize that. That's why I canceled all my appointments and blocked out fifteen minutes for you people . . . and my assistant will hold all calls."

"Fifteen minutes," Grissom said, moving his head again. "Very generous."

Harrison removed his arm from Grissom's shoulder, gestured graciously for the CSI to enter the office, which he did, and in fact held the door open for all of them, though it was Woo who finally shut the door behind the mayor.

The office, not unexpectedly, was spacious. The facing wall—behind a kidney-shaped desk that was itself no larger than a Caribbean island—consisted of tinted windows offering a hazy, filtered view out on the downtown activity. A large, round worktable sat off to the right side of the desk and, beyond that, a sofa hugged the wall. A quartet of chairs were arrayed facing the desk and Harrison waved a hand toward them as he circled his desk and sat down.

The CSIs and the detective exchanged various glances, then finally—Grissom going first—took the chairs.

"Coffee?" Harrison asked. "Soft drinks? Bottled water?"

Brass said, "No thank you."

Actually, Warrick could've used some water. . . .

The mayor folded his hands, prayerfully, and his expression became business-like, almost somber. "Then what can I do for you, Jim? . . . Gil?"

Brass fielded the question: "I told your secretary . . . that is, Mr. Woo . . . that this concerned the Candace Lewis case."

"I am aware of that. And I'm of course aware that you've taken over the investigation, now that it's . . ." He swallowed, and Warrick wondered if this was acting or actual emotion. ". . . now that it's a murder case."

"That's right," Brass said, and slipped the search warrants out of his jacket and set them on the edge of the mayor's desk. The mayor, himself a former district attorney, looked at them with a steady gaze; he did not need to be told what the documents were. He leaned a bit on his elbows, his clasped fingers tented, providing a slight barrier between him and his guests, as he peered over his knuckles.

The voice seemed flat, now—that melodic friendliness gone. "Just tell me one thing, Jim. And I expect an honest answer."

"You'll get one."

"Is Mobley behind this?"

Sitting forward, Grissom, his voice quiet and authoritative, said, "This is *my* doing, sir. I requested these warrants."

"I see."

"I hope you do. If you do know anything about me, you'll know I've never been accused of doing Sheriff Mobley any favors, personal or otherwise."

"I have heard about . . . certain tensions."

"Yes, sir. But I will say, Brian has behaved himself professionally, thus far. Starting with recusing himself from this case."

Harrison's eyes narrowed. "That's not just lip service?"

"He seems sincere."

"This . . . Anthony, this political advisor of Mobley's. He's a bad apple. Did Brian really fire him?"

"He did."

"Do you know why?"

Grissom shrugged. "I presume he was dissatisfied with the man's services. Beyond that, you'd have to ask the sheriff."

The mayor nodded, as if to say, *Fair enough.*

"My question now is," Grissom said, in his oddly pixie-ish way, "are you prepared to be as professional and cooperative as Brian Mobley?"

A smirk dug a small cynical groove in the mayor's cheek. "Why—have you served *him* with a search warrant?"

Grissom smiled angelically. "Yes."

The mayor shifted in his seat. He laid his hands out on the table, palms down. "Well, of course, Gil—I'll do whatever I can to help you catch the madman who killed Candace."

That sounded a trifle rehearsed to Warrick.

But Grissom seemed prepared to accept the response at face value: "That's what we were hoping to hear, Mr. Mayor. To start with, I'd like you to go over those two warrants on your desk."

The warrants were just out of reach and Sara picked them up and handed them to the mayor; she smiled, a little embarrassed, and Harrison gave her a small meaningless smile in return, as he took the documents.

He withdrew reading glasses from his inside suit-coat pocket, put the glasses on as he picked the papers up. He read them, then looked from Brass to Grissom. "My house? Why my house? . . . Candace worked here, at the office."

"You can read the specifics in the warrant," Grissom said. "But know that the judge, who shared your concerns about the sheriff's intent, didn't grant these lightly. . . . And if you don't mind, I'd like to send Warrick and Sara over there, to your home, now."

Harrison sighed. The documents were on the desk before him. He raised a cautious finger. "A question, first."

"All right."

"Is the media going to hear about this?"

Grissom half-smiled. "You're the mayor of this city, and you weren't aware that we'd served the sheriff a warrant."

"True."

Then Harrison's eyes traveled from face to face, stopping on Grissom's. A small smile played on the mayor's lips. "Gil—Jim . . . any of you. Do you think your job will be harder, or easier, should Brian Mobley leave the sheriff's office and take this chair from me?"

Grissom said, "I haven't given that any thought, Mr. Mayor. It has nothing to do with how I approach my job."

"The sheriff has been a thorn in your side for some time, Dr. Grissom."

Grissom's shrug was barely perceptible. "Another politician will replace him. Meaning no disrespect, I will find a way to do my job, and do it well, despite the best efforts of any and all politicians."

Sara couldn't seem to suppress a smile, and Warrick didn't even try to. Brass looked grave, and Grissom just wore that damn innocent expression of his.

The mayor studied Grissom for a long time; then he laughed. "By God, you really mean it. . . . Might I call Mrs. Harrison, just give her a 'heads up,' you're coming?"

Grissom and Brass exchanged quick alarmed looks.

Brass fielded that one. "We'd prefer that you didn't, sir—the intent of a warrant isn't to give a 'heads up' to anybody, with the exception of the police. . . . I'm sure you understand."

Sighing wearily, Harrison nodded. "I do. I do. I just hate to put my wife . . . It's just . . . how do I say this delicately? Mistakes were made."

Grissom said, "We know. I have a lab report putting your DNA in Candace Lewis's bed."

Harrison whitened. "Oh Christ. . . . When can I expect the press to get their hands on *that?*"

Brass said, "Well, when we do find Candace's killer, a defense lawyer will likely use your relationship with her to muddy the waters, and try to help clear a client. Your Honor, you need to prepare yourself for the day when this comes out."

"I understand. I appreciate the counsel."

Grissom, champing at the bit, sat forward again. "Now about Warrick and Sara . . ."

Harrison waved a dismissive hand, like the pope granting a reluctant blessing. "Send them. There's nothing to find. All I ask is that they not intrude on my wife any more than necessary. Jeanne and I are trying to hold the marriage together—she knows about my . . . indiscretion; but having the media pummel her with it, 24–7, has become a little . . . wearing."

"She needn't be present," Sara said, "when we do the search."

"Thank you, Ms. Sidle." Harrison said. "She may not be home, at any rate. She's not been spending much time at the house . . ." His expression turned glum. ". . . particularly when I'm there."

Warrick asked, "It would be helpful if someone's there to let us in."

The mayor nodded. "I'll alert our maid."

Grissom said, "That's fine." He paused, and seemed to be making a decision. He was: "Mayor, you can let your wife know my people will be dropping by. But a mention of the search warrant would, frankly, be a breach, Your Honor."

"I understand." And made the call right in front of them, short and sweet, to a servant named Maria.

After the mayor hung up, Grissom gave Warrick and Sara a nod; Warrick already had a copy of the search warrant.

They were at the door when Brass called out, "Call Conroy," referring to Detective Erin Conroy, with whom the team had worked on several occasions. "Have her go with you."

"Got it," Warrick said, then they were out the door and gone.

Gil Grissom settled back in the chair and allowed Brass to do his job.

"Now that the kids are gone," Brass said with wry humor, "I have a few more questions . . . questions that need asking that I thought you might feel more comfortable answering with . . . a smaller audience."

"Go ahead, Jim," Harrison said, only a hint of caution in his voice.

"I have to ask—how did your DNA get in Candace Lewis's bed?"

"It got there," the mayor said, "just how you *think* it got there."

"Had the two of you had a falling out, before her disappearance?"

"No—we had a warm, friendly relationship. Neither one of us thought it would be . . . lasting. We were two professionals who spent a lot of time together. My marriage was rocky, she was unattached. . . . Such things happen among adults."

"So there was no talk of divorcing your wife and—"

"Jim, I told you—our relationship wasn't like that. It was mostly about . . . well, companionship, yes, sex, where I was concerned. I was sort of . . . mentoring Candy. Discussing ways she could get ahead." Grissom thought, *I am so glad Jim is handling this.* . . .

"No talk of divorce at all? Could your wife have seen Candace as a . . . threat?"

Harrison shook his head. "Why do you keep harping on this. . . . My marital problems predated my relationship with Candy. And—" Finally it dawned on him; his eyes widened with alarm and he lurched forward. "You don't think *Jeanne* could have done this? . . . You've really taken a wrong turn, there."

"How so?"

"My wife may be quite capable of making my life a living Hell, but she would never physically hurt another person."

Grissom felt Mrs. Harrison an unlikely suspect, himself; he found it difficult to imagine a scenario that would include the mayor's wife killing the woman and someone else acquiring the corpse for recreational purposes.

Another ten minutes of questioning accomplished little else. As they left the mayor's office—little of the politician apparent in the shellshocked man now—Grissom hoped Warrick and Sara would have better luck at the mayor's home.

* * *

If Mayor Darryl Harrison's office was grand, his home was opulent. Situated on Lake Las Vegas, a gated community for the truly wealthy, the plush digs of Mayor and Mrs. Harrison were just down the road from the multimillion-dollar estate of pop singer Celine Dion.

Warrick had gotten Conroy's voice mail, leaving a message where he and Sara would be; as they parked in front of the mayor's palatial house, they still hadn't heard back from the detective. The one truism about Vegas was: traffic could be a problem, any day, any time of day.

The rambling castle-like brick structure would have looked out of place in any other part of the city; here it was just one more grandiose homemaker statement. Hell, for this area, Warrick thought, the place was downright downscale—there wasn't even a helipad! Five white pillars held up a widow's walk between the two main sections of the many-windowed house, which was seventy-five hundred square feet, easy. Four or five bedrooms, Warrick would bet, and more bathrooms than a small hotel.

They were just getting got out of the Tahoe when Warrick's cell phone rang; it was Conroy: "You guys inside yet?"

"No," Warrick said. "Just pulled up."

"Be there in five."

"Don't mistake the driveway for the freeway."

"Try not."

Crime scene field kits in hand, Sara rang the bell with Warrick just behind her, bearing the warrant.

The doorbell's echo sounded as if a cavern awaited beyond the white metal door.

When the attractive twenty-ish Hispanic maid, in light-blue uniform, answered the bell, the foyer glimpsed behind her was indeed cavernous, though few caves were outfitted with crystal chandeliers. The interior—or at least this expansive entryway—was the opposite of the exterior, where the brown brick was broken up by the white woodwork of windows; within the walls were white, trimmed in brown oak. Already Warrick sensed a chill, even clinical vibe suitable to a marriage in ongoing cold storage.

The day was just warm enough to make the air conditioning rolling out to them a refreshing greeting. The maid's response to them was cool in another way.

"You're the police?" she asked, her words lightly accented.

"We're part of the police," Sara said. "The ones Mayor Harrison called ahead about?"

"I would like to see your badges."

Warrick could not stop his brain from saying, *Badges? We don't need no stinking . . .*

But Sara was already indicating her I.D. on its necklace, saying, "Is this sufficient?"

The maid looked from one I.D. to the other and said, "I suppose so."

But she made no move to allow them entrance.

Warrick said, "You're Maria, right?" Just trying to warm her up.

The woman nodded. Her black hair was tied back in a ponytail and her brown eyes were grave and unblinking—the effect was severe and uninviting.

Getting irritated, Warrick said to the woman blocking their way, "Do you need to see the warrant? Is Mrs. Harrison here?"

Maria was still searching for answers to those two simple questions when another car—one of the LVMPD's ubiquitous Tauruses, this one dark green—pulled up and parked behind the Tahoe. Conroy came clipping up the slight slope of grass, and—perhaps sensing that the CSIs were stalled at the door—she withdrew from her purse what Maria seemed to crave: a wallet with an actual police badge.

A pretty green-eyed brunette with high cheekbones and luminous model's skin, her hair pulled back in a loose ponytail, Erin Conroy wore a light gray suit over a darker gray silk blouse, the jacket bulging on her right hip where her pistol rode. As she approached, she held her shield out in front of her, Van Helsing warding off Dracula with a crucifix.

And, at the sight of the badge, the maid stepped meekly aside and—Detective Conroy now in the lead—they all swept in.

Immediately Warrick noticed how immaculate the place was, adding further to a sterile aura—there was something almost institutional about it.

This time Sara was the one to ask: "Is Mrs. Harrison here?"

"*Si*," the maid said. "She is upstairs."

And the maid just stood there.

With a roll of his eyes, and a sigh, Warrick asked, "Well, could you let her know we're here?"

Maria was still thinking about that when they heard a voice from the wide oaken stairway at their left.

"Is that the police, Maria?"

"Yes, Mrs. Harrison," the maid said over her shoulder.

Warrick and Sara traded looks over the odd formality of that; neither seemed quite sure whether or not to be amused.

Footfalls on the steps further announced a middle-aged blonde woman, electric blue eyes in a face that was both haggard and strikingly, even delicately beautiful.

Conroy displayed her badge and introduced the three of them.

"I'm Jeanne Harrison," the woman said, shaking hands with all of them. "I'll do my best to help in any way I can, but I *do* have a tennis date I was on my way to. . . . Will that be a problem? Should I postpone it?"

Warrick answered that by handing Mrs. Harrison the search warrant.

"What's this?" She began to read it, and immediately knew. "No one said anything to me about this. Searching my home!" A hint of red appeared on her cheeks and near her ears, but otherwise she showed no reaction.

"That's the procedure?" Sara said, falling into the up-talking Valley Girl lilt that came upon her occasionally, particularly when she was nervous. "Just letting you know we were coming was a courtesy most people don't receive."

"Well, I thank you for that, Ms. Sidle."

Warrick tried to find sarcasm in the reply, but couldn't.

Turning to the maid, Mrs. Harrison said, "Maria, give these officers whatever they require."

"Yes, Mrs. Harrison."

"If you don't need me here," Mrs. Harrison said, her voice just a trifle icy, "I'd like to keep that tennis date."

"Please go ahead, ma'am," Conroy said. "We may still be here when you get back. If we have any questions, we can ask you at that time."

"Fine." She went over briskly and picked up a purse from a small, round table at the bottom of the stairs, and disappeared into another part of the house—most likely, Warrick thought, headed for the garage to escape from this embarrassment.

They split up—Sara taking the upstairs and basement, Warrick the first floor and garage. Conroy split her time between the two CSIs, observing and helping out.

The living room seemed white at first, too, but on closer examination was a pale, pale yellow; the oak trim continued and the floors were polished hardwood. The furnishings were contemporary, tasteful and sparing; frankly, "living" room or not, it didn't look like anybody lived here.

Warrick didn't know what he was looking for, much less what he expected to find in a room that had been cleaned like a surgeon's operating room. From there he moved on to the den, which also served as Harrison's home office. He found some long black hairs that might be Candace's (the maid was another possibility), but nothing else of interest.

It was the same for the whole house. They went through every drain looking for hair or blood, took out every trap and cleaned them out; used alternate light sources on the walls, baseboards and floors searching for blood stains; but, after three grueling hours, the two CSIs and the detective met up in the foyer with nothing but a few stray hairs to show for their time.

"Find anything?" Sara asked.

He shook his head. "Not to write home about. You?"

"Plenty of nothing. If Mayor Harrison's involved in this crime, he didn't commit it here."

Mrs. Harrison appeared from the kitchen, her tennis dress still immaculate, not so much as a drop of perspiration on it. "Hello. Are you finished?"

Conroy met her, saying, "Yes, ma'am—thank you for your cooperation."

How the hell, Warrick asked himself, *do you play tennis and not sweat?*

Mrs. Harrison gave them a friendly if cool smile, as if she'd come to terms with their intrusion while she was gone. "Anything Darryl and I can do, just let us know. No one wants this cleared up more than we."

Unable to restrain himself, Warrick asked, "How was tennis?"

Her smile turned faintly mocking. "I won. . . . I almost always do, Mr. Brown."

"Cool," Warrick said, but found himself wondering what sort of game she had been playing at the tennis club.

As they approached their vehicles out front, Conroy asked, "Should I interview her, do you think?"

"What about?" Warrick said, with a humorless half-

smirk. "We didn't find a damn thing. You could ask
her if she knows her husband was running around on
her with Candace Lewis, which we already know she
knows, and which'll only serve to irritate her. Then
she complains to her husband and we get less cooperation from the Mayor's office, so yeah, sure, interview
her, if you want."

Conroy gave him a look. "You could've just said
'no.' "

"Better check in," Sara said. She looked a little
tired, and glum.

"Better." Warrick used his cell to call Grissom.

"And you found?" Gris asked.

"Nothing," he said. "Couple of Candace Lewis hairs,
maybe."

"And His Honor already admits she was in his
house, from time to time. Any DNA in the bedrooms?"

"None. . . . It's not a loving household."

Warrick could hear Grissom thinking over the line.
Then Gris said, "Well, we had to check it out. No
stone unturned. . . . Hold on."

Grissom was gone for a few seconds and, as Warrick
held, Sara asked, "Anything new on his end?"

"Not that he said," Warrick said, and then Gris was
back on the line.

"That was Brass. He said the NLVPD patrol car says
there's still no sign of life at Cotton Gum Court."

"Maybe the guy signed a full confession and then
hung himself."

" 'Hanged' himself, Warrick. And I doubt we'll have
any such luck. . . . Come on back and call it a day."

"But, Gris—"

"No buts, Warrick. Let's eat up the overtime when we're actually accomplishing something. . . . Start over tonight."

". . . Okay, Gris. I could use a meal. I could use some sleep."

"Go wild," Grissom advised dryly, and clicked off.

Alone in his office, Gil Grissom contemplated how this important case was shaping up, and was not over-joyed.

The CSI supervisor had hoped for better news from either Warrick or Brass; and they did have a possible suspect located. That was a start. What was there left to do, today?

And he knew.

Grissom knew the time had come to place the phone call he'd been avoiding, even dreading, since his meeting with Mobley and the showdown with Ed Anthony.

After digging out the number from his old-fashioned Rolodex—this particular number was too distasteful to carry around in a palm pilot—Grissom punched it in and waited, hoping that he might reach voice mail and not have to actually speak to a human being.

He wasn't that lucky: the familiar oily voice came on the third ring: "Special Agent Rick Culpepper."

"Agent Culpepper, Grissom."

A stunned silence crackled over the line for an end-less five seconds.

"Hey, buddy. Something I can do for you?" The caution in the special agent's voice seemed tempered with suspicion.

Grissom worked at casualness as he said, "Just making sure you're in the loop on the Candace Lewis case, Agent Culpepper."

" 'Rick.' Call me Rick."

Grissom flinched. "Rick—did you get the crime scene report from Candace Lewis's apartment?"

"Hard copy, Gil, or electronic?"

Hearing Culpepper call him "Gil" made Grissom shudder. "Hard copy."

"Just a second . . ."

Grissom could hear the FBI agent riffling through some papers.

"I've got the prelim from the day after the search, but I don't see the final report."

"Thought you might not have that," Grissom said, lightly. "I'm messengering over a copy today. Some sensitive data, there. You suffering any press leaks?"

"No. We're a tight ship. We *use* the media, they don't use us."

"Good to hear. I'll have an officer drop it off right away."

Culpepper hesitantly said, "Thanks. Anything of mine you need?"

"Copies of your case files would be appreciated."

"Want to get together for a powwow?"

Shuddering again, Grissom said, "We may need to do that. At some point. I don't have any new major developments, yet."

"Why so amenable . . . Gil?"

The scientist kept it nonchalant. "Just sharing information . . . Rick. You said you wanted to be kept in the loop."

Culpepper's suspicion seemed to fade. "Well, buddy, I'm glad to hear that. I'm glad we had that little come-to-Jesus meeting the other day. Relieves me you're finally seeing the light of cooperation."

Grissom tried to find something positive to say, but all he could muster was, "The report will be over there yet today."

"Thanks, Gil."

Grissom hung up, looking at the phone as if it were the devil's friend.

He was by nature honest, too honest if some opinions were to be believed; overly frank, perhaps. Having to pose with the likes of Rick Culpepper was singularly distasteful to Gil Grissom.

Sighing, he picked up the receiver and punched in another number. Mrs. Mathis put him quickly through to Sheriff Mobley.

"Yes, Gil?" the sheriff asked, his voice as dry and indifferent as Culpepper's had been oily and patronizing.

"I think it's time to bring charges against Ed Anthony."

Mobley seemed to consider that for a moment, if the silence on the line was any indication, then he said, "I don't think he stepped over that line. He's been fired. He's paid for his misconduct."

"I just spoke to FBI agent Rick Culpepper."

"Lucky you."

"You're not the only one Ed Anthony kept that file from—he didn't forward it to the FBI, either."

". . . Christ."

"That's obstruction of justice, Brian. Possibly aiding and abetting. Federal charges, perhaps."

His voice colder now, Mobley said, "Gil, I think Ed's suffered enough. His firing was his punishment. I've refused to write him a letter of recommendation."

"You are strict."

"Save me your sarcasm. I don't think there's any reason to embarrass him further."

"Or the department? Or yourself?"

"Grissom—take your own advice: stay out of politics."

"You don't want this played out in the media. I understand that. But—"

"There's nothing more to discuss, Grissom."

"All right. But I'm putting what I know in writing to you, as a memo."

"Now who's political?"

"Just practical. Be advised that I'm sending the crime scene file to the FBI."

"That's the correct thing to do, of course. But you needn't point out—"

"If Special Agent Culpepper catches the discrepancy in the date, I'm not going to lie, Brian. If the FBI charges Anthony, your mayoral run will be over before it begins. You might want to face this head on, and bring the charges yourself . . . before the FBI does."

Dryly Mobley said, "Thanks for your advice, Gil."

"Well, you will get it in writing—so you can ponder it at your leisure."

"Is that all?"

"It's enough."

"For once we agree," Mobley said, and hung up.

9

SITTING IN THE LOCKER ROOM, RELISHING THE SILENCE, lulled by the absence of activity, Nick Stokes was about to call it a night—or, more accurately, a morning. Overtime had been piling up for him and Catherine, not only on this case but over the last couple of weeks, which put the CSIs seriously at odds with department budget directives. And the hours and energy they'd invested in their investigation—they were four mornings into it—had left them both approaching burnout level.

Earlier this very shift, however, the same two CSIs had been lolling in the euphoria of a case that was coming together, and a suspect who looked to be on the fast-track to going down.

That was before they struck out on the fingerprint front: Gary Randle's prints were on neither the zip disk from his office nor the laptop in his home. This was consistent with the suspect's claim that he'd seen neither the disk nor the laptop before.

This didn't really surprise either criminalist: child

pornographers were, after all, notoriously careful criminals. Though many of their ilk asserted that their particular desire wasn't a crime at all, the vast majority
went to extreme lengths to keep from getting caught—
of this Nick was well aware. Two stories, in particular,
had stayed with him. Both involved elaborate plans to
destroy hard drives in the event computers were seized.
One predator he'd heard about from a buddy in Los
Angeles had rigged a small bottle of acid to his hard
drive prompting, when a particular series of keys was
inputted, an acid bottle falling over to spill its contents
all over the hard drive. An even more aggressive vari-
ant on this protection plan—told him by a CSI from out
east—utilized a small dot of C-4 in place of the acid.

So the notion of Randle wearing gloves, or wiping
the disk clean, to keep from leaving fingerprints
seemed pretty mild by comparison.

Nick already had his shirt off, was just unlacing his
shoes when his cell phone rang.

"Nick Stokes."

"Hey," Catherine said.

"Hey. I was just getting ready to head home.
Something up?"

"Nunez just called and gave me an update."

Nick groaned. "I don't think I can take any more
'good' news."

"Then you better hang up."

"What is it, Cath? What now?"

"Nunez finished his preliminary read on the zip
disk and it's blank."

"Blank. Like what we've been shooting on this
thing."

"Actually, it's not as bad as it sounds—despite somebody's best efforts, Nicky, we *do* have twelve 'bullets.' "

Nick perked up; that was the number of pornographic images found in the ad agency printer. "But you said the disk was blank."

"I'm starting to learn that you can't erase *anything* from a computer. . . . Meet me at the break room and I'll fill you in."

She had a cup of coffee waiting for him. Accepting it gratefully, he sat next to her and sipped the steaming brew and said, "Just like I like my women . . ."

Catherine arched an eyebrow.

Nick gave her his patented boyish grin. ". . . strong and bitter."

That drew a chuckle from her. "Our computer guru used that Encase thing of his to scan the disk— he's still working on it in fact—and he found all twelve 'deleted' jpegs. At one time they were on that disk."

The weariness evaporated from Nick's body; energy spiked through him, and it wasn't the caffeine. "We got enough to make the arrest?"

She nodded. "I ran it past O'Riley—he's picking up the arrest warrant. He'll meet us over there."

Grinning, Nick swung a fist at the air in "yes" fashion. Then he looked at his watch. "You suppose Randle is at work yet?"

"Probably, or on his way. Wanna meet him there?"

"Why don't we?"

As Nick navigated the morning rush hour, Catherine called O'Riley on her cell to confirm the

CSIs were on their way to Newcombe-Gold. O'Riley had the warrant and would meet them there, which he did, the Tahoe and Taurus rendezvousing in the ad agency parking lot just before nine.

Getting out of the Tahoe, Catherine said, "Get a load of the Sarge, Nicky—looks like we're not the only ones putting in too much overtime."

O'Riley was lumbering out of his car, expression chipper, though his suit was even more rumpled than the norm and the bags under his eyes would've set off an airport security alarm.

Nick said, "I think he wants this one as bad as we do."

They had been inside the ad agency so much in the last three days, Nick felt like he ought to go in and pick up a paycheck at the receptionist's desk. Nick was holding the door open for Catherine and O'Riley, who were inside when Nick heard a car door slam and glanced behind him.

Randle was climbing out of a black Lincoln Navigator, about halfway down on the other side.

"Guys," Nick said. "He's out here. . . ."

O'Riley and Catherine stepped back into the morning sun and the glass door whooshed shut behind them. Randle strode toward the entry, briefcase in one hand, a folded *USA Today* in the other, his head down as he had a look at the headline.

The ad man was almost on top of them before he looked up and caught startled sight of them. He did a deer-in-the-headlights freeze, which quickly shifted into the fight-or-flight reflex Nick had seen on the faces of so many about-to-be-collared perps.

Please break and run, Nick thought, *please*.

But instead Randle just stood there, looking from official face to face with open defiance. *"Now* what do you fine public servants want with me?"

O'Riley stepped forward. "Gary Thomas Randle, you're under arrest," and went into the standard recitation of Miranda rights, even as he withdrew the handcuffs.

At the sight of which, Randle whitened. "You can't be serious." His wild gaze went to Nick and Catherine, back and forth. "That laptop isn't mine—the zip disk either! I *told* you that."

"Turn around, sir," O'Riley said. "Hands behind you."

"That's not necessary. I'll go with you. I'll answer your questions. Haven't I been cooperative?"

"You've been a dream," Nick said.

O'Riley said, "Do I have to give you the 'hard or easy' speech?"

"This is false arrest. This is going to mean one hell of a big law suit."

"Hard, then?"

A huge sigh left Randle and much of the life seemed to exit him, as well. Zombie-like, he handed the newspaper to Catherine. She took it, then Randle gave her the briefcase.

Suddenly, oddly, Randle said to Catherine, "Are you a parent?"

She stiffened. "Yes."

"I'm telling you, on my daughter's life, I didn't do this."

Catherine said nothing.

O'Riley, cuffs in one hand, with the other made a

little turning motion with his finger, and Randle nodded and showed his back to the detective, thrusting out his clenched fists, offering his wrists rather melodramatically, Nick thought. O'Riley clicked on the cuffs.

Then O'Riley took the man by an elbow and ushered him toward the Taurus.

"Big mistake," Randle was muttering. "Big mistake."

"Yeah, it was," O'Riley said flatly.

Randle looked over his shoulder at Nick, still seeking a sympathetic audience: "I swear to you I had nothing to do with this."

As if in absurd response, Catherine's cell phone rang.

As she was responding, Nick's rang, too; and a beat after, so did O'Riley's. Then the three of them moved apart from one another, to find minimal privacy for their individual if simultaneous calls.

As Nick punched the cell button, he heard Catherine saying, "You gotta be kidding!"

Into the cell, the confused CSI said, "Nick Stokes."

"Grissom."

To one side of him, Nick heard O'Riley saying, "Yes, sir," and go back to listening; the words "Yes sir" seemed to be about O'Riley's entire end of the conversation, as Randle stood beside the detective looking as flummoxed as Nick felt.

In Nick's ear, his supervisor was saying, "I just talked to Tomas Nunez, Nick. I hope you haven't made that arrest."

"Well. We sort of just did."

"Sort of Nick? Do we 'sort of' arrest people, now?"

"O'Riley arrested him."

"Really. We may have a problem with that."

Nick glanced over at Catherine, whose eyes were wide with unpleasant surprise as she continued her own cell phone conversation.

"What problem could there be, Gris? Evidence says he's the guy."

"Does it? Get back here. We need to talk."

"Oh-kay."

Nick replaced the cell on his belt just as O'Riley was undoing the handcuffs, freeing the suspect.

"What's this?" the ad man asked. "Cuffs not enough? Bringing out the shackles?"

O'Riley said, "Mr. Randle, we'd like to request you to accompany us back to headquarters."

Randle looked understandably confused. "Request? I'm *not* under arrest?"

"Not at this time," O'Riley admitted. "We would appreciate your cooperation in helping us straighten this matter out."

"And accompanying you will help do that?"

"We hope so, sir. Yes."

Nick felt anger rising within him. Grissom had been unspecific and yet Nick felt he'd been accused of something, unfairly accused, at that.

"Then I'm not required to go with you," Randle said, making a show of rubbing his wrists.

Catherine stepped forward. Her tone was almost friendly. "No, sir, you don't—but if you would cooperate with us maybe we can help get you out of this situation."

"It seems to me you're the ones who put me *in* this situation!"

She shook her head. "The evidence put you in this position, Mr. Randle—and we do have a substantial body of evidence pointing in your direction."

His eyes tightened and his voice had a mild waver in it. "I'm not in the clear yet."

"No. But if you're innocent . . ."

"*I'm innocent!*"

". . . your cooperation can help explain this evidence, even possibly make it . . . go away."

Randle drew in a deep breath; this time life seemed to come to him. "I'll go with you. I'll show you I mean to be cooperative."

"Good," Catherine said, with a smile so strained it made Nick's face hurt.

"Over here," O'Riley said, pointing toward the Taurus, not taking the man's elbow this time.

The ad man glanced at the looming glass building behind them. "Can't I tell them inside? That I'm going to be late?"

"I thought you worked your own hours," Nick said. O'Riley gave Nick a look and said to Randle, "You can use my cell to call them on the way."

Nick and Catherine stood, shellshocked, watching the Taurus pull out of the lot and disappear. "Who called you, Cath?"

"Tomas—he says there may be a problem with the disk."

"Yeah, I gathered."

"Who called *you?* Grissom?"

Nick nodded. "And he had that very quiet measured calm thing going."

"In other words, royally pissed."

"Who do you suppose called O'Riley?"

She shrugged. "Mobley maybe? Brass?"

He turned and looked at her, hard. "Did we screw
up?"

Unhesitatingly, she said, "No. Absolutely not. We
have the right guy. This computer evidence is just so
highly technical, it's easy to run into snags."

"That's it," he said, nodding, "that's gotta be it."

At HQ, O'Riley led Randle into an interview room
and Nick and Catherine marched back to the garage
where Nunez had set up shop. Nick opened the
door and saw Nunez poring over his monitor, Grissom—in black polo and slacks—standing just behind
him.

"What's up, Gris?" Nick asked, trying to keep it
light.

Their supervisor turned and smiled at them in an
angelic fashion that chilled Nick's blood. "Gee, Nick—
that's just what I was going to ask you . . ."

"Hey," Catherine said, quietly defensive. "We were
in the midst of a righteous arrest when somebody on
this end got nervous. Why?"

Nunez appeared to be so hard at work he was neither hearing nor noticing what was happening
nearby; Nick didn't buy it for a second.

Grissom folded his arms; his head bobbed to one
side and his eyes were unnervingly placid. "Tell me
about the evidence you've developed for this case,
Catherine . . . Nick."

Nick and Catherine traded an uneasy look.

She had to be wondering, like he was wondering, just what the hell Grissom was so worked up about—though to anyone who didn't know him, Grissom's manner appeared calm, his two colleagues could feel the displeasure radiating off the seeming tranquillity.

"You," Nick said to Catherine, who nodded, and laid out what they knew so far. Nick studied Grissom's implacable face, looking for evidence of what was going on behind the unblinking eyes, with no success.

"You found the laptop in Randle's house," Grissom said, nodding once, then cocking his head again, lifting an eyebrow, "but no fingerprints."

"Yes." Catherine shrugged. "But that's not uncommon in cases like this."

"True, but a predictable lack of evidence is not in fact evidence."

She shrugged again, a little embarrassed. "True," she echoed.

Now both Grissom's eyebrows lifted. "Did you wait for Tomas to finish his analysis before you ran off to arrest Mr. Randle?"

Gesturing toward the seemingly oblivious computer expert, Catherine said, "Tomas hadn't even started on it—but he told us the scan showed that the pictures had been on the zip disk we found in Randle's office."

Grissom turned toward Nunez. "Tomas, would you care to stop pretending you're working, and tell my CSIs what you *did* find?"

Looking at least as exhausted as O'Riley had—and

as if he wished he were anywhere else—Nunez wheeled in his chair to face the trio, but his eyes went to Catherine. "Catherine, remember I told you that the print order came from work station eighteen?"

"Yes."

"Well, after we popped that bank hacker, I went back to it. There's no evidence that the photos originated from that computer."

"Well, it did come from the zip disk, right?" she said, sounding a little less sure of herself.

Nunez nodded. "That's true; but that's not the problem. I checked the MAC address of the NIC card."

Shaking his head as if trying to dislodge an insect, Nick said, "Whoa! I have no idea what you just said."

Nunez took it slowly. "The NIC or Network Interface Card is a piece of hardware inside each computer in Newcombe-Gold's office. It's what connects to the network cable and thus connects each computer to the network. Each NIC has a MAC or Media Access Control address that is unique to each machine. These MACs cannot be easily changed."

"Oh-kay," Nick said, glancing at Catherine, "we're with you that far."

"All right. Although information is routed by the IP address, that's the identifier I told Catherine about before . . ."

They both nodded.

". . . even though information's routed with this IP, it's sent and delivered by the MAC address."

"I think I need a couple aspirin," Nick said.

Catherine added, "I could use three."

Grissom said, "Layman's terms, Mr. Nunez."

Nunez said, "Think of the IP as the Post Office and the MAC as the mailman. Although the Post Office sorts the mail and makes sure it's all headed for the right box, the mailman delivers it. I found that the server log for the network showed the MAC address of the sending client computer to be this . . ."

He presented them with a sheet of notepad paper on which was written: "08:00:69:02:01:FC."

Nick shrugged at Catherine; Catherine shrugged at Nick. Grissom closed his eyes.

Nunez kept trying: "That MAC doesn't match up with the MAC address of the computer in work station eighteen, even though the IP matched."

A sinking feeling came over Nick—he not only followed this, he had a terrible feeling he was not going to like what Nunez had to say next. . . .

"The computer we *thought* sent the print order . . . didn't."

Nick winced, then suggested, "Maybe you put the wrong computer back in the work station."

Nunez shook his head. "No way—didn't happen. Besides, I had all the serial numbers from the original seizure of equipment."

Head tilted, eyes narrowed, arms folded, Catherine asked, "Just how were we fooled? Actually, Tomas . . . how were *you* fooled?"

Grinning ruefully, Nunez said, "Helluva question, Catherine. And I don't have the whole answer, but I know where the answer starts: somebody *wanted* to fool us."

Again Catherine and Nick traded glances, wide-eyed ones. Grissom's eyes, however, were still closed. Catherine asked, *"Who?"*

"That," Nunez said, "I don't know . . . yet."

Grissom's eyes opened and he said, "He does know *how*. . . . Tell them, Mr. Nunez."

Nunez presented them with a larger piece of paper, this time—with a rough drawing he'd made. "This box represents the computer in eighteen."

"Okay," Nick said.

"This box," he pointed to another square he'd sketched, "is a computer hooked to the network that was supposed to spoof eighteen."

"Spoof?" Catherine asked.

"Imitate. Simulate . . . And, from our being lost for so long, I'd say it worked. Anyway, the print order originated there."

Feeling sick, Nick asked, "Which leaves us where?"

Nunez sighed, sat back in his wheeled chair. "I already checked the MAC addresses we had from Newcombe-Gold—it doesn't match any of their computers."

Catherine's head lowered and she covered her face with a hand.

"Please tell me we're not back to square one," Nick moaned.

"Not all the way back," Nunez said, trying to minimize their woe. "But when I couldn't find any trace of the photos on the network server hard drives, I ran an E-Script to carve out all the jpegs—since that's the most popular format of most kiddie pornographers. In unallocated space, I found the pictures angel1-

angel12.jpg. The reference file indicated that they had been accessed from the D drive—a zip disk. I ran the MD5 hash algorithm and noted the hash values of the pictures."

Nick, who'd just been thinking he was actually following this, held up a "stop" hand. "Hash value?"

Nunez nodded. "It's like a digital fingerprint. The value for Angel12 is . . ." He checked his notes: "E283120A0B462DB00CEAFA353741F5E9. When we find another file with that hash value, we'll have our source material."

"Near mathematical certainty," Grissom said.

Nodding emphatically, Nunez said, "It's like I told Catherine—the odds against two files having the same hash value and not being identical are astronomical."

Catherine asked, "Have you done the laptop we found at Randle's house yet?"

"No—I'll get to that next. I'm not on anything but this right now. But that was why I called Grissom. I didn't want you thinking you had an airtight case when we're really not even close."

"Go ahead and get back to work, Mr. Nunez," Grissom said, and motioned his CSIs to the other side of the room. They stood on either side of him as he held court, arms folded, eyes serene . . . terribly so.

"What other suspects," he asked, "have you looked at?"

"Randle is still the guy," Catherine said.

"You know this to be a fact."

"The evidence says so."

Gary Randle and his wife were swingers, living a group-

sex lifestyle, with the hardcore pornography collection to prove it: videotapes, photo albums, magazines. Perhaps out of some hypocritical consideration for his daughter, he doesn't want to print his kiddie porn pictures out on his computer. So he takes them into the office, and when his computer doesn't work, he chooses to use Ben Jackson's, since the new kid trusts everyone at Newcombe-Gold and his password is easily accessible.

But instead of printing the stuff off on Ben's computer, the print order is sent to Ruben Gold's printer—since that's where Ben Jackson had sent the last thing he'd worked on Friday to the boss. Figuring he was having trouble with that computer as well—and that his photos hadn't printed any-where—a pissed-off Randle went home for the weekend, not realizing that his filth was lying in the printer tray in his boss's office.

"And this erotica collection of his," Grissom said. "Any pictures of children? Possible underage teens?"

Catherine and Nick traded a long look before they both shook their heads.

"So," Grissom said, with a tiny smile that Nick considered mocking, "you've isolated a male suspect who likes to look at pictures of naked women."

"Gris," Nick said, "it goes way beyond that—the lifestyle, the snapshots!"

"So you have a suspect who likes sex. That would create a substantial suspect base, even just at this ad agency."

Neither Nick nor Catherine said anything.

"What we have in this case," their boss said, "is a lot of circumstantial evidence. Nothing concrete."

Nick didn't like it, but he knew Grissom was right. "Yes."

Catherine said nothing.

Grissom gave them his innocent look. "How do you two feel about child pornography?"

Neither replied.

"Is it possible that in your zest to nail this suspect, you made the crime fit the evidence instead of letting the evidence speak for itself?"

Nick considered that but Catherine immediately said, "No, this guy's been avoiding dealing with us, withholding information . . ."

Nick heard himself blurting, "The guy's a prick!"

"If that was a crime," Grissom said, "we'd all have cause for concern."

Catherine actually smiled at that.

Grissom's voice remained as calm and cool as a Mount Charleston stream. "Could the suspect have been trying to protect himself? Because he thinks he's being railroaded?"

Catherine seemed to be staring into nothing.

Nick had a sick feeling.

Grissom's tone lost its lecturing quality. "How hard have you looked at your other suspects?"

"There really weren't any," Nick said with a shrug, and knew it came out too fast.

Grissom didn't hesitate. "There's at least one other."

Nick said, "Who?"

Catherine was covering her face, but she said, "The first person on the scene."

Nick instantly recalled the axiom Grissom had

pounded into all of them, from the very beginning: *first on the scene—first suspect.*

"Her name's Janice Denard," Catherine said. "She's the personal assistant of Ruben Gold."

"It was his printer the images were found in, right?"

"Right."

"And you checked her out?"

Embarrassed, Catherine shook her head.

Grissom's eyebrows flicked up. " 'What can be done with fewer assumptions is done in vain with more.' "

"What's that mean?" Nick asked.

Catherine gave him a grim little smile. "It means, Nick . . . back to square one."

A hint of a smile tightened around Grissom's eyes.

"And this time," Catherine said, "we're going to look at everybody at Newcombe-Gold."

Suddenly Grissom didn't seem to be listening; his eyes were distant, his expression strangely grave.

Nick said, "Gris—you okay?"

Catherine asked, "What's the matter, Gil?"

Their boss grunted a near-silent laugh. "I was just thinking . . . maybe I should be taking my own advice." His attention snapped back to them; looking from one to the other, he asked, "You two going to be all right?"

"I think my head's screwed on straight," Nick said. "Now."

"Good."

And Grissom left them in the garage with Tomas Nunez and his big pile of computer data yet to be gone through.

Strolling back over to the computer expert, Catherine asked, "How long do you need to get through Randle's laptop?"

Nunez looked at his watch, then at his monitor. "Four, maybe five hours . . . depending on what's on it."

"Can you track the address of the computer that actually sent the print order through Ben Jackson's machine?"

"If it's here, I'll find it," he promised. Then he hedged: "Otherwise, could be hard."

"And this case has been so easy this far," she said dryly. "We'll be back later."

In the corridor, Nick smiled over at Catherine. "This is starting to feel like another double shift."

"That's because it is one. Let's go help O'Riley interview Randle and see where that takes us."

They found Randle and O'Riley seated across from each other in an interview room, the ad man's hands beating a gentle rhythm on the metal table. Both looked up when the CSIs came in, and O'Riley glanced at his watch.

"Mr. Randle's attorney should be here any minute," the detective said. "We'll not start the interview until Mr. Austin is present."

The detective's demeanor had done a one-eighty since this morning and Nick could only wonder what Mobley (or Brass) had said to him on the phone.

Soon a soft tap on the door announced the arrival of Jonathan Austin. The gray-haired, rather elegant lawyer—tan suit, white shirt and dark brown tie—carried a large leather briefcase, which he deposited on the floor as he took a seat next to his client.

Austin's blues eyes had a nasty sparkle as he asked, "And to what do we owe the pleasure of another meeting with such dedicated law enforcement officers?" The lawyer obviously knew from his client that an arrest had been made . . . and retracted.

Catherine glanced at O'Riley for permission to take the lead, and the detective nodded.

She said, "We need to clear this matter up before it turns embarrassing. And we're hoping your client can help us."

"Before it *turns* embarrassing?" the lawyer asked. "Singling my client out from everyone at Newcombe-Gold for this kind of intensive investigation hasn't already embarrassed him? How about arresting him right out front of the agency? Perhaps you take such things lightly, and don't consider any of that an embarrassment."

Leaning against the wall, Nick thought, *Well, this is already going well . . .*

"Of course, since you couldn't arrest him," Austin was saying, cold blue eyes focused on Catherine, sitting next to O'Riley, "it might seem reasonable to assume that this matter *has* been cleared up, as least it does . . . or rather, *doesn't* . . . pertain to my client."

"Mr. Randle is still a suspect," Catherine said. "But he is not our only suspect."

The attorney nodded. "Thank you—that's what I needed to know. And, since you're not arresting him, I see no reason for this conversation to continue." Picking up his briefcase, the attorney rose. "Gary?" His client stood, as well.

"Slooow down," O'Riley said, raising a traffic-cop palm.

But Austin and Randle were already halfway around the table and heading for the door.

Catherine called out, "If your client *is* innocent, he should also be interested in clearing his name. . . . And maybe even helping us solve this."

Stopping at the door, Randle seemed about to speak, but Austin silenced him with a gesture, and said, "With the treatment he's received from you people, why should he help you in any way?"

"Good citizenship?"

Austin made a face and began to open the door for his client.

"Try this then, counselor—how easy will it be for your client to make a living in his field, in this or for that matter *any* town, after the media finally finds out he was suspected of either dealing in, or using, child pornography?"

"I hope," the attorney said, "that's not a threat to leak such information."

"Absolutely not. But, the questions will remain—*unless* we find the actual guilty party. Our best bet at retaining the reputation and integrity of your client—and Newcombe-Gold—is for this case to be closed as quickly as possible, with your cooperation . . . And I *am* a parent. If you were sincere before, please help me find whoever's responsible for those photos."

Soon the attorney and his client had returned to their seats.

But Austin was not through: "I want it known from

the outset that, although my client is cooperating, if for a second I believe you're trying to get him to incriminate himself, this interview is over."

"Fair enough," Catherine said. Then, turning to Randle, she asked, "You've said from the beginning that you're innocent."

"Because I am."

"You may be able to guess how many guilty people have said as much to us, over our years of experience. But giving you the benefit of the doubt, if you are innocent, do you have any idea who would or could have done this?"

Randle just shook his head. "No clue. But then, speaking from my own experience, nobody at the agency knows about my . . . interests."

"In erotica. The swinger scene."

"That's right."

"No one from Newcombe-Gold was involved in—"

"No one."

Catherine folded her hands. "All right, Mr. Randle—walk us through Saturday. The whole day."

The adman collected his thoughts, then said, "I got up early that morning. Went for a run around the neighborhood. Heather, my daughter, slept in. When I got back to the house, I took a shower, got ready for work and woke her."

"What time did you get to the agency?"

"Eight-thirty, nine o'clock maybe."

"Which?"

He shrugged. "You know I have loose hours. Just can't be sure."

"Try. Think back."

"Well, I stopped at a convenience store and grabbed a cup of coffee on the way in . . . so probably closer to nine."

From the sidelines, Nick said, "I thought Janice Denard made coffee in the office every day."

"I hate that pseudo-Starbucks swill," Randle said, with a disgusted look. "The coffee at Terrible Herbst's is better than that piss Janice brews."

What a charmer, Nick thought. "All right," Catherine said. "What then?"

"Went into my office, read my snail mail, looked at my messages, then turned on my computer. I originally thought that's what this whole fuss was over—me using Jackson's computer."

"Why did you end up using his machine if you turned yours on?"

"I mentioned this before, right? I turned mine on, but it wouldn't let me onto the network. I don't know what the hell was wrong with it, but I tried to boot it half a dozen times, before I gave up."

"Have you used it since?"

He nodded. "Sunday I was off, of course, and Monday I was out of the office, but Tuesday, before you buttonholed me, I had it on." A shrug. "Everything was fine."

"So," Catherine said, "you don't have any idea why the computer was malfunctioning over the weekend?"

"None. But everybody who uses a computer knows the things just kinda misbehave, sometimes."

"Did you tell anyone at the agency it was on the fritz?"

"Yes—Roxanne Scott. She's Ira Newcombe's assistant . . ."

"Right."

"I told Roxanne. Well, she was going on vacation, said she'd leave a note for Janice to get it fixed, first thing Monday morning. And I figured Janice did, when it worked on Tuesday."

Catherine shifted in her chair. "Your computer wasn't working, and it occurred to you that you could use Ben Jackson's."

"Yeah, he was sloppy about his password."

"You went to his cubicle—then what?"

Another shrug. "I did the work I came in to do, and went home."

"What about the work you did? Did you print out anything?"

He thought a moment, then said, "No, I didn't print anything out. You see, the work I did was confidential—for a client. Honestly, it had nothing to do with what you're investigating."

Nick said, "And we should trust you about that?"

Austin said, "My client's being cooperative. That tone isn't necessary."

Catherine shot Nick a look that said she agreed with the lawyer. Then she said, "Tell me this, Mr. Randle—how did you save the file, or files, you were working on?"

"I burned it to a CD and took it with me."

Nick asked, "Not a zip disk?"

Randle gave Nick a nasty grin. "Oh, you mean like the one you 'found' in my office?" To Catherine, he said, "I don't use them—antiquated technology. If Ian and Ruben would spring for it, and they will soon, I'll have a DVD burner, and these zips and CDs'll all fall by the wayside, like the obsolete crap they are."

Catherine said, "You have a strong opinion on the subject. Why?"

Randle seemed looser, now. "Because even though I'm always hearing that size doesn't matter, with information storage? Size is about the only thing that does matter. A zip disk will hold 250 megabytes, the old ones only a hundred. A CD 700 megs, a DVD holds almost five gigs—there's just no comparison."

"Where is that disk now, Mr. Randle?"

"In my office—or, at least, it was until you seized all my equipment."

Nick said, "So we already have a copy of it."

"Yes, I suppose you do," Randle said. "Are you people getting what you need? Is this going anywhere?"

"Only toward helping prove your innocence," Catherine said. "If the time/date stamp matches between your disk and Ben's computer, that would go a long way toward telling us you're not lying."

"*I'm* telling you I'm not."

Nick said, "We'll ask the machines."

Catherine said, "If you're not lying, Mr. Randle, then someone else did this."

"Hell," Randle blurted, "I've said that all along!" Austin nodded approvingly next to him.

"For example," she said. "We found Ben Jackson's fingerprints on the keyboard and in the cubicle. After all, it's his work station, right?"

Both men nodded now.

"But Mr. Jackson was out of town when this happened . . . so it wasn't him. Then we found your prints and you claimed you only used Ben's cubicle for work."

"Which is the truth," Randle said.

Catherine gave him a little smile. "If it is the truth, someone at Newcombe-Gold must've been wearing gloves on Saturday—notice anyone like that?"

"Gloves? You're kidding, right?"

"The only prints on that keyboard belonged to you and Ben Jackson—how do you explain that?"

Austin sat forward, his eyes intense. "It's not my client's job to explain it—it's yours."

Catherine held up a hand to silence the lawyer. "Let's slow down. If you're telling the truth, Mr. Randle, there's a third party involved here."

Both Randle and his attorney looked at her blankly.

"And if somebody wore gloves, using the keyboard," Catherine said, her tone one of thinking aloud, "that means they—"

Nick jumped in. "*Expected* the keyboard to be fingerprinted!"

He and Catherine shared a tense look. Randle and Austin suddenly looked lost, the conversation having taken a turn they had neither expected nor could follow.

Nick, moving to Catherine's side, said to her, "And the only reason a third person would know that the keyboard was going to be fingerprinted would be if they were trying to . . ."

". . . frame him," Catherine said, eyes tight.

They both looked at Randle—as if for the first time.

"*Frame* me?" he asked, his voice barely a croak.

"Anybody at work hate you?" asked Catherine.

Randle seemed to really consider that before answering; finally, he simply shook his head.

Catherine pressed: "No one at work has a reason to dislike you?"

"Not that I can think of . . . and, frankly, I can't think of a reason why anybody would."

Yeah, Nick thought, *you're so lovable, it's out of the question.*

"No professional jealousies?" Catherine tried. "Any personal relationships? Affairs? Please be frank, Mr. Randle—it's for your own benefit."

Randle looked at the lawyer, who was no help.

The adman said, "Not really. Nothing professionally. And my private life is separate from my professional one."

"Anyone outside of work?" Catherine asked. "How about from your swinger days? Any enemies at all?"

"Well, the only 'enemy' . . . Only real enemy I have is my ex-wife, Elaine."

Catherine frowned. "Does Elaine have access to Newcombe-Gold?"

He shook his head vigorously. "No, no, not now. Oh, she met a few of the old-timers, who were there back ten years ago or so—Ruben and Ian, Janice and Roxanne, a few more. But the truth is, with her drinking getting so out of hand back then, I'd already stopped taking her to office functions a year or two before our divorce . . . and after that she wouldn't have seen any of those people."

"You don't believe there's any way she could be behind this?"

"Well, hell! She definitely hates me enough to do this. But there's just no way she could have gotten into the office."

"Anyone else you can think of?"

"No one—not neighbors, not any parents of Heather's friends, nobody at the church . . . no."

Catherine heaved a sigh of finality. "All right, Mr. Randle. . . . I do want to thank you, sincerely, for this interview."

He beamed at her. "So then—"

"You can go, but don't leave town."

His face fell.

"No, Mr. Randle, you're not in the clear, yet; but if you're innocent, knowing we're going to keep investigating should provide some reassurance. And if there's evidence to exonerate you, you . . . and your attorney . . . will be the first to know."

Almost humbly, he said, "Thank you."

She smiled tightly. "Of course, if we find out you're guilty, you'll be the first to know that, too."

Randle merely shrugged.

After the adman and attorney had made their exit, the two CSIs and the detective remained in the interview room; they sat silently for several minutes, each on his or her own mental track.

Nick finally said, "So—first, we look at the rest of the staff."

O'Riley sat immobile, staring into the wall; it was just possible he'd lapsed into a coma.

Catherine laid it out: they would spend the rest of the day digging into Newcombe-Gold, the financial reports of the company and records of Ian Newcombe,

Ruben Gold, Janice Denard, Roxanne Scott, Gary Randle, Ben Jackson and Jermaine Allred. They would do background checks on those seven as well, and have Nunez concentrate on their computers first. If those inquiries didn't turn up anything, then the investigators would pick another group of employees and start on them.

"But just to give Grissom his due," she said, "we'll begin with the best first suspect: Janice Denard."

10

THE CARPET FIBERS FROM THE REMNANT IN WHICH THE corpse of Candace Lewis had been wrapped were polypropylene olefin, used in less than a quarter of carpeting in the United States.

Sara Sidle had tracked down the ten stores locally selling that variety of carpet, though she had yet to find out how much each one had sold of this particular type and pattern.

"But as ugly as it is," she told Warrick Brown in the Tahoe, parked across from the Kyle Hamilton residence, "they can't have sold much."

"You never know," Warrick said with a wry smirk, sitting behind the wheel. "Underestimating the bad taste of people can get you in trouble."

"No argument there. Anyway, I'll get on that when I get back to the lab."

"More overtime?"

"Well, I can't call stores during our shift. Even in Vegas, carpet stores keep regular hours."

This was one of the hassles of working night shift,

aggravated by their poor relationship with Conrad Ecklie's personnel on days: some contacts you needed to make just couldn't happen on graveyard.

They'd been sitting in the Tahoe—he sipping coffee, she drinking tea—for fifteen minutes. It was a little before six A.M.; Brass was on his way. Despite the hour, Brass had gone to a judge to obtain a search warrant for Kyle Hamilton's white Monte Carlo with the busted taillight.

They had relieved the North Las Vegas patrol car, who'd been watching the residence on Cotton Gum Court. The NLVPD reported no signs of activity at the two-story, orange-tile-roofed stucco. The odds that the car would be in the garage—which sat forward, the front door recessed to its left—were slim; but just getting in the garage would be a start. The sun had already peeked over the horizon, but the night hadn't yet given up the ghost, the sky a cobalt gray, early rising residents in surrounding houses still depending on electricity to guide their way.

Warrick sat up, almost spilling his coffee. "Was that light on before?"

"What light?"

"Upstairs. Second window over. I don't remember that being on."

She shrugged. "I'm sorry. I wasn't paying attention. Just sitting here zoned, waiting for Brass."

Around them, the neighborhood was slowly coming to life. The houses may have been cookie-cutter, but morning rituals varied, at least a little. Here a car backed out of a garage, the driver eyeballing the black man and white woman in the Tahoe as his own SUV rolled slowly out of the court. There a thir-tyish guy in a business suit came out and picked up the paper, quick-scanning the front page as he strolled back inside without even noticing the parked CSIs. And the Hamilton home remained life-less.

But for that one light . . .

Frowning, an alert Warrick was staring at the house as Brass pulled up behind them. Then the captain was leaning at Warrick's window like a carhop.

"Like we thought, gotta confine ourselves to the garage," Brass said, waving the warrant. "Didn't have enough to justify the house."

"I think somebody might be home, after all," Warrick said, and pointed at the second-floor light.

Brass squinted over at the house. "You sure that wasn't on when you pulled up?"

"No," Warrick admitted.

Otherwise, the house on Cotton Gum Court still looked deserted—curtains upstairs drawn, downstairs blinds pulled tight, double garage door down. No barking dog, no one had even taken in the morning paper. Only that one light on, upstairs . . .

"I'll ring the bell, as a precaution," Brass said, and watched the house as he waited for Sara and Warrick to climb down from the Tahoe, and secure their silver crime scene suitcases from the back.

They had just started up the sidewalk when an-other upstairs light went on in a small window, white-backed curtains glowing yellow.

They took a step and that light went out and Sara got the bizarre feeling that somehow the lights were linked to their movements—a security system of some kind?

When they were almost to the house, another light came on, downstairs, illumination flooding through the glass panels that ran down either side of the front door, as if the lights were on a course to intercept them at the entrance.

A frowning, cautious Brass raised his finger to ring the bell, but before he pressed the button, the door swung open and a tall, skinny white man in glasses, cotton running shorts and a Cowboy Bebop T-shirt jumped back a step, yipping like a watchdog.

Then the guy dropped into a martial-arts stance and yelled something in Japanese. Sara's response was not fear, rather to raise a hand to her mouth to keep from laughing.

Still in his combat pose, the man—who had a scruffy day-or-two's worth of beard—shouted in a nasal voice, in English, "Who the hell are *you* people?"

"Relax, Jackie Chan," Brass said, adding "LVMPD," even as he reached into his pocket for his badge wallet.

The man's only break from his stance was to use one hand to push the black horn-rimmed glasses further up his nose. "Take that ID out slow," he demanded, his voice still booming.

Brass held out his badge. Sara and Warrick pointed to the plastic ID necklaces. She noticed that their reluctant host wore old, un-laced-up running shoes that would have gone flying in any karate attack.

Was this buffoon their killer?

The skinny guy, swallowing, finally rose out of his stance and looked over each of their I.D.s, comparing their faces to the pictures on the cards.

"Sorry," he said, a little sheepishly. "Have to be careful, these days. Lotta psychos out there. . . . And you startled me."

Brass gave him a facial shrug. "We didn't think anyone was home."

"Well, I am home," he said, pointlessly. "But I have a bad cold. I've been in bed on NyQuil since yesterday morning, dead to the world. . . . A little better now."

That explained why no one had answered the bell on Warrick and Brass's first stop by the house.

Brass finally got around to asking, "Are you Kyle F. Hamilton?"

The guy nodded. "Listen, I'm a big supporter of law enforcement. I didn't mean to scare you."

Warrick's mouth twitched as he fought a smile and Sara turned her head and coughed to cover her laugh.

"How may I be of help, officers?"

Brass said, "Your car has come up in an ongoing investigation. It appears to be routine, but we'd like to talk to you about it."

"My car? Well, I haven't even been out since yesterday. I was following up on an installation at New York New York, and this cold just did me in."

With his narrow face and high cheekbones, his wide blue eyes darting from one to the other of them, Hamilton had a confused, vaguely victimized expression that reminded Sara of several other nerdy, paranoid types she'd met who'd gone into security work.

Brass was saying, "Mr. Hamilton, can we come in? This should only take a minute or two."

Hamilton said, "Of course," then to Warrick, Hamilton added, "Could you get the paper? That's why I was going outside in the first place."

"Sure thing," Warrick said with a smile, and did, then followed Brass into the house, Sara trailing them both.

The front door opened into a modest entryway with a smallish living room to the right. The hardwood floor was covered only in the very center by a small round rug depicting the yin and yang. A white futon hugged the back wall and a small television perched on a low table against the front wall with DVD and VCR beneath. A cloth wall hanging of Bruce Lee hung prominently in the center of the far wall.

"So what's my car got to do with anything?" Hamilton asked, his face revealing a thousand dire scenarios unfolding themselves in his paranoid imagination.

"We got a report that your vehicle might have been at the scene of a crime earlier this week. We can check that out easily enough. We'd just like to take a look at your car."

The skinny guy considered that for a moment, knuckles of one hand unconsciously riding up and down scruffy whiskers. "Please don't misunderstand. I support you guys, but I know my rights. I'm a real bug about procedure. You need a warrant."

Brass withdrew the warrant from his inside coat pocket and handed the papers forward. "Here you go."

Eyes wide, horrified, Hamilton leaned back like he expected Brass to slap him with the papers. "I didn't mean you had to *have* a warrant! I'm happy to cooperate. I just wanted you to know I was familiar with my rights. I can waive that warrant."

"Why don't you take it. Look it over."

"All right." He grinned nervously. "It's just that . . . well . . . it's early, I'm sorry. I still have a NyQuil hangover—that stuff puts me out! Hey, I know you have a tough job and I want to help. You just surprised me."

"Fine," Brass said.

Hamilton studied the document for a long moment, then, taking a step toward the back of the house, said, "It's this way. What makes you think it's my car? At this crime scene of yours?"

Warrick said, "The car spotted at the scene had a broken right taillight."

Hamilton stopped and the three of them nearly piled into him. Turning back, he said with a frown, "Well, then you're wasting your time."

Sara asked, "Why is that, Mr. Hamilton?"

He shrugged. "I don't have a broken taillight."

"We need to check," Brass said. "Procedure."

With a little nod, Hamilton turned back toward the rear of the house.

"So you guys are CSIs?" Hamilton said to Warrick.

"That's right."

"That must be an exciting job."

"It has its moments."

To Sara, Hamilton said, "Meet some real oddballs, I bet!"

"Now and then."

When their host got to the kitchen, he turned left and opened a door that led into darkness. Pushing open a screen door, he flipped a light switch and the two-car garage was bathed in light.

The '98 white Monte Carlo sat directly in the middle. On this side of the car, a heavy punching bag was chained to the crossbeam of the ceiling. Next to it hunkered a weight bench, with a barbell on the rack supporting about the same amount Sara could bench-press.

Hamilton led them to the back of the car and looked down at the taillight.

"What the hell!" Hamilton blurted, his head tilting to one side, as he tried to comprehend the broken light on the right rear fender of his car.

Actually, the taillight was mostly intact, a small piece broken out near the bottom, as if something had smacked against it and cracked off a piece, like Candace Lewis's body maybe.

After setting his crime scene kit on the concrete floor with a clunk, Warrick opened it and fished out the evidence bag with the piece of red plastic inside.

"What's that?" Hamilton asked, hovering, his voice unsteady.

Sara said, "Piece of a taillight found at our crime scene. We just need to see if it fits the break in yours."

Hamilton looked pale as death, and Sara didn't think it was the man's cold. He shuffled back, out of the way, as if every bad thing in his past, real or imagined, had caught up with.

Taking the piece out of the bag, Warrick fitted it into the hole in the Monte's taillight.

From the sidelines, Hamilton said, "It fits perfectly!"

"Yeah," Warrick said, dryly.

"What's it mean?"

Brass showed their host the hint of a smile. "It means, Mr. Hamilton, you're going to be answering a lot more questions and these criminalists will be searching both your house and the car."

Hamilton seemed to crumple in on himself; Sara wondered if the man was about to faint.

Then he hauled himself up straight and said, "I haven't done anything. You're welcome to search all you want—you don't have to go out and get another warrant for my house or anything. But there's nothing to find."

Warrick gestured toward the broken tail. "You don't remember doing this?"

"No. Unless . . ." His eyes flared; paranoia danced in them. "Maybe somebody's trying to frame me!"

"Frame you for what, Mr. Hamilton?" Brass asked pleasantly. "Why don't we let our CSIs work their magic, while you and I go have a talk."

"All right. I'm here to cooperate. I hope I've made that clear."

"Crystal."

Sara and Warrick rolled their eyes at each other and got to it: she took the car, he took the garage.

After an hour in the trunk, she had found no blood, no fibers, no hair, no leftover adhesive from the duct tape, no anything. She climbed out, perspiration matting her hair to her forehead and the back of her neck.

"This is the wrong car, Warrick," she said, matter of factly. "There's never been a body in this trunk."

"You're sure?" he asked, crossing from the workbench on the far side of where she stood. "Guy's a law enforcement freak. Maybe he cleaned it."

"Does he strike you as savvy enough to obliterate each and every trace of evidence?" She pointed to the Monte Carlo. "If Candace Lewis's body had been in this trunk, there would be *some* evidence of it. Blood, fibers from the carpeting, a hair, something. Instead, there's nothing but trash. What did you find?"

"Diddly," Warrick said.

Sara gestured with both hands. "You think maybe that's because there *is* nothing to find? I mean, geez, we found more at the mayor's house. At least those hairs confirmed Candace had been there."

Warrick mulled that for a while; then, tilting his head toward the house, he said, "Let's go have a talk with Brass."

They packed up their gear, lugged it through the house and Warrick signaled for Brass to meet them in the front yard. A moment later, Brass joined them.

"What have you got?" he asked.

They both shrugged.

Brass frowned. "Meaning?"

Sara said, "Unless this guy is the Dr. No or Professor Moriarty of crime scene cleanup, Candace Lewis was never in that trunk."

"You're sure? Didn't that taillight match?"

She nodded. "It did, and that's a significant puzzle

piece, a literal one. But other than that, I can't find anything. What's Hamilton saying?"

Brass sighed. "He claims he never heard of her until she made the papers."

"You believe him?"

The detective gave a half-hearted shrug.

"He have an alibi for that night?" Warrick asked.

"Yeah—he says he was at the All-American Juke-box casino, all night."

"Gambling?"

Brass shook his head. "Installing a new security system."

"He's not a security guard?" Warrick asked.

"No," the detective said. "He installs stuff. Works for a company that handles a lot of the casinos."

Warrick frowned. "Security systems. Doesn't that ring a bell?"

Sara's mind was elsewhere. "So, he should be on videotape somewhere, sometime, night of the murder?"

"Should be," Brass said.

"Helpful," Warrick said.

Hamilton peeked tentatively from his doorway, then came outside; he was holding a cup of coffee. "Are you guys done in there?"

They traded looks, then shrugs, and finally, Brass nodded to Hamilton.

Hamilton approached them and, in a confidential manner, asked, "So, are you allowed to tell me who claimed my car was at your crime scene?"

Slowly, Brass shook his head. "Sorry."

Hamilton took a slug from his mug, swallowed, and

looking Brass in the eye, asked, "I was just wondering . . . Was it David Benson?"

Their eyewitness!

And Benson was also an installer of security systems. . . . That was the ringing bell none of them had been able to answer!

Brass kept his cool. "Why do you ask, Mr. Hamilton?"

"Oh, I don't mean to be rude—anybody want coffee?"

"Thank you, no, Mr. Hamilton," Brass said. "Benson?"

His voice icy, Hamilton said, "The little bastard's been my nemesis for a couple years now. See, I work for Spycoor, and Benson works for Double-O Gadgets."

Warrick said, "You're competitors?"

"Sort of. We work the same territory for different outfits. We've had a couple of run-ins over clients and he's tried to blackball me with customers, by trying to get me in trouble with the cops."

"Can you give us the details?"

"Sure. Chapter and verse."

Sara turned to Warrick and whispered, "Grissom's mantra."

With a pained expression, Warrick replied: " 'First on the scene, first suspect.' "

"So. We've been played?"

Moving closer to her, keeping his voice low, Warrick said, "We have been *played*."

Brass was still talking to Hamilton. "Thank you for your time, sir. I'm going to send another detective out to get the details on Benson's other . . . pranks on you. But in the meantime, you've given us a real lead."

The skinny man's eyes danced behind his glasses. "Have I? Great! I can't imagine anything cooler."

"Pardon?"

"Helping break a big case, and getting Benson's ass in a sling! You know—I'm feeling better!"

The trio practically sprinted to the street and around to the back of the Tahoe where Sara and Warrick loaded in their gear. Then they moved around to the far side, so the vehicle was between them and Hamilton's house.

"What do you think?" Brass asked.

Warrick still kept his voice down. "So who checked Benson out?"

They all took turns looking at each other.

Warrick groaned.

Sara was getting her cell phone out, to fill Grissom in, when it twittered on its own.

"Sara Sidle."

"We overlooked something," Grissom's voice said.

She glanced around the neighborhood as if he were somehow shadowing them. "We just figured that out too."

"Kyle Hamilton's car may be a wild goose chase," Grissom said, "the killer sent us on."

"That's right. The broken tail matches, but the car is cleaner than Martha Stewart's sink. How did you know?"

"I was just talking to Nick and Catherine about their case, and how they'd neglected a key aspect . . .

and it dawned on me we'd made the same fundamental mistake . . ."

And in unison, Sara and Grissom said: "First on the scene, first suspect."

Sara said, "Hamilton's a rival of Benson's in the security installation game."

"Now we know why Benson was such a great eyewitness. Get back here."

"We're on our way," she said, but it was too late, as Grissom had already hung up.

Within the hour, they were all working different angles, trying to learn more about David Benson. Warrick was tracking the man's work history while Sara dug into his past, looking for a connection between Benson and Candace Lewis. Grissom spent the time dealing with the various labs about the physical evidence they had, such as it was.

He was, in fact, the first one to announce any progress when he came into the room where Sara was working.

"Mobley's in the clear," he said. "Greg reports the sheriff's DNA doesn't match any of the other samples we have."

"How about Ed Anthony?"

"Clean, too. He may be our favorite suspect, but he's not the guilty one."

"Pity. How's Warrick doing?"

"Nothing so far. How about you?"

She glanced up from the monitor and gave him a small shrug. "We know Candace was a workaholic and spent very little time with friends or family. Benson's sort of a cipher, himself. Bought his house two years ago, pays his bills, seems like a regular guy."

"He may be a regular guy whose hobbies include necrophilia and framing the competition for murder. Keep digging, there's got to be something."

"You know, Gil, our eyewitness may not be the killer. He could have just used this opportunity to cause trouble for this business rival."

"I don't buy that. There's no way he fit Kyle Hamilton for a frame without having something to do with this."

"What's that," she asked innocently, "a hunch?"

He just looked at her blankly; and then his expression turned into a little grin. "Okay, that's one for you. Get yourself another, by finding the link between Candace Lewis and David Benson."

And he was gone.

Warrick Brown finished Benson's work history and came up with nothing; but rather than just sitting around, he tracked down Grissom, finding his supervisor in the trace lab bent over a work table.

"What have you got, Gris?"

"If we've learned one thing in this case, it's not to ignore the basics. So I'm going back to the one thing that can't lie."

"The evidence," Warrick said.

Peeking over his boss's shoulder, Warrick saw a strip of duct tape on the table.

"I already did the smooth side and got nothing," Grissom said. "But I thought maybe we might get lucky on the adhesive side."

"Gentian Violet?"

Grissom shook his head. "What makes duct tape strong is the fibers running through it. Those fibers absorb Gentian Violet, and if we do raise a print, we wouldn't be able to tell what it is."

"Sad but true."

"Well, I remembered this detective I met at a conference a few years back, from the Midwest—Jeff Swanson. He told me he'd been experimenting with small-particle reagent on duct tape. We haven't really had a chance to use it until now."

SPR, or molybdenum disulfide, Warrick knew, was a physical development procedure that involved the tiny black particles adhering to the fatty substances left in fingerprint residue. Though it had been successful on many different surfaces—glass, metal, cardboard, even paper—Warrick had never heard of it being used on duct tape.

"Is it working?"

"Yes. I photographed it as it was, then put on a small amount of SPR, which gave everything a charcoal color. Then I rinsed it with just a tiny bit of tap water, and that made the print appear to be floating in the water. The SPR helped remove the fibers and other background noise."

Pulling out his Polaroid MP4, Grissom took three shots in quick succession.

"What kind of film?" Warrick asked.

"Six sixty-five positive-negative."

That meant prints in less than a minute. Warrick almost patted Grissom on the back. Almost.

The boss was saying, "Swanson even said that if we

use lifting tape when it's not saturated, but still moist, we can lift the print. I've been wanting to try this for some time."

The man was giddy with the science, and Warrick couldn't help but smile.

When Sara Sidle found what she needed, it was so obvious she almost tripped over it.

She printed two pages, then tore off down the hall in search of Grissom and Warrick. She found the two of them in Grissom's office, both looking beat, which was unusual for the CSI supervisor, who sat behind his desk, his shoulders hunched, arms heavy on the desktop before him. As for Warrick, he leaned against a set of shelves, likely to slide down the front and fall asleep right there.

Understandable that even bricks like Grissom and Warrick would show the strain: few cases in recent years had inspired more overtime, more double shifts than the Candace Lewis case. But Sara was about to wake her colleagues up. . . .

"And you're this chipper why?" a sleepy-eyed Warrick asked her.

"I *found* it," she said, holding up the pages.

Grissom sat up, instantly alert. "The link?"

"They were neighbors," she announced, and handed her boss the sheets. Then she leaned on his desk with both hands, grinning, unabashedly pleased with herself.

"Who were neighbors?" Warrick said, coming over beside her.

She looked from Warrick to Grissom. "Before

Candace moved into her condo, and Benson bought his house, they were neighbors in an apartment complex in Green Valley."

"What kind of neighbors?" Warrick asked.

"The next-door kind," Sara said.

Im midday traffic, it took a while to get there, even with Grissom giving Warrick *carte blanche* behind the wheel.

The apartment complex—a sprawling series of three-story buildings near the corner of Green Valley Parkway and Pebble Road—had been the latest thing, twenty years ago. Now it was a weathered roost for those unable to manage a down payment on a house trailer.

The manager—a middle-aged man with short, dark hair cut up over his ears and collar—looked to be ex-military; probably put in his twenty, Sara figured, retired and took the job of managing this place in trade for rent. The man seemed happy to see them—prospective renters, possibly—right up until Brass flashed his badge.

The office was small and cramped, the air stale despite the best efforts of a window air conditioner about ten years past its prime. Howard Thomas—as he'd been announced by a scruffy brass nameplate on his forty-dollar do-it-yourself-kit desk—sat grumpily drumming his fingers on the desktop.

"Let's make this short," he said. "I'm a busy man, and some of my tenants are allergic to police."

"Perhaps," Brass said, "they can build up a tolerance, if we have a patrol car stop by here, on the hour. Maybe they'll feel a little safer."

"You don't have to be unpleasant."

"We need to talk to you about a couple of your ex-tenants."

Thomas shrugged. "If you mean Candace Lewis, she was a model tenant—everybody liked her, everybody got along with her."

None of them was surprised that the manager had skipped a step and gone straight to Candace Lewis—as big as the story was in the media, as important as the case had been, this manager had no doubt already answered more than his share of questions about the mayor's late personal assistant.

But the manager explained anyway: "She's all you cops want to talk about. You and the TV and the papers and the FBI, you guys are sniffin' around here, every other day, seems like—and I can't get a decent renter to walk through the door."

"I hear life's a bitch," Brass said. "Now, let's talk about another former tenant—David Benson."

Thomas shrugged. "That's a new one. Who the hell is he?"

Sara said, "Lived here for two years. Left about two years ago?"

Grissom said, "That's four years, Mr. Thomas."

"Hell if I know."

Brass asked, "You keep records, don't you?"

Thomas pointed at a file cabinet. "You don't expect me to take my time sorting through there, do you?"

Sara was starting to understand why Grissom preferred insects to people.

A lanky guy in his thirties strolled into the room; he wore threadbare jeans and a tan workshirt with the name Kevin stitched in an oval over a breast pocket.

"Finished 4B," Kevin said, oblivious to the crowd in the tiny office.

"What about the bum washer in building six?"

"I don't wanna start that till after lunch."

Thomas waved dismissively and "Kevin" slipped back out the door. After Grissom shot them a look, Sara and Warrick were on the guy's tail.

The sun was high and hot, but a breeze from the west made it cooler out here than inside that stuffy office. Kevin strolled through the parking lot; he climbed into a red beater of a pickup, the box stacked full with plywood, two by fours, empty pop and beer cans, and some loose hand tools. He didn't start the pickup up, however; he was brownbagging it.

And as he unwrapped a sandwich from what might have been an evidence bag, Sara came up on the driver's side, Warrick looping around to the passenger side.

"Are you the maintenance engineer?" she asked, reaching for the most complimentary term she could muster. She gave him a nice smile.

He had just taken a bite of his sandwich, and looked up—ready to give hell to whoever'd interrupted his alfrecso dining—but then apparently liked what he saw, including her gap-toothed smile. He nodded slowly, still chewing, closing his mouth while doing so, indicating chivalry wasn't dead.

"Mind if I call you 'Kevin'?" she asked, gesturing to the name on his workshirt.

He swallowed a bite, then grinned. "Call me anytime."

Then the maintenance man seemed to sense Warrick, on the other side, and glanced at him with a frown. Warrick gave him a friendly nod.

The maintenance man returned the nod, guardedly, then turned back to Sara. "So who are you guys? Saw you talkin' to Howard."

She lifted the I.D. on its necklace. "Sara Sidle and that's Warrick Brown. We're with the crime lab? Can we talk to you while you eat?"

If Warrick had been the one asking, the maintenance man might have said no; but Kevin seemed intent on keeping Sara happy. "Sure, if you don't spoil my lunch with some gross-out shit from the morgue or somethin'!"

Kevin chortled at his own witticism and Sara managed a light laugh.

"What do you guys wanna talk about?"

"A couple of former tenants—Candace Lewis and David Benson."

"She was a babe," he said. "He was a dork. Anything else?"

Sara said, "Didn't they live next door to each other?"

"That's right."

"Did they get along?"

He shrugged. "She was nice to him. Hell, she was nice to everybody. Real doll. But Benson, he followed her around like a lovesick puppy. Carried her laundry up and down to the laundry room. Brought her groceries in for her and stuff. I always thought it was so he could try to get a whiff of her panties, pardon my French, but she thought he was harmless."

Sara frowned. "How do you know that, Kevin?"

He shrugged. "You can just tell. You know, some dorks fall for anything a babe hands out."

Warrick smiled a little, for Sara's benefit.

Kevin was saying, "That nerd had the hots for her, big time. Man, I told her she should've got a restraining order against him, but she kept sayin' he was 'sweet.' "

Reading between the lines, Sara said, "And she thought you were kind of . . . jealous?"

He straightened in the pickup seat. "Hey, we weren't an item. But we talked, 'cause I'm the maintenance guy, I helped her out, fixed stuff."

"And she was a nice person?"

"Yeah! I mean, she *knew* she was a babe. Babes know when they're babes, know what effect they have on gullible guys. Right?"

Sara didn't know how to answer that.

"But she also seemed kinda . . . naive. Like she didn't know she was playin' with fire. A weirdo like Benson, leadin' him on, that's dangerous, man."

Sara asked, "Did you ever talk about this with any other police, or possibly the FBI?"

"That guy Culpepper?" He shook his head. "None of them ever asked about Benson—you're the first ones." His eyes tightened. "You think the tabloids'd go for this?"

"They might," Sara said. "You could call them, if you don't mind Benson suing you."

"I don't need that shit!"

Warrick asked, "Would it be possible to see her old apartment?"

"Can't. Somebody's living there now. You'd have to get their permission, and they ain't home."

Sara asked, "What about Benson's old apartment?"

"That I could show you. Tenant after him just moved out last week."

The maintenance man finished his sandwich quickly and Sara kept an eye on the office door; but Grissom and Brass were still in there with the manager.

She and Warrick followed Kevin two buildings over and up two flights of concrete stairs to the third floor. The maintenance man led them around the building to an apartment almost at the far end of the walkway.

"Benson lived here," Kevin said, pointing to the door in front of them, "and she had the apartment on the end."

Using his passkey, the maintenance man let them in. As promised, the apartment was vacant. Tan carpeting covered the floor except for tile floors in the kitchen and bathroom. All the walls were painted white, the kitchen/dining area, the living room, the two bedrooms and the bathroom, all painted that chunky white textured paint that showed hardly any wear.

"Doesn't look too bad," Warrick said.

Kevin shrugged. "Not now. Guy that lived here last left it spotless. Even got his security deposit back."

Picking up on the implication, Sara asked, "What about Benson? Not so spotless?"

The maintenance man snorted. "You don't know how much time I spent in this dump, patching it up!

Thomas charged that dork a couple hundred over the deposit."

"Why?" Sara asked.

"The asshole had holes drilled everywhere!"

"Holes? What for?"

"His goddamned shelves and video equipment."

Warrick asked, "So he had a lot of video stuff?"

"Yeah, he was really into it. See, he sold the shit, so he got it at cost. He put holes in the walls to support these metal shelves all over the place—the joint was lousy with them." He walked over to the wall and pointed to a couple of spots where there were obvious patches.

The two CSIs both looked around the apartment and finally Warrick called the maintenance man over to the far wall of the dining area where a patch was on the wall, almost at ceiling level; the patch looked larger than the others.

"Kevin, did Benson have shelves all the way up there? Be hard to reach."

"Naw, below that. I don't know what the hell he was doin', drillin' holes so high."

Sara felt something tense in her stomach. "Did you have to patch any holes in Candace's apartment, Kevin, when she moved out?"

"Few nail holes from some pictures."

Warrick said suddenly, "These shelves—Benson had lots of equipment, right? Or were the shelves mostly for videotapes?"

"Videotapes."

"Tapes, like big movies? Or homemade videos?"

"Homemade, mostly. Just plain old VHS in black

sleeves . . . They were everywhere, shelves full of 'em, boxes of 'em."

A chill ran through Sara.

"What's on the other side of this wall?" Warrick asked, gesturing to where the high hole had been drilled.

"Other side?" The maintenance man stared at the wall, like Superman exercising his X-ray vision. "Lemme think . . . That would have been Candace's bathroom. Yeah—shower stall."

11

NEXT SHIFT, CATHERINE WILLOWS AND NICK STOKES SPENT most of their time working a murder on Marion Drive.

A drunk had chased his wife down the street before finally catching and stabbing her to death at the edge of Stewart Place Park. It wasn't exactly a locked-room mystery—the man still at the scene, cursing his dead wife, covered in her blood when the responding officers had shown up.

Nonetheless, a crime scene was a crime scene and required due and proper processing. Collecting the evidence from the murder site and all along the chase route back to the couple's house had made for long, tedious toil on an unseasonably warm (supposedly) spring night under the gently mocking soft-focus glow of streetlights.

Now—the two CSIs sitting in the IHOP on the Strip—they were finally getting the chance to read the financial records of their child-porn suspects, over breakfast.

Catherine had Janice Denard's payroll information

in front of her, and Nick was proving his walk-and-chew-gum proficiency by alternating bites of pancake with reading Roxanne Scott's payroll history.

They had picked up Newcombe-Gold's paperwork on the seven employees on whom they zeroed in, as well as the disk that Randle claimed to have been working on last Saturday, which they'd already turned over to Tomas Nunez.

Nick—after taking a long pull on a glass of orange juice, not quite as tall as the nearby Stratosphere—nodded toward the file. "I told you advertising pays."

"Wow," Catherine said, eyes wide as she took in Denard's yearly salary.

"Roxanne Scott makes almost twice what a CSI3 makes."

"Tell me about it. Ever think you made the wrong career choice, Nicky?"

Nick grinned. "Like last night, dancing with that drunk? . . . Ahh, I wouldn't know what to do if I had real money."

"Well, you probably wouldn't ever have anybody shooting at you on the job," she said, alluding to a case they'd worked together a while back. They had gone to a house to collect evidence and wound up ducking gunfire.

"At least we know that's a possibility," Nick said with a shrug. "Most people who get shot at their workplace don't get a warning." He glanced down at Roxanne Scott's payroll record. "How many hours d'you suppose *we'd* have to work, to get a five-grand bonus?"

Her brow furrowing, Catherine looked at Janice

Denard's history again. "Five thousand? . . . When did Roxanne get that bonus?"

"First of this month."

"That's funny," Catherine said, and licked a muffin crumb off her finger before tracing a line on the sheet of paper in front of her. "That's when Janice Denard got a *ten*-thousand-dollar bonus."

Nick frowned. "I thought these women had identical jobs."

"So did I." She handed him the sheet of paper.

He studied it for a moment and said, "Maybe Janice worked more hours or something."

"Seniority?" Catherine offered, but she didn't like the feeling in her gut. She had worked with Grissom long enough to know she shouldn't always trust that feeling; and this case had already confirmed that tenet, in spades. *Evidence, not intuition . . .*

But unconsciously allowing yourself to be impacted by bias was one thing, and heeding a gut instinct—developed over years and years of on-the-job experience and just plain living life in the real world—well, that was something else again.

Nick was saying, "Could be the size of the bonus is discretionary, on the boss's part."

"We better make sure to ask Ian Newcombe about that."

"Or maybe Ruben Gold—we haven't even *talked* to him yet. When *is* head honcho number two due back in town?"

Catherine shrugged. "Another good question for us to ask when we go back there."

"Which will be . . . ?"

She glanced at her watch. "They're not even open for another forty-five minutes."

"Do I detect another double shift coming on?"

"See, Nicky? You are going to have real money. Let's go back and see how Nunez is coming along, and then head over to Newcombe-Gold."

"It's a plan."

Still encamped in the air-conditioned garage, Tomas Nunez sat hunkered at a keyboard and monitor, his hair slicked back like a black helmet. Today's black T-shirt touted a gringo girl group—the Donnas—and the lanky, biker-esque computer guru had already worked up some sweat stains, despite the coolness of the concrete bunker. His black jeans had blown a knee but were otherwise intact, while his eight-thousand-buck forensic computer whirred quietly on the floor next to him as he studied a series of images rolling hypnotically across his monitor.

"Morning, Tomas," Catherine said, holding out a cup of coffee in a Styrofoam IHOP cup.

"Morning, Catherine, and *gracias*." Nunez accepted the cup and took a long sip through the hole-in-the-lid.

"Is it?" she asked. "A good day?"

"We've had worse on this case," Nunez said, casting an eye toward Nick. "What, no donuts?"

"Hey, treat us right," Nick said, "and I'll make a run."

"You found something?" Catherine asked.

"You could say that. . . . Have a seat. Have two."

They drew up chairs, on the same side of him, with a good view of the monitor.

"The laptop you brought in? Found a bunch more pictures . . ."

The CSIs sat forward.

". . . the twelve you've seen and maybe a hundred sad little brothers and sisters."

"So," Catherine said, with an eyebrow lift, "Gary Randle's back on the radar."

"But we still don't have his prints anywhere on that laptop," Nick reminded her. "The whole thing's been wiped clean."

"Nick, it was in his possession!"

Nunez cut back in. "Chill, you two . . . let me give you a few more facts to chew on, before you jump to your next conclusion."

"Ouch," Nick said.

"I ran a search for angel12.jpg and found reference to that file in unallocated space. Guess where the reference indicated it'd been downloaded from?"

"A kiddie porn website," Catherine said hopefully, "that you traced to Gary Randle?"

"How about a website . . . in Russia."

"*Russia?*" Catherine blurted.

"*Si.* Since the Cold War ended, all kinds of crime has flourished in the former Soviet Union, as capitalism flowers in various interesting and often vile ways."

"Less commentary," Nick said. "More data."

"Fair enough. I was able to resolve the Internet address to an IP address using a Domain Name Server Resolver; then I traced the IP address using a Trace Route site on the net, which sends a PING message to the IP, and waits for a response. It'll then trace the route the PING takes to the destination server and show where the destination—or host server—is, for the IP address."

"Soooooo," Nick said, "if we want the actual ped-dlers of this smut . . ."

". . . you'll be flying Aeroflot to Moscow, then hop-ping a train to East Armpit, Siberia."

Catherine asked, "How does this help us?"

"It helps you. Not directly, but it gives us something to hand over to the Feds."

Processing the info aloud, Catherine said, "This means that Randle, or someone else at Newcombe-Gold, is *not* a child pornographer, rather a consumer of the product."

Nick said, "I have to admit, I never really thought Randle had a camera and was taking photos . . ."

"A guy in an ad agency," Catherine said, flaring, "with his skills and smarts? With his sexually deviant tastes? With a teenager daughter in the house? *I* thought he might be."

"Till now."

"Till now," she admitted. "So he's a user, not a dealer. Either way, it's still 'drugs.' "

"*If* it's Randle."

"If it's Randle," she granted.

Nunez said, "Hey, kids—if you're through, I got a little something from that laptop to make you smile."

Catherine said, "Don't tease me, Tomas."

"No tease: I ran E-Script, which carved out the Internet history to an Excel spreadsheet, showing websites visited, along with the dates and time of each visit . . . and logged on user for each site."

And, as the computer wizard had predicted, Catherine and Nick traded smiles.

"That Russian website," Nunez was saying, "was

last visited Friday at four o'clock P.M., local time. The logged-on user was Randyman."

After glancing over at Nick, who seemed suitably impressed, she asked, "You got all that from the laptop?"

Nunez nodded. "Like they say on the infomercials . . . *but that's not all*: the laptop had AOL software. I got O'Riley to get a search warrant for the subjects of the AOL logs—account history, billing history and website history, along with saved e-mails. The AOL logs matched the laptop's Internet history log, so that'll stand up. Anyway, I tried to access the website, but like a lot of these child porn sites, it's password protected."

"Does this mean Gary Randle really *is* guilty?" Catherine asked, trying not to give in to the spinning-head feeling she always seemed to get during Nunez's explanations.

"Not necessarily," Nunez said. "All it means is those twelve pictures that you confiscated from Newcombe-Gold were downloaded from the Internet using *this* laptop."

"Smoking gun," Nick said.

"But who was holding it?" Catherine asked. To Nunez, she said, "Next step?"

"You need a search warrant for Randle's local telephone records, to see if the AOL access number was dialed during the times this machine was online, and the Russian website was accessed. If they match, he's your guy."

Nick took a sideways look at the laptop. "Could this machine be the one that was plugged into work station eighteen, and used to mimic Ben Jackson's computer?"

"No. The MAC address of the NIC card doesn't match the server log."

Catherine sat with arms folded, eyes narrowed. "So—there's still a computer somewhere that sent that print order . . . and we haven't found it."

"You haven't found it. But there's one more puzzle piece I can give you."

"Which is?"

He withdrew a sheet from his printer tray and held it up for Nick and Catherine to read. There was only one paragraph:

Given this opportunity, we will help turn Doug Clennon's All-American Jukebox into the biggest attraction in Las Vegas. By launching a major media blitz, including using our contacts at the above-mentioned publications, we can guarantee you market awareness rivalling the All-American Jukebox TV show itself.

"Some kinda letter," Nunez said.

"Pitch letter," Catherine said, slowly, eyes half-shut. "But where's the rest of it?"

Nunez shook his head. "One of the Angel jpegs got overwritten on the other sector this file was in."

"*Que?*" Nick asked.

Nunez smiled a little. "The memory is broken into sectors. Some files take up one, some take two, some take a lot more—it just depends on the size. But if a file is four and a half sectors, it will claim five. That half sector of unused space is called file slack. That's where I found this piece of this file."

"And this was on the same zip disk as the pictures?" Catherine asked.

"Yeah."

"What about Randle's zip disk that he was working on last Saturday?"

"Log numbers all match. He seems to have been doing what he said he was doing, when he said he was doing it . . . but that doesn't mean he wasn't in *earlier.*"

"Oh-kaay," Catherine sighed. She turned to Nick. "Time to split up and search different parts of this haunted house. . . . You get the phone records and see if we have a match. I'll go talk to the folks over at Newcombe-Gold, and try to widen this investigation beyond just our one favorite suspect."

"Sounds good." Nick frowned. "Cath, bring O'Riley in. We don't want to overstep."

"Not on this one," she agreed. She took the piece of paper, with the partial paragraph, from Nunez. "Thanks, Tomas."

Forty-five minutes later, Catherine walked into Newcombe-Gold, Detective O'Riley at her side. They started to display their credentials to the receptionist, but she just waved them back down the big hall— their presence, however intrusive, was starting to be perceived as routine around the agency. In fact, the receptionist even smiled a little.

As they walked down the corridor toward the conference room, Catherine pondered whether to talk to Janice Denard, first, or Gary Randle; she had questions for both.

But when she turned the corner, and glanced through the glass wall of Randle's office, seeing him behind his desk, telephone in hand, the suspect made the decision for her.

He slammed down the phone, jumped out of his desk chair and ran into the hall, his face red. But his rage came out only in a word, albeit a forceful one: *"You!"*

He had stopped inches from her face, and Catherine—normally cool in just about any situation—was genuinely alarmed.

"Not your business!" O'Riley shouted, as heads popped up over cubicles, then just as quickly disappeared.

"This is *your* fault," Randle said, trembling with rage, almost in tears, stabbing the air between himself and the CSI with a finger, coming within millimeters of Catherine's chest.

O'Riley took Randle by the arm, firmly but not rough, and said, quietly, "We're not having a scene, Mr. Randle. Step back into your office. Now."

Randle swallowed, backed up, knocking into the door frame; he composed himself, as best he could, and stumbled into his office.

He was getting back behind the desk when O'Riley—shutting the door behind himself and Catherine, just inside the office—said, "Mr. Randle, I suggest you settle yourself down."

"Settle down?" He held his middle finger up, thrusting it toward Catherine. "That *bitch* ruined my life!"

O'Riley pointed at the adman, who reacted as if it were a gun and not a forefinger aimed at him; Randle almost fell into his chair.

Gingerly, Catherine approached. "Mr. Randle— what are you talking about?"

He covered his face in his hands. He was weeping.

Catherine glanced at O'Riley, who shrugged helplessly.

The CSI drew a chair up close to the desk; she leaned forward, handing him Kleenex from her purse. "Please, Mr. Randle. Tell me what's wrong."

He snatched the tissues from her hand and dried his face of tears and snot and then, almost comically, said, "Th-thank you."

"Mr. Randle. Please talk to me."

"That . . . that was my ex-wife on the phone. Somehow she and her asshole lawyer got wind of this child porn crap, and now she's suing to regain custody of Heather!" His red eyes were pleading in a face wearing hurt beyond description. "Elaine . . . Elaine's claiming I'm an unfit parent. She drove drunk with our daughter in the car and almost *killed* her. Now *I'm* the unfit parent?"

"I'm sorry," Catherine said, and to her surprise, she meant it.

"Please . . . please, just leave me alone. . . ."

"I know this is a bad time . . ." Catherine began.

"Bad time! Do you *think?*"

". . . but we have some more questions."

Randle's ravaged eyes widened. "Why, anything I can do to help, just *ask!*"

"If you don't want to answer, that's your option," she said. "Believe it or not, I do understand how you feel . . . and I only have two questions."

The ad man sat there; he might have been dead, but for a twitching around his mouth.

"Did you work on the All-American Jukebox account?"

The query so came out of left field that it seemed to jar him back into a more mundane reality. He stared at her, then said calmly, "There wasn't an All-American Jukebox account—they went with Stevens, Hecht and Thompson . . . or as we call them around here, S-H-i-T. We pitched the Jukebox; that was it. Now, I'm sure that piece of vital information will clear everything up. Please go."

"We will, shortly. But, Mr. Randle, we're close on this. If you're guilty, you're smart enough to know that sooner or later we're going to catch you."

"Go to hell. Please just go to hell."

"But if you're innocent, you *need* the guilty party caught—it's the only way to prove your innocence, and demonstrate that you really *are* a fit parent."

This seemed to get through to him. At least, he was thinking.

Finally, he said, "That . . . that makes sense, I guess."

"Good. If you're really innocent, and you help us, I promise you—as one parent to another, as one *single* parent to another—I'll do everything in my power to help you keep your daughter."

Their eyes locked and he looked at her for what felt like a very long time. "How many kids?"

"Like you: just one. An eleven-year-old daughter."

His eyes tightened—just for a moment—and then he said, "So that it's . . . that's why you've hung me out to dry."

"Pardon?"

"You have a girl the age of the kids in those photos, some of 'em. You looked at me, and saw a guy into 'porno' and you just hung me out to dry."

They stared at each other.

"Maybe I did," Catherine said.

O'Riley looked at her, stunned.

"Thank you, for that much," Randle said, simply. ". . . What else?"

"You worked up the All-American Jukebox pitch?"

"Yeah—it was a big deal. I was part of it. Huge disappointment."

She held out the page with the paragraph on it. "Did you write this?"

He read it. "No—this is an introductory letter. My input was more specific, including preliminary artwork; that kinda thing isn't my deal. I came in at a later stage—too late to do any good, frankly—and we didn't get the account."

"Do you know who did write it?"

"Ian or Ruben probably—that's the kind of thing they'd handle themselves, at least with big clients, like casinos."

Catherine rose. "I have other people to talk to, here," she said. "If you're going to be around, I'll come back and keep you posted."

"I will be," he said, nodding slowly. "I have plenty to do—on the phone with *my* lawyer, to see what we can do about Elaine."

"With luck, I'll have ammunition for you."

She extended her hand.

He looked at it; then shook it.

She and O'Riley stepped back into the corridor.

"I almost felt sorry for the guy," O'Riley said.

"I do feel sorry him," Catherine said.

The CSI led the detective to the break room, which was empty. O'Riley plopped down at a table; he still looked like he hadn't had a good night's sleep this century.

Catherine said to him, "I need to talk to Nick, then we'll go talk to Janice Denard."

He nodded, got up, and lumbered over to a soda machine.

Nick answered on the second ring.

"Nicky," she said, "tell me you got the phone records from Randle's house?"

"Yeah, I did—weird though . . ."

"They don't match."

"That's right!"

"Nick—I don't think Randle did it."

"Playing hunches again, Cath?"

"Don't tell Grissom."

"Hey, *I* plan to duck Gris for maybe a month!"

She paced as she talked. "We're going to need two more search warrants, and Tomas is going to have to do some more digging."

"Warrants for who?"

Catherine went on for the next two minutes about how her thinking had changed—including the new suspect for whom she needed the warrants—and how they should proceed from here.

"And one last thing," she said.

"Yeah?"

"Ask Tomas about Randle's computer from the agency. Is there any sign that it's been worked on by anybody, and can he tell if something was really wrong?"

"These are better ideas than any I've had lately," Nick admitted. "I'll get right on it."

Catherine, putting her cell away, turned to O'Riley, who sat with a Coke can in one hand, the other hand flopped on the table, his expression almost as numb as Randle's. He looked like a weary king waiting for an angry mob to depose him.

"You look refreshed," Catherine said. "Shall we?"

"I didn't come here for a good time," he said, using the table to push himself up.

"It's working."

Surprised to find no one in Janice Denard's office, Catherine checked her watch: ten A.M.; too early for lunch—Denard should be here, somewhere. The CSI was still pondering her next move when the door to Ruben Gold's office swung open and Janice Denard appeared.

The attractive blonde's eyes widened, but any surprise and/or displeasure was momentary, a pleasant smile accompanying her greeting, as she stepped out, closed the door, and approached them.

"Ms. Willows—nice to see you again. Detective O'Riley. You two are here so often we should get your social security numbers."

Catherine didn't bother with a polite smile. "I'm following up on a few details."

Denard gestured to the chairs in front of her desk, sitting behind it. Catherine sat, while O'Riley stayed on his feet, arms crossed, hovering in the background like a harem guard.

"I can't imagine what information I might have left to share with you," Denard said, her own smile more strained than polite.

"I'd like to ask you about the bonus you got, first of the month."

The woman's eyes narrowed just a bit. "That's a little outside the scope of your investigation, isn't it?"

"Is it? Your bonus was double the next highest, which was that of Roxanne Scott, your counterpart."

"What's the point of this line of inquiry, Ms. Willows?"

"In fact," Catherine said, with a tight smile, ignoring the question, "it's higher than any bonus the company has *ever* paid."

Denard stiffened. "Mr. Gold values my services."

"That's the feeling I'm getting."

"What I mean to say is, he was very generous. Which I don't believe is a crime."

"No, Ms. Denard, that's not a crime. But that doesn't answer my question, at least not fully."

Denard shifted in her chair; annoyance tugged at her eyes and mouth. "Each partner has a discretionary account that no one else has access to. They pay bonuses for cost-saving ideas, a job well done—any number of things."

The door to the inner office swung open again and framed there stood a tall, thin, mostly gray-haired individual in his vague fifties, with boyish features that seemed somehow wrong for a man his age; he began to say something, but it caught in his throat, upon seeing the two people in the outer office.

"Excuse me," he said, smiling. "I wasn't aware you had company, Ms. Denard."

"These are the police investigators I was tell you about, Mr. Gold," she said. She also smiled, hers less convincing than her boss's.

Gold wore a bright blue shirt with a black tie and suit. His eyes were dark blue, half-lidded but alert, giving him a look of perpetual caution; not a man you'd care to play poker with.

The co-owner of the agency stepped deeper into Janice's office and shook hands with Catherine, who had risen, and with O'Riley, saying "Ruben Gold . . . Ruben Gold."

Catherine introduced herself and O'Riley. "I'm pleased to see you're back in the office," she said. "You're one of the people we've been needing to talk to."

"Really? I was under the impression this . . . unfortunate incident took place while I was away."

"That's my impression," Catherine said sunnily, "but the fact remains, you and Roxanne Scott are the only two people we haven't interviewed or fingerprinted."

"Fingerprinted?" he asked.

"Yes, we've fingerprinted all your employees."

"Well, I'm aware of that," he said, with an inappropriate chuckle. "But why would you need mine?"

His voice was mild—he might have been asking her to pass the butter.

"Routine elimination. Your prints are bound to be here and there, at your own business."

He shrugged his understanding.

She went on: "Let's take this opportunity to get our few questions out of the way."

Gold turned to Janice and gave her an easy smile. "I have a little time available, don't I?"

The secretary checked her book. "Other than phone calls you need to make, Mr. Gold, you're open till lunch with Ian, right at noon."

"Good," he said, and smiled again.

It was a beautiful smile—caps, Catherine wondered—but stained faintly brownish yellow. A smoker.

"Step into my office, would you?" he asked the CSI and the detective.

They entered, Gold holding the door for them. As she slipped by the exec, Catherine noticed the scent of a citrus-based cologne. She and O'Riley took seats across from the huge mahogany desk, while Gold settled into his leather throne. Behind him was the printer where the photos had been found.

Catherine gestured admiringly at the silver airplane on the C-shaped base on the corner of Gold's desk. "Aircraft enthusiast?" she asked.

"Something of one. Actually, that little number isn't all that different from mine." He smiled charmingly, adding, "Smaller, of course."

She returned the smile. "Company plane?"

"Yes," he said, pride in his voice, "a small Lear."

"Where do you keep it?"

"Pardon?"

"Your plane. Where do you keep it?"

"Oh. Henderson Executive Airport."

An easy drive, Catherine thought: south on Las Vegas Boulevard to St. Rose Parkway, then left, and HEA was just a short distance east.

She asked, "When did you leave for Los Angeles?"

Gold's expression turned business-like, indicating he was aware the chitchat was over. "Friday afternoon."

"And the trade show you attended started . . . ?"

"Well, there was a get-acquainted session Sunday evening, and the show started, for real, on Monday morning."

Catherine nodded. "And Friday evening?"

A little easygoing grin. "Giants-Dodgers game at Dodger Stadium. A chance to see some of the guys who'd started here."

Catherine was not a big baseball fan, but did know that the Las Vegas 51's were the triple-A affiliate of the Los Angeles Dodgers.

"And Saturday?"

"Slept in, had a late room service breakfast, played golf in the afternoon, dinner with friends in the evening."

"You traveled alone?"

"Unfortunately, yes."

"Why 'unfortunately?' "

"It's just . . . my job is not easy on relationships."

"Ah. I thought someone from work might have accompanied you. It *was* a trade show, after all."

Gold shook his head. "Ian and I've been doing this for quite a while. We're both comfortable working alone, and divide the duties, where these trade shows are concerned. Going to see the 'latest thing' can get to be old hat, in a hurry."

"You have a ticket stub from the ballgame?"

"Maybe at home."

"A receipt from your golf game?"

"On my Visa card."

"And the names and numbers of the friends you had dinner with, as well as the name of the hotel where you stayed?"

Gold's grin tried to be friendly but didn't make it; he shifted in the big chair. "You're acting like I'm a suspect."

"If you were, you'd be a suspect with his alibis all ready to go."

The grin vanished. "I'm well-organized. I'm used to a timetable, even where leisure time and socializing is concerned. . . . I don't appreciate this, treating me like a serious suspect." He grunted a laugh. "It's ridiculous, and frankly a little insulting."

"Child pornography is a serious crime," Catherine said.

Gold caught himself. "I didn't mean to imply that it wasn't."

"Then you will supply us with the documentation we need?"

"Yes, as soon as I can."

"May we fingerprint you now?"

"I have no objection."

She rose. "We weren't aware you'd be here today, Mr. Gold, so I'll have to get my case from the car. Sergeant O'Riley will wait here with you."

"No problem," Gold said, the picture of good citizenship.

Five minutes later, the CSI was back in the office, ready to go to work. She walked around the desk, tripping over something and almost falling into Gold's lap. When she caught herself, she looked down at what she had stumbled over.

"Oh, I'm sorry," Gold said, reaching down to up-right what Catherine had knocked into: a black leather bag that had been leaning against his desk.

"Your laptop?" Catherine asked casually.

"Yes. My personal one."

"Do you have a notepad and pen or pencil I could use, Mr. Gold?"

This surprised him mildly, but he said, "Certainly," and complied.

Catherine wrote down some quick instructions, and handed the little sheet to O'Riley, saying, "Take care of that, would you, Sergeant?"

He took the note, read it, and said, "Right away."

O'Riley exited, and Catherine went on with a leisurely fingerprinting of Ruben Gold, after which she handed him a paper towel to clean his fingers.

"A little undignified," he said good-naturedly.

"I know. Can make the best man feel like a common criminal. I do want to thank you for your time and cooperation, Mr. Gold."

"Glad to do it," he said. "I know how important it is to find the person responsible for this awful thing, and Janice tells me you people have been great about your discretion, where the media is concerned."

"It really could give your agency a black eye."

"A terrible one. Believe me, I never meant to mini-mize what was at stake here, either for the children involved or . . . and this of course is less impor-tant . . . our own business interests."

O'Riley entered and gave Catherine a curt nod.

"Serve it," she said.

The detective crossed the room and handed Ruben

Gold two search warrants—one for his laptop and one for his home.

Frowning, Gold flipped through the sheets, reading, saying, "What the hell is this?"

Pleasantly, Catherine said, "Your attorney will no doubt say your computer isn't covered by the original search warrant, since you weren't in town. That's b.s., but we've nullified that argument by getting you your very own personal warrant. We'll have your laptop back to you as soon as we can."

"These . . . these are *faxes!* These warrants were faxed to this agency!"

Catherine nodded. "Judge Madsen thoughtfully faxed them over, when Detective O'Riley called to explain the situation. By the way, thanks for the use of the company fax machine."

She picked up the leather bag by the strap. When she and O'Riley left, Gold was frantically punching numbers into his phone.

Back at HQ, Nunez worked on the laptop while Catherine and Nick handled more prosaic but vital forensic concerns; and it was just before five when the two CSIs, the computer guru, Sergeant O'Riley and two uniformed police officers made an impressive appearance at the Newcombe-Gold agency.

Their first stop was the office of Gary Randle. He was sitting at his desk and didn't even get up when Catherine led the parade into his office.

Obviously still numb, he could only manage to raise his eyebrows, in lieu of any question.

"I need to ask you something, Mr. Randle," Catherine said, standing at the front edge of his desk.

He looked up at her cautiously.

"How often do you see your ex-wife?"

Randle reared back, as if this were the most monstrous question of all. "Never!"

"She has visitation rights for your daughter. . . ."

"*Supervised* visitation. The last time Elaine and I were alone in a room together she tried to stab me in the eye with a ballpoint pen! Since then, at my insistence, the supervised visits with Heather all take place on neutral ground—a Lutheran church in Summerlin."

"And you don't see your wife at the church?"

"No. I come in one door with Heather, leave her with a court-appointed officer, and then I go out the same door. Elaine comes ten minutes later, through another designated entrance, and spends her hour with Heather. Then she leaves by the door she came in, and I come back ten minutes later, using the door I came in."

"So—you never see her, and don't know anything about her current social life."

"Just the little bits and pieces Heather drops, after their visits."

"What do you know about Elaine's social life these days? From what Heather has told you?"

"Supposedly Elaine has a new man in her life."

"Who?"

"I don't know, and I don't care. Heather doesn't know either, but you can ask her, if that's really necessary."

Catherine let a breath out. "Thank you, Mr. Randle."

His eyes were unbelieving. "That's all?"

"For now. I'll be back in a few minutes. Stick around, will you?"

"I'm not going anywhere."

"One more thing, Mr. Randle?"

"Yes?"

"You should shut down your computer for the day. Nick needs to dust the inside of it for fingerprints."

His chin began to tremble. "So it isn't over?"

"Very nearly," Catherine said. "Relax."

"Easy for you to say."

"Mr. Randle—we know you're innocent."

The adman looked more stunned than relieved, as Nick set to work, while Catherine led the rest of the law enforcement parade in a march down the hall.

The group stopped next at Janice Denard's office. "Is Mr. Gold in?" Catherine asked, standing to one side of the woman's desk.

"Yes, but . . ."

"Let's go in and see him then," Catherine said, gesturing to Gold's door. "Come along, Ms. Denard."

Catherine opened the door for the woman, who went in, with O'Riley, Nunez and the two uniformed cops following, the CSI the last to step inside the inner office.

Catherine strode to Gold's side of the desk, the executive looking up in surprised confusion, but saying nothing.

Denard, lamely, said, "I tried to tell them you were busy, Mr. Gold, but—"

O'Riley said, "Ruben Gold, you're under arrest on charges of child pornography and obstruction of justice."

Gold exploded out of his chair. *"What?"*

O'Riley turned to the man's personal assistant, his secretary, saying, "Janice Denard, you're charged with obstruction of justice."

While O'Riley recited the Miranda warning to them, Janice turned white and stumbled backward, then sat, clumsily, in one of the desk chairs, opposite Gold.

"This is absurd," Gold said. "The ramifications of groundlessly charging a respected businessman like myself of such heinous—"

"We have the evidence," Catherine said.

"Evidence that has nothing to do with me," Gold said.

"Oh, I'm not talking about the *planted* evidence you used to make us to believe that Gary Randle committed this crime. I mean, the real evidence."

Gold said, "I'm going to have to ask you people to leave my office."

Catherine laughed. "I don't think so."

"Mr. Gold," Nick said, walking in to join the party, "perhaps you'd like to explain your flight plans and fuel bills showing you flying to Los Angeles both Friday *and* Saturday."

As if punched, Gold staggered back; his expression hollow, he awkwardly settled himself into his leather chair.

"When I dust it," Catherine said, "your fingerprints will be on the network plug in Ben Jackson's cubicle where you disconnected it from his machine and hooked it to yours."

Gold's mouth was open, but he wasn't saying anything.

Nick said, "We were stuck on one little thing, though: how you sabotaged Randle's computer. Tomas couldn't trace that with computer forensics."

Nunez, on the sidelines, skinny arms crossed, said to Gold, "That was about the only thing you did halfway right."

"But old-fashioned forensics did the trick," Nick said. "Fingerprinting 101." He turned to the dazed-looking Denard. "Janice, your prints were on the inside casing of Randle's computer; and both yours and Mr. Gold's prints matched ones I just lifted from Gary Randle's network card. *That* was how you made his computer breakdown last Saturday: you loosened the network card. That's all it took."

Janice looked over at her boss, but he wouldn't, or perhaps couldn't, look back at her. They were both ghostly pale.

"That was fast," Catherine said to Nick admiringly, meaning the matching of the prints.

Nick shrugged. "Warrick was sitting at the computer waiting for my call. Matched 'em right away. Mr. Gold, your agency has one fast fax machine—it rocks."

Gold leaned on an elbow, touching his fingertips to his forehead.

Nunez said to the exec, "The MAC address of your laptop matches the one that sent the print order for the kiddie porn. Your address also matches up to the Russian porn site where this garbage was downloaded."

Now Gold covered his face with both hands; he might have been weeping, but Catherine didn't think so—hiding. Just hiding.

Nunez continued: "You also left a copy of a letter you wrote to the All-American Jukebox on your hard drive. It matched the letter from the zip disk the porn came off."

Gold looked up, his eyes wide but dazed. "But that was all deleted," he complained, incriminating himself.

Nunez's grin was a horrible thing. "Deleted like when you deleted your e-mails, you mean? Sorry—I found all those, too."

Gold looked stricken.

Catherine said, "You traded a lot of e-mails with your new girlfriend—*Elaine Randle*. Or is it an old affair, that got rekindled somehow?"

"She had nothing to do with this," Gold said weakly.

"She had everything to do with it," Catherine said.

"Elaine has already been served warrants for her house and phone records, Mr. Gold. I believe we already have her laptop in custody—that's what she sneaked into her ex-husband's house and left for us to find."

Catherine laid it all out for him.

You fly your private jet to LA on Friday, giving yourself a built-in alibi. Then you wing back to Henderson some time around dawn on Saturday and drive from the airport to your office. You hook your computer into Ben Jackson's cubicle and mimic his machine. Then, using your zip disk, you take the files you'd downloaded from the Internet and send them to your computer to print.

Before you leave the office, however, you get into Randle's computer and pull the network card, just slipping it out of its seat so that when Randle tries to log on the network, he won't be able to get on. Then you drive back to the airport, fly yourself back to LA, return to your hotel and order room service, so the receipt makes it look like you slept in.

Janice comes in early Saturday, as well, and takes the photos out of your printer, just in case anybody happens by, and sticks them in a locked drawer till Monday. In the meantime, Randle's come to work and the whole world knows that Ben Jackson's out of town, and where he keeps his password, so Randle naturally uses that machine, leaving his fingerprints there to be found by us.

Monday rolls around and Janice comes in, gets inside Randle's machine and reseats the network card, then puts the photos back in the printer tray and calls 911.

Then we come in, holding up our end of the charade, finding the planted pornography, and wind up busting Randle, just as we're supposed to. Elaine sues him for custody and will get her daughter back, once Randle's ruled an unfit parent.

Gold looked completely deflated and defeated.

"Did I leave anything out?" Catherine asked.

"Downloading the porn," Gold said. He seemed almost in a trance, staring, staring. "Elaine . . . Elaine did that. She used her laptop, and mine too." He laughed, an empty, racking thing, almost a cough. "Come to think, she probably did that to have something on me as well."

"I should have known from the start," Catherine said. "If I hadn't been blinded by my own distaste for child porn, I might have nailed you, days ago."

Gold's eyes tightened. "Why?"

"Janice calling the police—that was the first really suspicious thing."

Denard sat up; she'd apparently been preparing something to say, and now she said it: "I didn't have anything to do with this. I just came in and found those printouts and did the responsible thing."

Catherine turned to the woman and gave her a withering smile. "Oh, but you *wouldn't* do the responsible thing. The thing you would have done would be to contact your boss, Mr. Gold, not 911."

Denard shook her head. "I don't even follow you. Don't even know what you're—"

"Sure you do. Big ad agency like this this kind of situation calls for, requires, a cover-up."

"I just thought it was my duty," Denard said.

"Your duty was to Mr. Gold," Catherine said. "And to that ten-thousand-dollar bonus he paid you for aiding and abetting."

Catherine gestured, and O'Riley and the uniforms handcuffed Gold and Denard.

And led the boss and his personal assistant down the corridor, past cubicles and offices and framed award-winning advertisements.

Nick and Nunez still had crime scene work to do.

Catherine returned to Randle's office. As she entered, he sprang to his feet, wild-eyed.

"Ruben? Janice? You arrested *them?* I saw your guys dragging them out in *cuffs!* What the hell could—"

"You deserve the whole story," she said, and sat down across from him and told it to him—chapter and verse.

Randle didn't get angry; he seemed past that, sharing the numbness that had overtaken Ruben Gold.

"And Elaine will be arrested, too," Randle said.

"If she hasn't been already."

"Why . . . why don't I feel vindicated? Why do I only feel empty?"

"The good news," Catherine said, "is you get to keep your daughter."

He arched an eyebrow. "You're implying there's bad news, too?"

She nodded, somberly. "This is going to make the papers. Your agency will be in trouble. Newcombe is in the clear, but this won't be easy to weather."

He waved that off. "I'm good at what I do. I couldn't care less about the business end. Need be, I'll find work. The important thing is my daughter."

He sighed, shook his head. "Leave it to Elaine to figure the best way to spend more time with her daughter was to ruin the life of the girl's father."

"Mr. Randle," Catherine said, rising, with a regretful smile, "nobody's perfect."

12

LESS THAN AN HOUR AFTER SARA HAD INFORMED GRISSOM OF their disturbing discoveries in David Benson's former apartment, a CSI Tahoe and Captain Brass's Taurus descended on Benson's current residence on Roby Grey Way. They parked in the street, noses of the vehicles facing the house, blocking passage.

Warrick Brown jumped down and headed to the rear of the vehicle. The sun loomed high now—dry and hot and not at all like spring—and those not at work in the neighborhood peeked from windows and occasionally came out, to see what all the fuss was about.

A compelling case for a search warrant for Benson's house and car had been made based on the discovery of a hole in the apartment wall, through which Benson—the witness who had "found" the body—had apparently snaked a camera to spy upon, and surreptitiously videotape, showering neighbor Candace Lewis.

Benson's two-story home was typical of middle-class, upper-middle-class Vegas, reminiscent of Kyle Hamilton's residence a couple miles to the west—stucco with a tile roof, red this time—except where Kyle's lawn was well-tended, Benson's lawn was a scruffy brown whose little green bumps were like grassy pimples on the desert's face.

And, like Hamilton's, the house appeared to be empty, though everyone on this trip was well aware that last time they'd been wrong. Warrick, Sara and Grissom approached the house, their crime scene kits in hand, Brass leading the way.

On the cement front stoop, Brass withdrew his nine millimeter. No one questioned that: if David Benson was the homicidal necrophiliac the evidence was indicating him to be, such a precaution seemed prudent. On the other hand, no backup had been called: this was one suspect, and the CSIs were, after all, armed.

The doorbell went unanswered, and the peculiar sensation of tension and tedium, common working cases like this one, permeated the atmosphere.

Brass said, "Warrick, let's check out the back. Gil, take out your handgun, would you?"

Grissom's expression turned sour, but he complied, shifting the field kit to his left hand.

Warrick and Brass went around the house from opposite sides, Brass to the right, Warrick around the garage, the double door of which had no windows. A side window was covered by a cream-color curtain you could almost see through—almost. The CSI made his way around back, where he found Brass had climbed a few stairs to a small deck. After checking curtained

windows as best he could, the detective shook his head
and they headed back to join the others.

"I don't think our man is home," Brass announced.

"Doesn't look like he's been here for a few days,"
Warrick added, pointing to the overflowing mailbox
next to the front door. "*This* guy's not in bed with a
cold."

Sara scowled darkly. "I'd rather not think about
who or what he's in bed with."

"Time," Grissom said, "to serve the warrant."

Brass needed no convincing: he was the one who'd
gone to the judge with their evidence. "Warrick, get
the ram, would you? . . . Trunk."

The detective tossed Warrick his car keys.

"Gil," Brass said, "you cover us."

"Cover you?"

"Cover us."

"With the gun."

"That's right."

In moments, Warrick returned to the stoop with
the battering ram from the Taurus. The ram was a
black metal pipe with an enlarged flat head and a handle about halfway up on either side, providing an easy
grip. The heft of it felt good to Warrick, natural—this
baby had never failed him once.

Warrick took one side of the ram and Brass the
other, as Grissom and Sara backed to the edge of the
porch. Then, lining it up with the deadbolt, Warrick
glanced at Brass and they swung the ram away from
the door, straight back, then propelled it forcefully forward. . . .

The head hit with a satisfying, explosive crunch,

the jolt shooting up Warrick's arms through his whole body as the door burst inward, the jamb splintering into kindling.

Brass allowed Warrick to return the ram to the Taurus while he stood in the doorway, nine millimeter in hand again, and peered carefully inside.

When Warrick returned, Grissom was saying, "I'm putting my gun away."

"You do that," Brass said. Then he turned to the CSIs with a tiny rumpled grin. "Open house, gang. Refreshments later."

Brass again drafted Warrick, who drew his own sidearm, as they went through every room of the house, making sure the suspect really wasn't home.

After the detective pronounced the house clear, the CSIs went from room to room, checking drawers, closets, drains, carpeting, everything. For the next two hours and then some, they turned the house upside down and inside out, and when they were finished, they met in the foyer amid the detritus of the broken front door.

"What have we got?" Grissom asked.

Sara said wryly, "The only evidence of a crime? Looks like some people broke in here."

Grissom was not amused.

Warrick said, "If anything this place is cleaner than the mayor's place *or* Hamilton's"

"No blood, no hair, nothing," Sara said, then she addressed Grissom and Brass: "What about videotapes? Did you find any?"

Grissom picked up an evidence bag from his

open crime scene suitcase. "Only three home-recorded: labeled *NYPD Blue*, *Without a Trace*, and *Lexx*. Everything else is prerecorded DVD, horror movies mostly."

"Porn?" Warrick asked.

Grissom shook his head. "Nothing rated NC-17, let alone triple X . . . We'll check them when we get back to the lab, but it doesn't look promising."

They loaded their gear inside and hauled it out to the Tahoe. An aura of dejection and confusion hung over them, and few words were exchanged. Sara, Brass and Grissom gathered near the vehicles while Warrick went back and put crime scene tape up across the broken door.

Nearing them, Warrick heard Brass saying, "I'll take the heat for this—Mobley's gonna be *very* pissed if we broke down the wrong door and the department gets sued."

"I think this is one case," Grissom said, "where Brian will cut us some slack."

Feeling movement more than hearing it, Warrick turned to see a forty-something couple sauntering over from the house next door.

In shorts and Miller Beer T-shirt, the man was tall, balding and trimly bearded, with the look of a one-time football player whose paunch said most of his sports were conducted in front of the tube, these days; his wife was a petite brunette with a ready smile and bright brown eyes, wearing a yellow sundress. They approached with a confidence that was a relief, considering how many neighbors and witnesses were wary of the police.

"Are you looking for our neighbor?" the man asked. "David Benson?"

Grissom met them halfway. "We are. Do you know where he is?"

"He works a lot," the woman said. "Very dedicated. Gone at all hours. He's in the security business."

"I'm Gil Grissom with the crime lab. And you are?"

"Judy and Gary Meyers," the wife said, as her husband slipped an arm around her shoulders. "We've lived next door for the last five years. Of course, David has only been here a couple of years. . . . He prefers 'David,' doesn't care for 'Dave.' "

"And you think David's at work?"

Gary shook his head and said, "I don't think so. We haven't seen him for a couple days. He's probably out at that cabin of his." He checked with his wife: "Don't you think, honey?"

"He *calls* it a cabin," Judy said, nodding, "but it's really a second home. *Very* nice."

Her husband picked up on that: "He's got all sorts of high-tech gear out there."

Warrick glanced at Gris, but the man's attention was fully on the couple.

Brass stepped up to Grissom's side, introduced himself and told the couple he'd be making a few notes; they said they wouldn't mind.

"Sounds like you've been there," Grissom said, meaning the cabin.

"Yeah, just once, though," Gary said. "He invited us out, 'cause Jude's a photographer, and David found that interesting—said he was a camera buff, himself. Told us there were some desert birds and rodents around out there, if she wanted to take some interesting shots."

"That was right after he moved here," Judy said. "But we must have overstepped, somehow."

Grissom frowned in interest. "Why do you say that?"

The woman shrugged. "Well, he hasn't invited us back since."

"You notice his video equipment," Gary said, "when I tried to talk to him about it, he got kinda close-mouthed and said it wasn't any big deal. Most people with a hobby, you know, if you're *into* something, you usually you wanna talk about it. Try to get *me* to stop talking about the Dodgers."

Grissom smiled. "I've been a Dodgers fan my whole life . . . and I see your point."

Warrick and Sara traded glances; Grissom connecting with a human being was always worth noting.

Grissom was asking, "Could you give us directions to David's cabin?"

Judy shook her head. "I'm directionally dysfunctional. You remember the way, Gary?"

"We only went that one time," her husband said, "but I think so . . . if you don't arrest me, if I steer you wrong. . . ."

Brass jotted the route down.

"I hope David's not in some kind of trouble," Judy said. "He's nice, in kind of a quiet way."

Yes, Warrick thought, *the rule of the "nice, normal" serial killer next door always seemed to pertain. . . .*

But then Gary Meyers contradicted it: "Yeah, honey, but to be honest with you? He's got a streak.

Guy's an oddball. Not that that's against the law. Has he done something?"

Brass said, "We don't know yet. Just following up on a lead."

"Must be some lead," Gary said. "You busted down his door."

"Thank you for your help," Grissom said, bestowing his fellow Dodgers fan a curt smile, then turning his back on them.

Dismissed, the couple headed to their own homestead, and the CSIs and the detective huddled in the street, between parked vehicles. Brass got on his cell and called to post a patrol car to watch Benson's residence while he and the CSIs took their excursion to the country and the cabin.

Then Brass suggested, "Let's take one vehicle."

Warrick opened the driver's side door, saying, "Always room for one more, Captain."

"Why don't I drive," Brass said, holding his hand out for the keys. "I'm the one with the directions."

"You can navigate."

"Warrick, I've seen you drive."

Shaking his head, Warrick got in back with Sara.

They were at the far north end of the city; Benson's cabin was south and west out Blue Diamond Road, down some back roads, almost to the county line. After a stop downtown at the courthouse for a search warrant, the drive took the better part of an hour; but it was time well spent, much of it on their various cell phones.

Grissom talked to the County Recorder and discovered that Benson had purchased both the house and his cabin about the same time. This also provided them with an exact address, which seemed to fit the neighbor's directions.

Warrick leaned up from the back. "Why is this guy so flush all of a sudden, Gris?"

Grissom said, "See what you can find out, Sara."

And Sara got a dayshift intern to help her dig into Benson's records to find out what else they had missed. The intern told her that an aunt of Benson's had died and left him a good chunk of money, explaining his sudden move from renter of a nondescript apartment into multiple-property owner.

Warrick phoned Benson's place of employment, Double-O Gadgets, and spoke with a receptionist who seemed more than happy to talk about Benson, as long as she mistook Warrick for a security-system client.

After he clicked off, Warrick said, "Our guy's on vacation this week, and they have no idea where he is."

"On vacation at his cabin?" Sara asked.

"Didn't know. He could be in the Bahamas, or in Cleveland."

Sourly, Brass said, "Or on the run."

Grissom shook his head. "No reason to think he's made us, Jim."

Brass ground the wheel to the left and everybody leaned to one side, comically, as they headed up a dirt inlet that seemed to Warrick more like a path than a road. The Tahoe jumped and bucked and a cloud of dust that could be seen in Arizona trailed them like a jet plume.

"Really sneaking up on the guy, Jim," Warrick said, still nursing hurt feelings over the general disregard for his driving abilities.

Half-smiling into the rearview mirror, Brass said, "Still a couple more miles before we're even close enough to worry about it."

Grissom looked back at Warrick. "Consider this an intervention, Warrick—where we demonstrate what it's like to be driven by a maniac."

Brass flicked a frown at Grissom, obviously not liking the sound of that any better than Warrick.

But any criticism of Brass's driving did not prevent the detective from jostling them around several more times before turning off onto another dirt road, this one even more dubious and less forgiving. Then, once he'd made the turn, Brass took what seemed like a firebreak at a more manageable speed.

They were winding up into the foothills now and—despite what Benson's neighbors had said about the cabin being more a second home—Warrick began conjuring visions of this trip ending outside a run-down, ramshackle tacked-together hovel purchased from the Unabomber.

When they popped up over a rise, however, and got their first look at Benson's "cabin" in the distance, Warrick's notion of a shack dissolved and he realized that couple back on Roby Grey Way had not exaggerated. The house perched on a low hill to the west, a long, low-slung stucco ranch-style with a typical Vegas-area tile roof.

Grissom said, "Most people have a cabin to 'rough it,' get away from civilization. Why does David Benson need two houses, roughly the equivalent of each other, only miles apart?"

Sara said, "Do I have to answer that?"

Their supervisor went on: "He's not next to a stream, for fishing. There's nothing to recommend this location, other than its . . ."

"Splendid isolation?" Warrick offered.

Grissom nodded.

Only one way up the hill to the house: a curving dirt driveway that—no matter how slow they took it—would give Benson ample opportunity to spot them coming. Nonetheless, Brass took the hill slowly, kicking up a minimum of dust, though if Benson was home, they were made, no question.

They pulled up in front, in a small graveled area extending from the garage's gravel drive. A propane tank sat off to one side of the house, and next to it a large generator chugged right along, little wisps of exhaust disappearing skyward.

"Okay," Grissom said, almost to himself. "So he's a survivalist—that's one reason to have a second house, in the boondocks. . . ."

They got out and no one made a move to unload the Tahoe. Unholstering his sidearm, Brass gave the CSIs a look that had all of them—even Grissom—unhesitatingly unholstering theirs.

Even if David Benson wasn't their homicidal necrophiliac, he was a loner in the security business who had the earmarks of a survivalist, and when the cops showed up, that type of individual sometimes . . . overreacted.

They went to the door, with its cement-slab stoop,

the detective in the lead, Warrick right behind him, feeling beads of sweat on his brow, and not just because they were no longer in the air-conditioned vehicle.

Brass tried to peek around the curtains of the front window with no success, then turned and gave Warrick a had-to-try shrug.

Poised at the front door, with Grissom and Sara off to the sides of the stoop, weapons in hand, Brass signaled Warrick to go around back.

Which Warrick did, the gun heavy if reassuring in his hand as he skirted along the side of the structure. With no lawn out here, the desert floor seemed to crunch under his feet like broken glass, as if the ground itself were a security alarm. With his left hand, he rubbed the perspiration from his face, particularly away from his eyes, drying his hand on his shirt, and crept along. Three windows on this side—as heavily curtained as the one in the front.

In back, a twenty-foot-wide flat space extended to where the scrubby hill sloped steeply up. More windows—four to be exact, two on either side of a screened backdoor, each as heavily curtained as the others. Beyond the screen, the rear door was steel with a peephole but no window.

Warrick pounded hard on the metal border of the screen, but got no response; and it proved to be locked.

To the far side of the house, the CSI noticed three small bushes, their leaves brown and withered . . . and Warrick realized he'd likely located the source of the crushed leaves found in Candace Lewis's carpet cocoon.

He didn't know how far Brass and the others were—or weren't—getting, out front; but he figured if Benson did happen to be inside, and Brass succeeded in chasing him out, this was the way the suspect would be exiting . . . so Warrick decided this was exactly where he ought to be.

Nerve endings on alert, Warrick imagined he could feel every molecule of the breeze slipping past him. The gun now felt more heavy than reassuring, and the impulse to drop his arms down to his sides beleaguered him; but he fought it, and kept the gun up, barrel pointed at the sky.

If he leveled it, it would be for one purpose only.

Warrick took a position off to one side, preparing himself for whatever came through that door. His back was against stucco, shirt cool and damp against his back, bumps of the wall digging into him, reminding him he was alive. A good way to be . . .

Nothing to do but wait.

Then his cell phone trilled, and he felt himself jump a little—no one was around to see that, thankfully— and he jerked the phone off his belt, about to shut it down when he recognized the incoming number as Brass's.

"What?"

"We don't think he's here," Brass said without preamble.

"He could be burrowed in," the slightly amped Warrick reminded the detective, "just waiting to jump out and say 'boo.' "

"Is there a car, any kinda vehicle, back there?"

Warrick glanced, then felt silly for not putting it together sooner: no car out front, no car in the back, middle of nowhere, equals . . .

No Benson.

"No vehicle out back," Warrick said.

"Join us," Brass said, sounding laidback. "We'll do our deal with the door, you and I, then while you CSIs start working your wonders, I'll move the Tahoe around back of the house. Assuming there's room . . . ?"

"Plenty," Warrick said, taking in the flat space.

Warrick circled the building and met Brass at the rear of the Tahoe. They fetched the battering ram and lugged it to the stoop, to repeat the action from the other house. This door proved more secure, and it took a second blow to send the puppy sailing in, this jamb splintering, too, survivalist measures or not.

After leaning the battering ram against the side of the house, Brass told Grissom and Sara to stay put and keep a watch for Benson, should he return.

Then Brass went in first, Warrick after him, guns drawn. Warrick held a flashlight in his left hand and the weapon in his right, fanning them both around.

The single curtained picture window shrouded the room, but sun spilling through the open door aided the flashlights, if also creating dancing shadows. A certain strobe-like effect resulted, and Warrick had trouble adjusting for a few moments, not able to recognize even familiar objects.

The room was air-conditioned—cold in here, which explained why the generator was working with nobody (apparently) home. Warrick recalled Doc Robbins saying Candace Lewis's body had been preserved for some time, and a chill ran through him that had nothing to do with air conditioning.

Brass clicked the light switch and revealed a medium-sized living room that was at once cluttered and stark: parked in the middle were the only furnishings—a big lounge chair and a small, round table with a coaster and a remote control, opposite a huge projection TV against the far. The cluttered feel arrived by way of the right wall, which was consumed by shelving, the upper levels home to more electronic gear than the backroom at Best Buy—several VCRs, DVD players and recorders, laserdisc player, various cameras and more. The lower shelves were lined with hundreds of videotapes, all the homemade variety, with white spines hand-lettered in black felt-tip.

Even from across the room, Warrick could make out a row of tapes labeled CANDY, volumes one and two and three and on and on. . . .

Shuddering, Warrick glanced around the other, vacant walls—no pictures at all, not mom, not Jesus, not even a velvet John Wayne.

Brass and Warrick exchanged lifted-eyebrow glances, and the detective led the way through an archway into a dining room, each going down one side of a scuffed, secondhand-looking wooden table and two wooden chairs with spindle backs. The chair on Warrick's side was rubbed white on one of the spindles—could this indicate Candace had sat here, handcuffed, while her host fed her during her imprisonment?

Beyond the dining area was the kitchen, but Warrick couldn't move any further without exposing himself to a hallway at left. Brass indicated he'd take the kitchen, and Warrick nodded toward the hall, a choice Brass confirmed with a return nod.

Warrick had taken only a few steps down the narrow corridor when Brass whispered from behind him, "Kitchen's clear, too."

The first two doors in the hall faced each other.

As before, Brass went right and Warrick left, turning into a room bearing the fragrance of a relatively recent paint job, the walls a flat white; probably intended as a bedroom, this had been converted into a kind of office—devoid of furniture but for a swivel desk chair facing a TV monitor on a small desk. A cable behind the monitor ran up the wall, and out of sight. What appeared to be a closet had its door padlocked.

Again, Warrick felt Brass right behind him.

"Bathroom," the detective said, sotto voce, "clean."

"We'll be the judge of that," Warrick said.

"I meant empty," the detective said.

They traded quick smiles, which made Warrick, at least, feel less tense; he started toward the padlocked door.

But Brass touched Warrick's sleeve. "Leave it for now. First we clear the house."

"Okay."

Brass led the way into another probable bedroom, this one on the right, also minus any bedroom furnishings, again vaguely an office: chair, monitor with cable rising out of the back and padlocked closet. This one, however, lacked the scent of fresh paint.

The third bedroom, at the end of the hall, actually was set up like one: a bed with a cream-color spread, another shelf of homemade videotapes, and a TV/VCR combo atop a squat dresser. This closet door wasn't padlocked and, when Warrick opened it, he found only clothing—men's apparel, nothing fancy. The bed was king-size, but the tidy room had less personality than a Motel 6; again, the walls were blank—the only images in this house would be those appearing on monitor screens.

"Homey," Warrick said.

"Real dream house," Brass said, from the hall.

"Check the garage?"

"Yeah. Clear. Whole damn house is clear." Brass holstered his weapon, and Warrick followed suit. "Let's get you people started, before Benson gets back. I don't want Prince Charming seeing that Tahoe in back of the house, and bolting."

Warrick, Sara and Grissom unloaded their equipment and headed inside as Brass wheeled the Tahoe around back, parking it out of sight. Then the detective walked down the hill and positioned himself, out of sight among the scrub, to keep a lookout for their suspect. Brass and the CSIs would communicate via cell phone, if need be.

In the living room, Sara—field kit heavily in hand—was staring at the wall of tapes. She pointed to the row of tapes marked CANDY.

"No way I'm watching those," she said.

Grissom lifted his eyebrows. "Probably not an old

Marlon Brando/Peter Sellers movie. I've got Benson's bedroom. Sara, the kitchen."

"A woman's place?" she said archly.

"Not in this house," Warrick said, somber. "I'll start with bedroom office, number one."

The small room smelled antiseptic—not just freshly painted, but scrubbed, an olfactory cocktail of latex paint and Lysol. Warrick picked up his hooligan tool—a chrome bar with machined grooves to give it a non-slip grip, with a duckbill for forcing windows along with a pike, used to break locks and latches, while the other end had a standard claw used for locks and hasps. Weighing in at about fifteen pounds, the hooligan made just the ticket for tearing a padlock off a locked closet door. . . .

Coming down from the top, Warrick forced the claw behind the hasp and snapped it off, padlock dangling from the jamb.

The closet door slowly, creakily swung out to greet him.

Half expecting the Crypt Keeper to jump out at him, the CSI shined his flashlight inside the closet, which also appeared to have been recently scrubbed and painted in the same flat white.

Warrick set down the hooligan tool, got into his case and withdrew one of his newer toys, a Crime-lite. On loan from its manufacturer, Mason Vactron, the Crime-lite gave Warrick a compact alternate light source—no cables, no guides, size of a flashlight, with a lamp life of 50,000 hours.

He stepped into the closet and switched on the Crime-lite and the white-painted walls seemed to

throb with large black splotches . . . with many tinier
black dots around the doorknob . . .

. . . blood.

Benson may have cleaned the closet and painted it,
but he hadn't hidden Candace's blood from the
Crime-lite. If Warrick had even the slightest doubt
about Benson being their guy, it vanished under the
bright light of truth.

With his Mag-Lite, Warrick illuminated the upper
corner of the closet and could see the tiny snake-head
camera that was the tip of the black cable from the
monitor in the room. *The sick son of a bitch . . .*

Warrick took a few moments to let pass the non-
professional thoughts of what he'd like to do to this
guy; then he got back to work.

In bedroom/office number two, Warrick again tore
off the padlock on the closet with the hooligan tool. In
this closet, he found a roll of carpeting leaned against
the back wall. This gave him a momentary start, as at
first he thought they had another body on their
hands; but when he tipped the rug toward him, he
could see nothing was wrapped in it.

But the remnant seemed a match, and Warrick was
pretty sure the cut on this edge would correspond to
the piece already in evidence. He took a photo of the
carpet and used his Crime-lite on this closet as well;
but no sign of blood. He used luminol spray, and also
came up empty.

Glancing around at the little room, with the monitor and its snake camera extending to this second
closet, Warrick had to wonder: had Benson prepared
this second station for another victim?

But the thought went no further, as a sharp explosive sound from outside caught Warrick's attention . . .

. . . *a gunshot!*

Warrick was already at the front door, when Grissom came up behind him and Sara stepped out from the dining room, having been in the kitchen, asking, "Was that a shot? . . . That was a shot."

Then they heard two more quick reports, and Warrick yanked open the front door and rushed outside into a day that had turned into dusk. In the shadow-blue twilight, he could see down the winding drive a car had been approaching the house, a dark-blue Corolla—Benson's . . . but the vehicle was sagging to one side, both the front and rear tires shot out!

The driver's side door flew open, and a lanky figure emerged—Benson, in a blue T-shirt and black jeans and running shoes, sprinting away from the car, at an angle between the vehicle and the house. Brass was running up from the scrub brush where he'd been on lookout, yelling for Benson to stop.

Warrick took off after the fleeing suspect. He knew he could pull his gun and fire at the guy, but Benson was empty-handed, which meant shooting an unarmed man, and a moving target at that, which Warrick wasn't sure he could hit anyway. Brass, in the meantime, had reached the car, shielding himself behind the passenger side, but Warrick didn't figure the detective could hit Benson at this range.

Benson probably knew this area well enough to elude them, at least for a while; this was rough country, unfamiliar. They could not let him slip away.

These thoughts flashed through Warrick Brown's brain as he cut toward the running suspect. The uneven ground threatened a turned ankle, but Warrick's only thought was taking this bastard down. His arms and legs churned and he swiftly lessened the distance between them.

Seventy yards now, and Benson seemed to be slowing, breathing hard, and Warrick closed the gap, sixty yards, fifty, twenty, ten, then twenty *feet* . . .

. . . and he could hear Benson gasping as he ran, all but spent. At ten feet, Benson zigged, only Warrick zagged, and caught up to his prey in three more steps.

Warrick launched himself, grabbed Benson around his skinny waist, and the two of them hit the ground hard and rolled, over jagged rock and hard dirt clumps and knobby plants, as the killer's glasses flew off into the underbrush, leaving huge scared animal eyes behind.

For a moment Warrick had him, but Benson was a squirmy creature, fighting for his freedom, flailing for his life, and then a sharp elbow came around—just luck, but the wrong kind—and caught Warrick in the right temple, dropping him to the dirt.

Unconscious for at most a second, the CSI rolled onto his back and as he looked up Benson was suddenly astride him, hovering over Warrick, as a knife seemed to materialize in the man's grasp, the handle held tight in a fist, ready to stab, to plunge into Warrick's exposed chest.

Pinned there, Warrick could neither move nor get

to his weapon. And as the knife began its deadly downward arc, Warrick Brown realized he could do not a thing about it—this was the end, then, on his back in the desert with a maniac's knife in his chest.

In the slowest two seconds he'd ever experienced, Warrick waited for his life to flash before his eyes, but instead a streak of scarlet did, erupting out of a red blossom in the midst of Benson's heart.

The murderer's mouth dropped open in surprise, and his eyes looked down at Warrick, as if for pity.

"*Hell* no!" Warrick cried, and the now slack figure astride him was easily thrust aside, flopping to the sandy earth with the eyes wide but no longer registering life.

Warrick got to his feet, breathing hard, leaning on his knees, shocked to be alive. He looked down at Benson, the blade loose in the dead man's hand.

Brass came running up, pointing the pistol at the fallen suspect; though it was obvious the man was dead, Brass kicked the knife away from the limp fingers. Like Warrick, the detective was breathing heavy.

"You shot him," Warrick said.

"Do you mind?"

Warrick leaned on Brass's shoulder. "You're . . . you're not such a bad guy, Captain."

"I have days. You okay?"

"Yeah. Oh yeah . . . how about you?"

Brass shrugged, looked down contemptuously at the corpse. "Great. Don't look for me to lose any sleep over this one."

Warrick checked the body; and it was a body: David Benson was dead.

Rising, running a hand through his hair, Warrick asked, "What the hell happened?"

"Son of a bitch made us," Brass said. "Was going to turn around and drive away." He gestured with the nine millimeter. "But without any tires, wasn't so easy."

"Hey!" Grissom called from over by Benson's car. "Over here!"

Brass and Warrick hustled over to join Grissom next to the slumping Corolla. Sara was coming up from the house.

"Pop the trunk on this, would you, Jim?"

Brass reached in next to the driver's door, to comply with Grissom's request.

The three CSIs looked down into the trunk to see the wide-eyed terrified face of a young woman, her mouth duct-taped, her hands and ankles bound with black nylon electrical ties. She was about twenty, and her brunette good looks were not unlike those of the late Candace Lewis.

They helped the woman out of the trunk, cut her bonds and removed her duct-tape gag, preserving all of that as evidence. Sara led the hysterical but grateful girl toward the Tahoe to check her over, physically, and then start interviewing her.

"The new girlfriend," Brass said.

"Nice," Grissom said, arms folded.

"How so?"

He turned his angelic, ever so faintly mocking gaze on the detective. "How often do we ever find a body at a crime scene . . . that's breathing?"

Brass grunted an appreciative laugh.

Watching Sara with the woman who would never have to suffer the way Candace Lewis had, Warrick Brown, meaning every word, said, "It is nice, Gris. Nice to save one, for a change."

Author's Note

I would again like to acknowledge the contribution of Matthew V. Clemens.

Matt—who has collaborated with me on numerous published short stories—is an accomplished true crime writer, as well as a knowledgeable fan of *CSI*. We worked together developing the plot of this novel, and Matt created a lengthy story treatment, which included all of his considerable forensic research, from which I expanded my novel.

Once again, criminalist (and newly promoted) Lt. Chris Kauffman, CLPE, Bettendorf Police Department—the Gil Grissom of the Bettendorf Iowa Police Department—provided comments, insights, and information that were invaluable to this project. Thank you also to Lt. Paul Van Steenhuyse, Certified Forensic Computer Examiner, Certified Electronic Evidence Collection Specialist, Scott County Sheriff's Office (whose assistance the dedication of this book can only partly repay); to Detective Jeff Swanson, Crime Scene Investigation and Identification Section, Scott County

Sheriff's Office; and to Todd Hendricks for his knowledge of cars.

Books consulted include two works by Vernon J. Gerberth: *Practical Homicide Investigation Checklist and Field Guide* (1997) and *Practical Homicide Investigation: Tactics, Procedures and Forensic Investigation* (1996). Also helpful were *Scene of the Crime: A Writer's Guide to Crime-Scene Investigations* (1992), Anne Wingate, Ph.D, and *The Forensic Science of C.S.I.* (2001), Katherine Ramsland. Any inaccuracies, however, are my own.

Again, Jessica McGivney at Pocket Books provided support, suggestions, and guidance. The producers of *CSI* were gracious in providing scripts, background material, and episode tapes, without which this novel would have been impossible.

As usual, the inventive Anthony E. Zuiker must be singled out as creator of this concept and these characters. Thank you to him and other *CSI* writers, whose inventive and well-documented scripts inspired this novel and continue to make the series a commercial and artistic success.

MAX ALLAN COLLINS has earned an unprecedented eleven Private Eye Writers of America "Shamus" nominations for his historical thrillers, winning twice for his Nathan Heller novels, *True Detective* (1983) and *Stolen Away* (1991). In 2002 he was presented the "Herodotus" Lifetime Achievement Award by the Historical Mystery Appreciation Society.

A Mystery Writers of America "Edgar" nominee in both fiction and nonfiction categories, Collins has been hailed as "the Renaissance man of mystery fiction." His credits include five suspense novel series, film criticism, short fiction, songwriting, trading-card sets, and movie/TV tie-in novels, including *In the Line of Fire, Air Force One* and the *New York Times* bestselling *Saving Private Ryan*. His many books on popular culture include the award-winning *Elvgren: His Life and Art* and *The History of Mystery*, which was nominated for every major mystery award.

His graphic novel *Road to Perdition* is the basis of the acclaimed *DreamWorks* feature film starring Tom Hanks, Paul Newman, and Jude Law, directed by Sam Mendes. He scripted the internationally syndicated comic strip "Dick Tracy" from 1977 to 1993, is cocreator of the comic-book features "Ms. Tree," "Wild Dog" and "Mike Danger," has written the "Batman" comic book and newspaper strip and several comics miniseries, including "Johnny Dynamite" and "CSI: Crime Scene Investigation," based on the hit TV series for which he has also written a series of novels and a video game.

As an independent filmmaker in his native Iowa, he

wrote and directed the suspense film *Mommy*, starring Patty McCormack, premiering on Lifetime in 1996, and a 1997 sequel, *Mommy's Day*. The recipient of a record six Iowa Motion Picture Awards for screenplays, he wrote *The Expert*, a 1995 HBO World Premiere; and wrote and directed the award-winning documentary *Mike Hammer's Mickey Spillane* (1999) and the innovative *Real Time: Siege at Lucas Street Market* (2000).

Collins lives in Muscatine, Iowa, with his wife, writer Barbara Collins; their son Nathan is a computer science major at the University of Iowa.

CSI:
CRIME SCENE INVESTIGATION™

THE FIRST THREE SEASONS ON DVD

EACH SPECIAL EDITION
BOX SET INCLUDES:

ORIGINAL UNCUT
EPISODES
AND EXCITING BONUS
FEATURES.

OWN THEM ALL

IN STORES NOW

LOOK FOR CSI: MIAMI™ SEASON ONE
ON DVD SUMMER 2004.

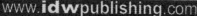

Not sure what to read next?

Visit Pocket Books online at
www.SimonSays.com

Reading suggestions for
you and your reading group
New release news
Author appearances
Online chats with your favorite writers
Special offers
And much, much more!

10421